THE LION of
LARK-HAYES
MANOR

THE LION of
LARK-HAYES
MANOR

AUBREY HARTMAN

LITTLE, BROWN AND COMPANY
New York Boston

Text copyright © 2023 by Aubrey Hartman
Illustrations copyright © 2023 by Christopher Cyr

Cover art copyright © 2023 by Christopher Cyr. Cover design by Patrick Hulse.
Cover copyright © 2023 by Hachette Book Group, Inc.
Interior design by Michelle Gengaro.

Little, Brown and Company
Hachette Book Group
1290 Avenue of the Americas, New York, NY 10104
Visit us at LBYR.com

First Edition: May 2023

Little, Brown and Company is a division of Hachette Book Group, Inc.
The Little, Brown name and logo are trademarks of Hachette Book Group, Inc.

The publisher is not responsible for websites (or their content) that are
not owned by the publisher.

Little, Brown and Company books may be purchased in bulk for business, educational, or promotional use. For information, please contact your local bookseller or the Hachette Book Group Special Markets Department at special.markets@hbgusa.com.

Library of Congress Cataloging-in-Publication Data
Names: Hartman, Aubrey, author.
Title: The lion of Lark-Hayes manor / Aubrey Hartman.
Description: First edition. | New York : Little, Brown and Company, 2023. |
Audience: Ages 8–12. | Summary: Twelve-year-old Poppy meets a water
nymph and exchanges her favorite book for a lion, but her deal has
unexpected consequences that Poppy must fight to correct.
Identifiers: LCCN 2022027121 | ISBN 9780316448222 (hardcover) |
ISBN 9780316448420 (ebook)
Subjects: CYAC: Books and reading—Fiction. | Lions—Fiction. | Nymphs (Greek
deities)—Fiction. | Family life—Fiction. | Fantasy. | LCGFT: Fantasy fiction. | Novels.
Classification: LCC PZ7.1.H3767 Li 2023 | DDC [Fic]—dc23
LC record available at https://lccn.loc.gov/2022027121

ISBNs: 978-0-316-44822-2 (hardcover), 978-0-316-44842-0 (ebook)

Printed in the United States of America

LSC-C

Printing 1, 2023

To Mom
for helping me discover my
Dream for the Taking

CHAPTER ONE

Far away but not long ago, there was a girl and a house.

The girl? Well, she was nothing special.

But the house . . . was *magic*.

A place filled with creatures and enchantments and even a portal to a secret land—much like the wardrobe to Narnia but not exactly the same because that would be copying. And inside, there lived all sorts of undiscovered creatures: fairies smaller than dust, monsters kinder than grandmothers, whispering keyholes and shadows made of light, satyrs and gnomes and a library full of memories. And even though the girl was not magic herself, she was—

"Penelope Woodlock! Stop there!"

Poppy froze, her imagination winding like a spool of thread.

She turned, halfway up the front steps of Lark-Hayes Manor. Apparently, she'd been so busy thinking up a story about this place, she'd forgotten to be invisible. Not *really* invisible, of course—that would actually be cool—but the boring kind of invisible she was expected to be during work hours, or in public, or whenever her parents were supposedly *not fighting, Penelope, just having a discussion.*

Three adults crunched down the gravel drive toward her— Mom, in her rain boots and pencil skirt; Dad, with his hands stuffed in his overalls; and Mrs. Mendoza, carrying an umbrella so wide it covered them all.

As Mom passed, she shot Poppy a *what's gotten into you?* look.

Poppy winced. "Sorr—" she began, but Mom pressed a finger to her lips.

"Did you say *untouched* since 1899?" Dad asked the city official as they climbed the remaining steps.

"The trust did its best to keep it protected from the elements, but yes, for the most part," Mrs. Mendoza replied. "According to Eliza's memoir, she built the estate in America to rebel against the royals. But after her death, her son took his inheritance back to England and left the place to ruin. We'll just take a brief tour for now. There are over fifty rooms, and I know you need to get your daughter to school."

Poppy gazed upward. Lark-Hayes Manor looked like it had grown here with the rest of the forest—its stone walls cloaked in moss, huge turrets mimicking the pine trees all around. It stretched as far as she could see in either direction, the size of a hospital or museum.

"Wait till you see inside," Mom whispered to Dad. She'd already toured it last month, when she'd flown out to accept the project. "You're going to die."

Dad peered at the rickety balcony above them. "That seems like a real possibility."

"Oh, don't worry, we have everything in fairly safe shape now," Mrs. Mendoza piped, though the word *fairly* was not said with much confidence. "Thanks for your patience while we fixed that foundation issue."

Even though the Woodlocks had moved into a cottage on the property two weeks ago, the manor had been off-limits until today. Something about *liability*—which Dad had explained to mean the city didn't want to be responsible if someone ended up dead inside.

Mrs. Mendoza drew a long brass key from her pocket. "And *now* you can finally start working your magic."

Poppy's parents' *magic*—not real magic, of course—was fixing up old buildings. Dad was an architect and Mom was a historic preservation officer, so they made the perfect team. A boarding school, an abandoned lighthouse, and two Victorian homes. Four jobs, four states.

And now Mom's dream project: Lark-Hayes Manor.

So once again, the Woodlock family had packed up and moved, this time to Chatlain, Oregon.

Mrs. Mendoza passed out yellow hard hats from a bin. "Just in case," she said.

The hat slipped over Poppy's eyes just as the front doors were thrown open. The scent of a hundred years of neglect rushed out.

Everyone shielded their faces, choking and coughing.

"What *is* that?" Dad wheezed. The odor was more than just decay, Poppy realized. It was a strange and suffocating mix, like cinnamon and fire and...*fish*.

"I don't think that was here yesterday," Mrs. Mendoza choked.

"Definitely not last month," Mom managed.

The scent coiled itself around Poppy, lifting the tiny hairs on her neck. She pushed up her hat, hoping they'd stumbled upon something creepy and awesome. But all she saw were her parents' backsides and Mrs. Mendoza's giant umbrella.

Mom waved a hand. "Whew. It's going away." She was right: To Poppy's disappointment, the scent was already leaving. Mom stepped over the threshold. "Hello again, beautiful."

Dad followed. "Oh...my..."

Poppy slipped between them and gasped.

Lark-Hayes Manor was just as magical as she'd hoped.

The foyer was two stories high and twice as wide, every inch paneled in elaborate wood. The floorboards splintered and bowed, punctured by so many weeds it looked more like a forest floor. Straight ahead, a grand staircase spiraled up to the second story.

"*This* is the well-preserved part?" Dad asked.

High above, the ceiling was a chessboard of skylight windows, but a giant sheet of plastic had been taped over it, muting the light. The plastic rustled and snapped in the draft.

"As we say in Oregon, stop moving for a day and you'll grow moss." Mrs. Mendoza used the handle of her umbrella to yank a vine from the doorjamb.

"No kidding," Dad said.

Mom dropped her voice. "Spencer, *please* be positive."

"You completely undersold the amount of work this is going to be, Cordelia."

"That's because I knew you'd react like this."

"Rationally?"

"Pessimistically."

Poppy drifted away from the bickering and deeper into the manor, her feet practically moving without permission. Run-down historical sites were like her second home. But *this* was different. Something about the muted light, the hushed air. The sudden stillness, like every insect and animal was watching.

Every old place had a secret past. But Lark-Hayes Manor whispered of a secret present.

Poppy's pulse quickened.

Maybe *this* was the feeling that had pulled Lucy Pevensie into the enchanted wardrobe. Or Mercy Johnson to the time machine. Or Hector Jenkins through the marsh where he discovered his powers.

All Poppy knew was that every one of her favorite stories

started this way. And the thing that made those plain old kids into heroes?

Magic.

A door built into the base of the staircase caught Poppy's attention. The knob was so rusted she had to use both hands to turn it, and when the dust cleared, it revealed a shallow closet.

A secret passage?

Poppy pressed the back panel.

Enchanted portal?

She stepped inside and shut her eyes.

"Poppy!"

Her eyes shot open, and she found she was firmly, depressingly still in Oregon. She hurried out, meeting Mom's irritation with her most innocent smile. "What? I'm *staying out of the way*, aren't I?"

Anyway, those had been Mom's exact words to Luca this morning. "Hold up!" Poppy's older brother had yelped. "You're going inside the manor? I'm coming."

"No, *you* are going to school," Mom had said, dropping a piece of toast onto his plate. "It's Dad's first time seeing it. I can't have you there distracting him."

"Then why's Poppy going?"

"For one, high school starts earlier than middle. For two, you'll have a million questions and ideas, Luc. You know Poppy. She'll stay out of the way."

Everyone knew what Mom meant. Poppy was the one who got quiet when everyone else got loud. The one who agreed when everyone else bickered. The one who *stayed out of the way*. Because someone had to do it. There were three big personalities in the Woodlock family and no room for a fourth.

Luca had looked ready to keep arguing, but Poppy had softly kicked him under the table, begging him not to ruin this for her. He'd groaned and ruffled her hair. "Fine, Weasel. Never say I gave you nothing."

Mom waited for Poppy beneath an overgrown archway. "Staying out of the way does not mean wandering off on your own. Stick with us or you're walking back to the cottage. And Pops"—she looked suddenly tired—"is that what you're wearing to school?"

"Yeah?" Poppy glanced down at her wool skirt, cardigan, and plaid stockings made from masking tape. "Why? You don't like it?"

"I just think …," Mom started, then seemed to change her mind. "Grab a coat before you go to school."

"A *coat*?"

Mom obviously hadn't thought that through. A coat would cover half of Poppy's outfit, and this was some of her best work.

She'd found exactly the right cardigan, then spent all night cutting tape for her plaid tights. Even now, the outfit required a certain level of commitment: She moved with a faint *shweep*-ing sound and kept finding random stuff stuck to her legs—dry grass, clumps of mystery fur, one of Luca's socks.

But it was all worth it this morning, when she'd looked in

the mirror and she was no longer Poppy Woodlock—she was Lucy the Valiant, the girl who'd discovered Narnia and Aslan's closest friend.

"I guess Lucy did wear a big coat in the eternal winter," Poppy said.

"What?" Mom asked, gazing upward. "Who?"

"Lucy Pevensie, from the Chronicles of Narnia. You remember, the—"

"Okay, not now, Penelope."

Poppy slunk back. *Be good, Poppy. Be quiet.*

"Spencer, you see this?" Mom pointed to a gaping hole in the ceiling. "What do you think?"

Dad followed her gaze. "I think there are more holes here than there is house."

Mom groaned, then swept off to catch up with Mrs. Mendoza.

Dad watched after her for a moment, then leaned toward Poppy. "For the record...I think that outfit is your best one yet." In his khaki overalls and sweatshirt, Dad wasn't exactly an authority on fashion, but Poppy grinned back anyway.

"Come along," Mrs. Mendoza called.

She led them through room after room. Mom kept muttering words like *stunning* and *magnificent*, and Dad kept cleaning his glasses and sighing, like he hoped the rot and rubble were products of his foggy lenses.

They passed an arched window facing the rear of the

property and Poppy slowed. Across the overgrown grass, behind a copse of trees, a rooftop glinted.

She hadn't known there was another house on the property. Was it part of the estate? Did anyone live there? She didn't dare interrupt the conversation, but Dad must have seen her staring.

"Sophia, what's that over there?" he called.

"The carriage house," Mrs. Mendoza replied, "where they used to park the horse-drawn coaches. But it won't be part of the renovation. Funding is tight enough already. This way, please. Watch your steps."

Poppy trailed behind, running her hand along the wallpaper in search of secret passages. She found nothing. But if she closed her eyes, she *felt* something: the walls pulsing with a magical past. She could nearly hear it—a live orchestra, swishing petticoats, the clink of glasses.

Another layer of sound emerged.

Croaking.

"Hats on, everyone," Mrs. Mendoza said. "*This* is where you'll have your work cut out for you."

This time, all three of them gasped.

If the other rooms pulsed with magic, *this* was the heart.

It was also, apparently, the source of that terrible smell. Poppy plugged her nose, surveying the room. It seemed it had once been an indoor swimming pool, but at some point a wall had collapsed, and nature had made itself right at home. Lily pads bloomed over the murky surface; ferns crept up the walls. Insects and frogs filled the room with droning song.

The water shuddered.

Something like a spindly octopus flashed beneath the surface. But unlike that animal, this one had bulging eyes and iridescent scales.

"Whoa!" Poppy shed her backpack and scrambled down for a closer look, but the lily pads suddenly drifted together, moved by some strange, invisible current. "Mom! Dad! Did you see that?"

"Oh, I see it," Dad replied, his attention elsewhere. He gestured to the excavator parked in the room, its claw left extended into the water. "Who did that?"

"That would be the flood team." Mrs. Mendoza rubbed her temple. "My nephew."

Dad's voice rose an octave. "He's going to ruin a hundred-thousand-dollar machine!"

"Apparently, he got spooked by some critter last night and made a quick exit." Mrs. Mendoza's voice dropped to a murmur. "That's the last time I stick my neck out for him, mark my words."

Poppy tried to see around the blanket of lily pads for another glimpse of that fish. But she swore they followed her, swaying gently in whatever direction she moved.

A hushed noise rose from beneath the surface—barely audible.

Like hissing steam.

A thousand whispers.

As quickly as it came, it disappeared.

Poppy's blood went cold. Her eyes stayed fixed on the pond. "Did anyone hear that?"

"How long will it take to clear out this room?" Mom asked Mrs. Mendoza.

"Maybe a week. Any idea on a timeline for the rest of the renovation?"

The hissing noise came again, this time sharper around the edges.

"Ssssave me!"

Poppy searched the water frantically, her pulse thundering.

"With the cooperation of the city, I think we could have this done in a couple of years," Mom said. "What do you think, Spencer?"

"A decade," Dad said.

"Spencer."

"I'm kidding. We'll have it done in two years, max."

Mom pecked his cheek with a kiss. "Thank you." She checked her phone. "Shoot! We need to get Poppy to school."

Poppy's head snapped up. "Wait! Did you guys hear that voice? I swear it said—"

"Don't fight with your mother." Dad scooped up her backpack. "Come on."

"But I—"

Mom pinned her in place with a warning look.

Poppy sighed and slung her bag over her shoulder. It was useless to argue with her parents, especially once Mom got that look. Still . . .

Poppy's gaze strayed back to the pond. She'd seen something. Heard something.

Her imagination was good, but it wasn't *that* good.

"Poppyseed." Dad took her by the shoulders. "I can see what you're thinking. But you are *never* to come back here alone. Parts of this place are barely standing. You could fall through the floor and *boom!* smack your head and never wake up. And that's to say nothing of venomous spiders and snakes."

Mom used her singsong voice: "You're giving her anxiety."

Dad sang back, "I'd rather have an anxious kid than a dead one."

"Are those my only options?" Poppy asked.

"Penelope," Mom and Dad said, no longer singing.

"Kidding," Poppy said, turning to hide her *very expressive face*. Because even though her parents refused to listen, she'd read enough books to know what was going on here:

Magic was hiding in Lark-Hayes Manor.

And she—Penelope Quinn Woodlock—would find it.

CHAPTER TWO

"Poppy? Is she not here today? Poppy Woodlock?"

"I'm here." She was sitting so close to Mrs. Bartholomew that the teacher's perfume choked the words.

"Oh!" Mrs. Bartholomew blinked behind her thick lenses. "Apologies, my dear. Seems I need my eyes checked."

Poppy had been at Chatlain Middle for two weeks now, and still Mrs. B seemed surprised every time she saw Poppy in her assigned seat. The teacher slapped the test results down on the desk as the bell rang.

Kids scattered. Poppy waited for the chaos to die down, her thoughts returning to the manor for the hundredth time. To the mysterious, creepy smell. The hissing voice.

Sssave me!

The more time that passed, the easier it was to believe she'd imagined it. It could have been the wind. Or frogs. Or maybe she'd wanted to find magic so badly, she'd summoned some sort of hallucination.

Poppy stuffed her test into her backpack and fished out her favorite book. She paused in the doorway at the edge of the crowded hall, turning the novel outward, hoping someone would notice. After a moment of nothing, she adjusted her grip—giving a better view of the cover. She glanced down, straightening the tape on her tights.

Soon someone would look her way. *Is that the first Narnia book?* they'd say. *You're kind of dressed like the characters. Did you do that on purpose?*

Duh! Poppy would reply. *It's my number one favorite book!*

And just like that, they'd dive into conversation about how much they love Aslan and hate Edmund, how the first book is the best in the series, and how the movies are awesome, even though they got the battle scene all wrong. Then they'd make plans to meet up at lunch, where they'd bond over everything else they had in common.

Poppy had started over at three different schools, and each time, this had been a sure way to find her people.

But strangely, no one seemed interested in the book clutched against her chest. They didn't even give her plaid tights or wool skirt a second glance. In fact, everyone *else* seemed to be wearing a variation of the same thing: hoodie, pale denim, sneakers. Was that a Chatlain thing? Or a middle school thing?

Back in Virginia, sixth grade had been in elementary school. Poppy had been the oldest. The top of the food chain. But here, sixth grade was middle school. She'd been launched into this new world without much warning at all. And suddenly she had a feeling like one wrong move and she'd be eaten alive.

Poppy joined the hallway stampede and ducked into her next class, where she found Mr. Thomas sitting on his desk, twirling an old-fashioned quill pen.

"Morning, Poppy, queen of fiction," he said.

He gave each of his students a nickname. Poppy's had been settled on her first day, when he'd caught her checking out his bookshelves. He'd been shocked—*and*, Poppy liked to think, impressed—by how many she'd already read.

"Hi, Mr. T."

He cupped his ear. "Sorry, what was that?"

Poppy laughed, trying to remember the rest of his title. "I meant hi, Mr. Thomas, almighty god of grammar... collector of stories... lover of bow ties... and"—she squinted at the plaque behind him—"enthusiast of ancient Greece."

"Get that memorized by next week or you owe me cookies. How's the book coming?"

Poppy tucked her Narnia book away and drew another novel from her backpack. It occurred to her that this was the reason her back hurt every night. But she couldn't think of a single book or notebook in her bag that wasn't completely necessary. "Finished."

Mr. T gaped. "Already?"

He'd just loaned it to her on Friday, but she'd had the entire weekend to herself. Her parents had been busy unpacking boxes, and Luca had gone on a student council ski trip. In typical Luca fashion, somehow he'd already become a class representative.

"Did you like it?"

"Totally. Loved it," Poppy lied. The characters were boring. The ending was predictable. But it was just easier to tell people what they wanted to hear.

"Nice," Mr. T said.

Poppy found her desk, offering a smile to the girl next to her. Annabelle was a "new-student ambassador" assigned to show Poppy around. She was chatty and smart, with coiled dark hair and dimples in both cheeks. And even though she had serious *real friend* potential and always saved Poppy a seat at the lunch table, her crew had been friends since kindergarten, so Poppy spent a lot of time awkwardly smiling like she understood their inside jokes.

Annabelle squinted. "Are you in a costume?"

Poppy adjusted the masking tape on her tights, which had gotten stuck as she'd slid into her seat. "Kind of. It's an outfit inspired by the Chronicles of Narnia."

"The books?"

"Yeah! You've read them?"

"No. I don't have time to read. Too much schoolwork."

"Oh." Poppy tried to tame her *very expressive face.*

"Are you doing a costume for the Lady Day Picnic?"

"Wait, do people do that?"

Annabelle shrugged. "Usually only old ladies. But since you're into dress-ups, maybe you should."

The Lady Day Picnic was this month, a Chatlain tradition every year on Lady Lark-Hayes's birthday. Everyone gathered in the grassy park right outside the manor gates and had a big party, with food and croquet and horse-drawn carriage rides.

This year was supposed to be bigger than ever, because the trust had finally given the go-ahead for the restoration of Lark-Hayes Manor. Poppy's parents had even been asked to speak.

The bell rang and Mr. Thomas called, "Holden, gum in the trash. Grace, Ziva, find your seats. We have some business to discuss before we start the unit we've all been waiting for."

The class rustled with excitement. The room had been decorated for the upcoming Greek mythology unit since Poppy had started here two weeks ago; fake ivy draped the walls, 3D columns flanked the doors, even a papier-mâché monster hung from the front of Mr. Thomas's desk.

"Our business is this: It's come to my attention that since Greyson Jager moved last month, Readers Club has fallen apart. I'm looking for a new president to get things rolling again."

Poppy looked around, but no one seemed eager to volunteer. Someone *had* to do this. Books were everything! She'd read fifty-two last year, and that didn't even include the three times she'd read the Narnia series.

Mr. Thomas added, "Whoever does it gets an extra point added to their grade."

Holden Cline called, "I'll do it."

Poppy had only been here two weeks, but it seemed obvious Holden was only volunteering for the extra credit. He was the soccer team captain, but not exactly Mr. Responsible—always begging for an extension on his homework.

"Thanks, Holden. . . . Anyone else? If we have multiple volunteers, we can put it to a vote. Anyone?" Mr. T sounded a little desperate. "Poppy? What about you?"

Poppy's eyes flew wide. Her? President of Readers Club?

Before she could squash the thought, ideas poured in. Posters in every hall. Flyers in every hand. Sleepovers in the library. Book discussions where everyone dressed up like their favorite character.

She could already see herself telling her family at dinner tonight. They'd be shocked. Poppy? President? That was more of a Luca move. But he'd be proudest of all. He'd hold out his knuckles for a fist bump. *That's my little sis*, he'd say.

"Wait, who's Poppy?" Holden called, right in her ear.

"The new girl?" someone else said.

The class telephone rang, a high-pitched trill that made Poppy jump. Mr. Thomas lifted a finger. "Hold that thought," he said, turning to pick up the clunky receiver.

Grace Jennings, who was always secretly checking her cell

phone, turned to Poppy. "Aren't you the girl who moved into the manor?"

Holden made a sound of disgust. "That place is a dump."

Poppy's family had been fixing up old buildings since she was born, and only people with pathetic imaginations talked like that. "It's not a dump," she said. "It's . . . it's . . ." She remembered the prickling feeling, the hissing voice. "It's magic."

Holden scoffed. "Magic?" He turned to the kid next to him. "What is she, like, eight?"

"Is that tape on your tights?" Grace asked.

Poppy reached down and felt the crisscrossed adhesive. It had taken her until midnight to get the plaid pattern just right. "Yeah. They're, like . . . from the Chronicles of Narnia."

"What is that, a store? So, you bought them like that?"

Kids snickered.

Clearly, no one knew the books.

Clearly, no one knew *anything* about the things Poppy loved.

Mr. Thomas returned. "All right. Poppy? What do you say? Would you like to run for Readers Club president?"

Poppy looked around at the kids in their hoodies and jeans staring at her like she was a nobody and what gave *her* the right to be in charge of anything? Holden, at least, seemed like a kid people listened to.

Poppy kept her hands spread at her sides, trying to cover as much of her tights as possible. She shook her head.

"Are you sure?" Mr. Thomas asked.

Poppy nodded.

He sighed. "All right. Holden, you're the new Readers Club president. See me after class." He told Annabelle to hit the lights, then flipped on the projector. "Our big project this quarter will be to create a poster board visual. Which character from *The Odyssey* do you relate to most? Goddess, god, mortal, monster—anyone from the text. Let's go over our cast...."

Magic? What is she, like, eight?

In the dark, Poppy dropped her head into her hands.

Whenever she'd moved before, kids had been excited to get to know her.

But being the new girl in middle school had earned her exactly zero points. Everyone looked taller, bigger, broader— and yet...smaller. Less excited about everything and less interested in anyone.

The game had changed, that much was obvious.

But for the life of her, Poppy could not figure out the rules.

By the time Poppy bought her usual Cheetos and juice from the vending machines, the cafeteria was packed. It was super nice of Annabelle to save her a seat every day—even if it was only because she was the new-student ambassador—otherwise Poppy would be stuck eating in the overflow with Mrs. Bartholomew.

When Poppy got to the table, Annabelle and Lexi were laughing so hard that Poppy found herself smiling, too. "What's so funny?"

Lexi waved a hand. "Inside joke."

"You wouldn't think it's funny," Annabelle said, still humming with laughter.

The two girls turned away, chatting about wearing matching outfits for next week's pep rally.

Poppy pulled the first Narnia book from her backpack to appear occupied. Lucy, Peter, Susan, and Aslan—the greatest heroes of all time.

But today, even though she opened up to her favorite part, she couldn't focus. She just sat there, blinking back her blurry vision, reading the same sentence over and over until the lunch bell rang.

Chapter Three

"How was your day, Poppy girl?" Mom leaned over the stove to taste her tomato sauce—a secret recipe from Grandma's journal. Grandma had died when Mom was a little kid, but she'd left behind a frayed green diary, where she'd written down a few recipes, too. Mom joked that in a fire, she'd save it first, then come back for the rest of the family.

Poppy peeled the last of the masking tape off her tights, balled it up, and threw it in the trash. "Day was fine."

"Oh, good." Mom wiped her hands down her apron, pulled it over her head, and tossed it to the counter. Dad always said Poppy was Mom's little twin. Olive skin. The same narrow nose. One big difference was their hair—Poppy's was chestnut, chopped into a bob, while Mom's was dark and long.

"Now," Mom said. "Dad and I have a little surprise for you. Actually, a big surprise! It's going to require some maturity on your part, because Dad wasn't exactly thrilled about the idea. But I convinced him."

Mom steered Poppy toward the back door, passing through the hall lined with faux-wood paneling. The cottage had been built forty years ago, a seven-minute walk from the main Lark-Hayes Manor, but still within the property gates. Before the move, Mom had shown Poppy a picture—a single-triangle roofline with a wide ivory porch—and Poppy had told all her friends she was moving into Hansel and Gretel's cottage.

But the inside, she'd discovered, was...less charming. Low ceilings, linoleum floors, cheesy wood paneling *everywhere*. It was no mystery why it had sat empty until the Woodlocks had moved in two weeks ago.

The screen door banged shut, and Poppy was met with a rush of cool evening air. Dad waited for them near the shed, beside a tarp-covered heap. He waggled his fingers like a magician, then tore the tarp away.

Despite the brand-new paint job, Poppy recognized it immediately.

Dad thumped the cracked leather seat. "I fixed up Luca's old dirt bike for you!"

A *dirt bike*? This wasn't her thing at all. It wasn't even Luca's thing, given how long this had sat abandoned in storage. "Wow, Dad. It's so...yellow."

"Painted it just for you..I thought yellow was your favorite. Was I wrong?"

Mom sighed. "I told you blue was her favorite. Look at her room. Do you see any yellow?"

"We're living in a rental house," Dad said. "No one's room is their favorite color."

Poppy's favorite color was neither yellow nor blue, but now was not the time. "I love it!" she said to squash her parents' bickering. She cranked the bike handle a few times. Rubber flaked onto her palm.

"Well, you deserve it, my girl," Mom said. "Because we know moving from Virginia wasn't easy. And starting midyear at a new middle school isn't exactly on anyone's bucket list."

"But listen," Dad said. "You can only ride on the forest paths. Don't go anywhere *near* the coast. And always wear your helmet. And take your cell phone. And—"

"Spencer. You're ruining the moment. Just show her how to use it."

Dad gave Poppy a quick lesson on how to ride, accompanied by a hundred more rules that would apparently keep her from dying.

Mom announced it was time to head in for dinner.

Dad squeezed Poppy's shoulder. "When construction starts next week, Mom and I will be spending a lot of time at the manor. Just a three-minute ride straight down this path." Dad gestured toward the dirt trail that cut through the woods.

Mom nodded. "But you probably won't even notice we're gone, with all the fun you'll be having on this thing."

"Yeah. It'll be great." Poppy gave them each a quick hug, then turned to hide her fading smile.

Not because she wasn't grateful. But because she loved her parents more than anything in the world. And tonight, they just felt like two more people who didn't get her.

Poppy brushed her teeth for bed, then headed down the hall. Sometimes she peeked at her parents in the living room before she closed her door for the night. They always looked so peaceful in the soft lamplight: Mom's legs draped over Dad's, a book in each of their hands. It felt like proof they actually did love each other, despite the bickering, and it gave Poppy a little more room in her lungs.

But their books were facedown in their laps.

"She'll grow out of it," Dad said, hushed.

Mom whispered, "She's just being so silly. Her outfits and all that. And I think she actually believes in magic."

"Oh, come on."

"No, really. I saw her at the manor sneaking into a closet. You know, like the Narnia kids? I'm sure that's what she was doing."

Dad blew out his cheeks. "Well. At least Luca seems to be transitioning well."

"I don't want Poppy to get left behind. You don't think we should talk to her?"

"And say what? We already put her through enough with the move. Just let it be. She'll figure it out."

Her parents sat in silence for a moment.

Then, as if that were a perfectly fine end to the conversation, they picked up their books.

Above Poppy's head, a rooster clock ticked seconds into a minute. But the heat on her face did not cool.

When had they decided Poppy's love of reading was a problem? And now they didn't like her outfits, either? Mom used to call Poppy her *creative cat*. She used to be the one clapping when Poppy emerged all dressed up, guessing what book her latest costume was from.

"Night, Mom. Night, Dad," she called from the shadows.

Mom's eyes shot to Dad, worried.

Dad called, "Night, Poppyseed. See you in the morning."

"Yep." Poppy took a few steps back.

"Do you think she heard us?" Mom whispered.

"No, she was in the bathroom." Dad picked up his book. "And you say I'm the anxious one."

Poppy crept back to her room and climbed onto the bed.

Without the glow of neighboring houses, her room was awash in an unfamiliar darkness. Cold seeped in from the cracked window. The empty moving boxes were still stacked against the walls, a reminder that this was barely even home.

Poppy drew her knees to her chest, stretching her nightshirt over her legs.

Her parents wanted her to grow up, but why did that feel like it meant giving up everything she loved? Mom and Dad were supposed to be on *her* side. Not the rest of Chatlain Middle's. Not Holden Cline's.

That place is a dump.

Poppy's curtains fluttered, moved by a breeze.

Magic? What is she, like, eight?

A glimmer of light flashed between the drapes, coming from somewhere outside. But there were no streetlamps near the property. No other houses for a mile.

She stood and parted the curtains.

A distant light winked through the trees, coming from the direction of Lark-Hayes Manor. Was someone over there? In the middle of the night?

A voice rose from the dewy grass. *"Ssssave me!"*

Poppy stepped back, the hairs on her neck standing on end.

Wind rushed forward and her gauzy drapes billowed upward, like flapping wings. Pine branches stirred and the mysterious light glowed brighter. Brighter.

Like a sign.

Poppy's heart galloped.

She'd go tonight and find that mysterious voice. Uncover the hidden magic of Lark-Hayes Manor.

And if she found nothing? Fine. She'd put on the plain hoodie and jeans. She'd be so easy and invisible and boring, her parents would forget she was even alive. Just like they wanted.

Poppy threw on a jacket, packed her backpack, and climbed out the window. The restless night whipped around her as she pushed the dirt bike to the edge of the property so no one would hear it start. The helmet smelled of stale sweat and squeezed her ears, muffling the sounds of night frogs and crickets.

She kicked the starter twice. The seat rattled and the headlight threw a puddle of light onto the rutted path. "It's real," Poppy said. "I'll prove it."

Then she drew a deep breath, twisted the throttle, and charged into the shadowy pines.

CHAPTER FOUR

Poppy cut the dirt bike's engine.

In the darkness, Lark-Hayes Manor looked nearly unrecognizable. The light she'd spotted was apparently coming from the other side of the house, and in the moonlight, the manor's roofline merged with the pines, sketching a serrated edge through the sky.

The mysterious light no longer felt like an invitation.

It felt like a warning.

Poppy unzipped her backpack, rifling past a rain poncho and her Narnia book. Her hands found the comforting, fuzzy cover of her quote notebook. It was filled with her favorite lines from her favorite stories. And usually, it provided just the advice she needed.

"Is this a terrible idea? Should I go home?" she whispered, then let the pages fall open. She clicked on her flashlight.

He was a wishing star. She was a wishing moon.

Well...that made no sense. She flipped through until another quote jumped out.

Quiet things keep the best secrets.

Her trusty notebook had done it again.

If Lark-Hayes Manor was keeping a secret, Poppy would find it.

She tucked away the notebook and trudged toward the house, keeping close to the path's mossy stone walls. Dad's warning echoed in her ears: *You could fall through the floor and boom!* *smack your head and never wake up.*

Poppy shook her head to clear it. Dad was always overprotective.

Mom's voice came: *She's just being so silly. Her outfits and all that. And I think she actually believes in magic.*

And Holden's: *Magic? What is she, like, eight?*

Poppy couldn't shake those voices so easily.

But she could prove them wrong.

She marched up the front steps with more resolve but found that the front door was fastened with a giant padlock. She shook it a few times, frustrated, then remembered that the swimming-pool room had a collapsed wall she could easily scale.

Poppy crept along the front of the house, nearly tripping over a long orange construction cable. She followed it, and ahead, the trees reflected the dull shine of whatever light source Poppy had spotted from the cottage. She turned the corner, and a huge floodlight blazed through the darkness, illuminating the room.

Apparently, Mrs. Mendoza's nephew had never come back to clean up the equipment, because the excavator claw was still dropped in the water.

A splash broke the silence.

Poppy froze. "H-hello?" she called.

The splash came again—more frantic, like a fish flopping on the water's surface.

Poppy drew a breath. She scaled the waist-high wall, then crept onto the plywood bridge. Once she reached the excavator's belted wheel, she crawled along it, moving toward the overgrown pool.

The chorus of night creatures surged around her—frogs croaked faster, crickets and night birds shrieked.

Poppy reached the end of the wheel and peered into the water.

Two white orbs met her gaze. The animal hissed.

Poppy screamed and scrambled back, barely saving herself from a cold, slimy swim. "Stupid possum!"

Poppy knew those creepy, glowing eyes all too well. An entire family of opossums had been living beneath the cottage porch when the Woodlocks had moved in. They were awful critters, mean and territorial, and it had taken two different exterminators to get rid of them.

The animal thrashed, water flying in every direction. It was stuck—its tail probably pinned under the claw.

Mean or not, Poppy couldn't let it die.

She climbed into the excavator cabin and studied the controls, which were cast in sharp shadow by the floodlight. She'd sat on Dad's lap in the Bobcat machine a hundred times, and these buttons didn't seem much different.

A small key was stuck into the ignition. She twisted it.

The machine rumbled to life.

A long lever rose between Poppy's knees. She pulled it and the whole machine lurched. Poppy cried out, jerking the lever back to neutral.

The machine steadied.

Her voice trembled. "Okay... not that one."

She reexamined the control panel, spotting a small joystick next to the ignition. She drew it back slowly, a hair's breadth at a time. The claw hinged upward.

"Yes! There we go... that's it... a little more..."

She released the joystick and the claw jolted to a stop, hovering above the water.

Poppy waited for some indication that the possum had left, so she could get back to searching for that mysterious voice. A minute passed. Two.

It had to be gone by now.

Poppy slipped out of the cabin and inched along the roller track, keeping a hand on the excavator for balance. She reached the end.

The pond fell eerily still.

The sound of night creatures died, as if the entire forest had sucked in a breath.

"Hello?" Poppy whispered.

The white-orb eyes appeared again. Glowing, frosty bulbs without pupils or lashes.

But that, Poppy realized, was no possum.

She sank to her knees, clutching the tire in her trembling hands.

Above the glowing eyes, hair like riverweed rose out of the pond, each strand bobbing upward as though still underwater. Slitted nostrils. Leathery green lips.

Poppy had to be dreaming. She'd fallen and smacked her head, just like Dad had warned. But even in her nightmares, she couldn't have imagined something so terrifying. The creature was shaped vaguely like a woman, with angular joints and skin the color of sun-dappled water. Clusters of iridescent scales coiled around her neck and arms.

Poppy's head buzzed like a severed power line.

Danger.

She should run. But she was paralyzed, captive to her own curiosity. "What . . . are you?" she croaked.

The creature bobbed halfway out of the murky pond. "What am *I*? What are *you*?" Her voice carried like an underwater echo.

Poppy's mouth opened and closed, then finally managed, "I...I'm a girl."

"A girl," the creature said, her barracuda teeth forming a smile. "A girl who knows nothing of water nymphs?"

Poppy, in fact, *had* heard of nymphs before. Many times—from the Chronicles of Narnia. "You're a naiad?"

The nymph's eyelids pinched. "So, the girl does know *ssssomething*."

Poppy felt a glow of pride. Yes! If anyone knew about enchanted creatures, she did. But this nymph was nothing like the descriptions in her book. This one looked more like the sum of a dozen different animals—tiny teeth and sleek eel skin and gills carved into her neck like a shark's.

"*Sssettle* the debt for saving my life, tiny-faced mortal," the nymph said. "*Sssay* what you wish."

"Wait. Wish? You mean...you do magic?"

"I *am* magic. From the Old World beyond this one, where magic is life and law and purpose."

Poppy's entire body hummed. This was it! What she'd been searching for, what she'd known all along. Magic was *real*! She wasn't silly. And now she could prove it. "What other creatures are around here? Mermaids? Fairies?"

"In this, the Minor World?" The nymph's green lips twisted.

"There is nothing of the Old World here. Only frail mortality and poisoned springs."

"But...but *you're* here."

The nymph's gills flared as she sucked in a breath. "The Keepers expelled me to this world."

"Wait, what are Keepers? Expelled for what? For how long?"

"For as long as I am required."

It wasn't exactly an answer, but Poppy sensed that this was a sensitive subject and didn't want to test the patience of those needle-sharp claws. "Oh. Well, my family is going to fix this place up soon. You need to find somewhere else to hide."

"I cannot *sssimply* leave, tiny-faced mortal. I am in exile. Bound within the gates of this mortal estate."

"But my dad is going to—"

"*Sssilence!*" The nymph gnashed her teeth. "You are a leech on my patience!"

Poppy winced. "Sorry. I'll shut up."

The nymph glared back. "*Sssettle* the debt or forfeit your wish."

"You mean I can wish for anything?"

"*Sssay it.*"

Poppy closed her eyes. It was happening so fast.

But she was ready.

"I wish to go to Narnia."

CHAPTER FIVE

The nymph drew farther out of the water, revealing
a band of iridescent scales spiraling around her torso.
"*Narn-y-yah?* What is this word?"

"Narnia," Poppy said. "The magical kingdom between
Ettinsmoor and Archenland."

"Where did you learn of this place, *Narn-y-yah?*"

"*The Lion, the Witch and the Wardrobe.*"

"A wardrobe spoke to you? What dark mortal magic gives
voice to *things* and *stuffs?*"

"No, I didn't talk to a wardrobe. It's the title of the book."

"*Narn-y-yah* is a place of make-believe? What do you think,
that I can magic an entire kingdom into existence for you?
That if I could, I *would?*"

Apparently, Narnia didn't exist. It wasn't surprising, but it had been worth a shot. "Then what about this Old World that you're from? Can I go there?"

The nymph laughed, a sound like cracking sheets of ice. "A mortal, in the Old World? The Chimaera would hunt your scent. Wraiths would drink your soul. Yes, tiny-faced mortal, if the Old World is what you wish..."

"Wait! No, wait." Poppy threw her hands up, suddenly feeling much less brave. "I changed my mind. What else can I wish for?"

"I can grant you *things*. All manner of *stuffs*. Is this not what mortals desire?"

It was depressing, and—Poppy realized—completely true. Most people would wish for a mansion or a fancy car or a million dollars. But Poppy lived in a perfectly fine rental house, she wasn't old enough to drive, and even if she could lug a treasure chest out of here, her parents would question where it came from. They'd force her to give it back to the Lark-Hayes trust. A wish totally wasted.

Poppy pressed the heels of her hands to her eyes. She had to *think*. She couldn't wish for anything that could be taken away. Which limited her options by a trillion. More depressing still, she couldn't go to Narnia. She'd never be surrounded by magic, never know the greatest hero of all time, Aslan. But then again—

She looked up, her heart hammering. "I wish for a lion."

"A mortal beast? This is your desire?"

"Not just any lion. A magic one, like Aslan."

"A *magic* creature? From the Old World? You . . . speak of the winged lion?" Before Poppy could respond, a sharp-toothed smile spread across the nymph's green lips. "Now *that*, fledgling mortal, is a *wish*."

A bubble of laughter escaped Poppy. *A winged lion*. A thing no one could take from her but that still proved the existence of magic. What would her parents say when they realized *they'd* been the silly ones? What would her classmates do when they saw her soaring over the school, a triumphant blur of wing and fur?

"Now." The nymph extended her hand. "Your offering." Water pooled in the taut webbing between her fingers.

Poppy stared at the claws. "My offering?"

"What did you think? I could summon your winged lion from air? From nothing? Magic isn't free. It *cosssts*." The word came out like a hiss.

"I . . . have to give you something? But . . ." Poppy's voice wavered. "Didn't you say you owe me? For saving your life?"

The nymph's mood soured further. "The universe demands balance, frail mortal." She scooped both hands into the water, then raised them, palms flat. Orbs the size of golf balls floated above each hand, suspended like rippling planets.

Poppy clutched the wheel beneath her, barely believing her eyes. Tadpoles darted around inside the floating orbs, as if con-fused by the sudden shift in gravity. Poppy's world tilted on its axis, too, threatening to pitch everything she knew about what was real. About what was possible.

"To bring something into this world," the nymph began, "something must be taken from it." A bead of water split from each sphere and floated toward the opposite. "An equal, simultaneous exchange."

Poppy nodded vigorously, eyes wide. Magic had a price. Of course. "But...I don't have any money."

The nymph closed her fists and the watery orbs burst, raining down around her. "I have no interest in money. You must give a thing of worth. Something you love."

Something she loved...

Poppy had read enough books to know she should be careful. Magical creatures—especially ones exiled for mysterious reasons—were usually trouble. Still, what was Poppy supposed to do? Say, *No, thanks. I've been dreaming of magic my entire life, but I'll pass*?

There would be no second chance, no redo, no backup creature waiting in the wings to grant another wish.

Poppy just had to be smart. Offer something she could replace.

"I've got it." Poppy whipped her backpack around and drew out the first Narnia book. There were thousands of copies in the world. "You can have this."

The nymph glared skeptically.

"It's a book," Poppy pressed. "You said something of worth,

and books are the most valuable thing on earth. Kind of like . . . like the magic of our world."

The nymph stroked the surface of the pond, sending concentric ripples over the water. "Mortal magic, you say?" Only now, Poppy saw that the nymph's eyes weren't completely colorless. They swirled with watery shadows, like bowls of milk being stirred. "Ah, yes. This will suffice, if that is what you wish. So then . . ." The nymph wrapped her claws around the novel. "The deal is sworn."

For one inexplicable second, Poppy's grip tightened on the book, some deep, subconscious part of her refusing to let go.

She scolded herself and drew her hand away.

"Return with the sun," the nymph said.

"In the morning? And my lion will be here? Wait! What time?"

The nymph did not respond. She clutched the book to her scaly chest and sank beneath the surface, the pool so still it was as though the water concealed her on purpose, the humming night creatures filling the silence in her wake.

Gray morning light seeped through the window above the toilet. Poppy had crept out of bed before the sun in order to make a very important and very secret bowl of oatmeal, but she was so nervous she wasn't sure she'd slept at all last night.

Dad's shuffling footsteps approached from down the hall. Poppy let out a whimper, just loud enough to attract his attention. She dumped the watery oatmeal into the toilet, cringing at its believability.

A knock came on the bathroom door. "Luca?"

"No." Poppy groaned. "It's me."

"You okay, Poppyseed?"

"I think I'm feeling better now. I'll just change my shirt, then be in the car."

"Open up."

Poppy stowed the bowl under the sink and inched open the door.

Dad spotted the chunks of oatmeal floating in the toilet. He stifled a gag. "Back in bed. No school today." He flushed the toilet with the toe of his shoe, then shuffled toward the kitchen, calling for Mom.

Poppy slunk back to her room and crawled beneath the covers.

"Yo." Luca appeared in the doorway. "Real or Quaker Oats, Weasel?"

Weasel was the latest evolution of her nickname. It had started off *Poppy*, then became *Pop*, then expanded to *Pop Goes the Weasel*, and now, well, it was just *Weasel*.

Poppy whispered, "Apple cinnamon."

"Ew. Chunky."

Today Luca wore jeans cut in a jagged hem above his ankles,

a striped yellow belt, and a faded Domino's polo from last summer. In typical Luca fashion, it was so ridiculous it was cool. He hadn't trimmed his hair for months and it curled below his ears, which drove Mom and Dad insane, but they only fought about it when they weren't fighting the bigger issue—which was always, *always* computer time. "Who taught you to be so sneaky?" he asked.

"Some weird guy."

"Never say I gave you nothing," Luca said, a thing he managed to tell Poppy once a day. He left, his backpack hitched high.

Mom came in to check on Poppy, leaving her with the infamous metal bowl dubbed *the retching pot*, a sleeve of saltines, and a promise to check in during her lunch break. For the last two weeks, Mom and Dad had been working in the Chatlain administration building, making plans with the city officials, but when construction started in a couple of days, they'd be spending all their time at the manor.

Poppy was supposed to call if she needed anything, presumably using the dinosaur-age cell phone on the nightstand. It didn't have internet or apps, and it had *actual* buttons. Her parents thought Luca's gaming obsession was a result of getting a smartphone too young, and they'd resolved to do better with Poppy. But honestly? If they were so concerned about her getting "left behind," this phone wasn't doing her any favors.

The garage door slammed and the house fell quiet. Poppy

waited. Someone always forgot something. Sure enough, the door opened and footsteps raced to the kitchen, then back out. Two cars started. The gravel drive crunched beneath tires.

They were gone.

Poppy threw off the covers and swung her backpack onto her shoulder, then burst through the screened back door.

That gift from her parents was proving useful.

Poppy and the banana-yellow dirt bike skidded to a stop in front of Lark-Hayes Manor exactly two minutes later. She parked in the trees—out of sight—then hung her helmet on the handle and began picking her way through the long grass.

The front door was hanging ajar.

It felt like a sign.

The hinges let out a long, low whine as she pushed the door open. The dim morning cloaked the foyer in shadow.

"Hello?" Poppy called. The sound of scrabbling mice echoed through the walls. The plastic sheet covering the skylights shuddered. She took a tentative step. "Hello?"

But there was no one else here, beyond the pale insects flitting through the floor weeds. What had she expected? A golden lion poised on the staircase? Napping across the floorboards?

She headed for the flooded room.

The pond seemed quieter than yesterday. And clearer—offering a glimpse of tadpoles darting beneath the surface. "Nymph?" Poppy inched around the perimeter. "Are you here?"

"Hey!"

Poppy startled.

A man in a plaid shirt climbed onto the collapsed outer wall. "What are you doing here? This is a work zone!"

Poppy backed into the doorway. This was probably the man who'd left the front door unlocked. *Duh, Poppy.* "Sorry, I... I was just..."

"Just what? Speak up!"

"Just wondering... have you seen anything strange around here? Like something that does not belong in a mansion in Oregon?"

"Yeah, I'm looking at her. How'd you get in here?"

Poppy laughed nervously. "I'm the Woodlocks' daughter. You know, the people who are restoring the house? We live right there." She pointed in the direction of the cottage.

"You're Spencer's girl? You homeschooled or something?"

Poppy fumbled for a response. If Mom and Dad found out she'd snuck into the manor, she'd be grounded for life. "I... uh..."

The foreman called over his shoulder: "Aaron! Is Spencer coming on-site?"

The man called back what Poppy already knew: "He's at the office today."

The foreman turned back to Poppy. "Spencer's girl or not, stay out of my work zone or I'll boot you myself."

Poppy backed away. "You won't see me again. Promise." She

searched the pond one final, frantic time. Something wasn't right. Where was the nymph? Where was the lion?

Mom had called her silly, but *this* was far worse. This was ridiculous. Had she hit her head last night? Why did she let herself believe in this stuff?

Something moved near the lilies, rocking the water.

Two white orbs appeared between the waxy leaves.

"Oh, thank goodness," Poppy said in a single exhale. Her eyes darted up to the foreman, making sure his back was still turned. The nymph lurked low in the pond. One of her claws broke the surface.

Poppy followed the nymph's finger to the mold-speckled ceiling. When she looked back, the nymph was gone. But Poppy had her answer.

Her lion was upstairs.

Chapter Six

Poppy took the stairs two by two, leaping over the missing treads, bracing herself on the creaking banisters. At the top, the landing split in either direction. Rubble and rat droppings coated the floor; shadows pooled in the corners.

She held her breath to listen. The steady drip of water echoed all around. But there was no rustle of a lion's mane. No floorboards creaking beneath heavy paws.

Poppy grabbed her flashlight, shook it a few times, then gave it a sharp whack. It sprang to life.

The corridor meandered and split, then split again, like the house was intent on losing her. Poppy ripped a vine from a broken window, then dragged the branch, leaving a trail in the dusty floor in case she needed to Hansel-and-Gretel her way out.

The rooms were empty, except for one, which had a three-legged chair and a bucket catching a leak.

Plink . . . plink-plink. Plink.

Poppy lifted her flashlight and scanned the room. Dark paper curled from the walls. Grime smothered the light from the window. Across from it, a closet door hung open.

Poppy wrinkled her nose against the odor of decay and something else. Something spiced and dark and out of place. Poppy inhaled, trying to place it, and the scent seemed to curl around her, filling her head. It was the scent that had rushed out of the manor that first day, the scent from the pond.

Her flashlight fluttered and failed.

Poppy yelped. She thumped it against her thigh and the beam snapped on, illuminating the closet, full of drifting cobwebs and lazy clouds of dust.

She exhaled and moved on.

Once she'd checked every room, Poppy retraced her steps and checked them again.

Nothing.

She leaned her forehead on the wall at the end of the corridor, defeated. Either the nymph had lied, or Poppy *was* losing her mind. Either way, she had no magic lion.

A floorboard whined in the room behind her.

She whirled around, her flashlight outstretched.

Her tiny arm hairs stood on end.

Something was watching her.

Poppy took a careful step into the room. The shadows

beyond her flashlight stirred. "It's okay to come out," she said gently. "I'm a friend."

Please, please, let the lion be real.

She'd made it to the center of the room when her flashlight died again. "Come on!" She whacked it against her hip, too hard. The compartment snapped open and the batteries tumbled to the floor.

Poppy fell to her hands and knees, groping.

Something furry scurried over her legs. Bigger than a rat.

Poppy screamed and scrambled backward, her hands falling on the missing batteries. She stuffed them into the flashlight and the beam shot across the room.

A small bundle of fur squinted against the light.

A lion cub.

His face looked smudged with ink. His fur was nappy and short. His wings were like the knobby, gray-feathered limbs of an ugly duckling.

Poppy's mind fumbled. "You're my wish?"

The cub backed farther into the corner, stumbling over his oversize paws.

Poppy's heart clenched. He wasn't the big, glorious lion she'd expected. But he was scared and alone.

She set the flashlight on its end, casting the room in a thin white glow. "I won't hurt you."

The cub tensed, his dark eyes locked on Poppy.

She extended her hand.

The cub pursed his whiskers, bared his teeth, and attempted to roar. But no sound came out. He raced out the open door.

"Wait!" Poppy snagged the flashlight and ran after him. "Come back!"

He ignored her, knocking into walls, his wings dragging behind him.

He veered into a room. Poppy began to follow, then stopped cold on the threshold. Of all places to hide, he'd picked the smelly room with the leaky ceiling.

She padded forward. "Little cub?" Her flashlight skimmed the floors, the closet, even the ceiling in case he knew how to use those knobby wings after all.

She heard a scuffling within the walls and aimed her flashlight into the crooked slats. Dark eyes flashed within.

If she borrowed a hammer from the construction workers, she could probably pry away the wallboards. But then what? The cub, scrawny as he was, had teeth twice the size of a dog's.

Poppy pulled out her cell phone to check the time. Her parents would be home soon.

Her parents, who'd doubted Poppy. Who'd thought she was going to get left behind.

Poppy threw back her head and released a clap of laughter, vindicated. She hadn't been wasting her time, wishing for the magic she found in her books. She'd been right. She'd even brought some of that magic into this world.

A winged lion.

Her winged lion.

She squatted, peering into the wall. "Since we're going to be best friends, I'll introduce myself. My name is Penelope. But everyone calls me Poppy. And you are…" She'd stayed up all night imagining names for the triumphant lion king she'd expected. But this was no king. This was a scrawny thing, scared of his own tail.

"Creighton? Whistlethorne?" She rattled off some names she'd loved from her favorite stories. But none of those felt quite right. "Theo?"

The cub seemed to grimace at those suggestions, too, wrinkling his whiskers.

She stared into his blue-glass eyes. Waiting for inspiration to come. Then, like a rush from the closet, a whisper on the wind—

It did.

"S-Sampson?" Poppy tried.

The cub's dark eyes sharpened, his head cocked. Poppy had no idea where that name had come from. It wasn't from any book she'd read. But maybe that was the point. Maybe this little lion was going to write a story all his own.

"All right." Poppy grinned. "We'll call you Sampson."

CHAPTER SEVEN

Poppy pulled on an oversize pajama shirt and slid into bed just as the garage door opened.

"Penelope?" Mom called, followed by her infamous jangling. She kept her keys hooked to the outside of her purse, so she sounded like an old-time jailer wherever she went.

"How you feeling, my girl?" Mom asked.

Poppy gave a little cough. "So-so."

Dad checked the empty retching pot. "Have you been able to drink anything?"

"No."

"That's not good. I'll get you some juice."

Dad left and Mom began twisting open the blinds. "Did you make it out of bed at all?"

Make it out of bed? Poppy had done a whole lot more than

that. She'd gone to the manor, saved a nymph, and wished a winged lion into this world. It was so unbelievable, Poppy *had* to say it aloud. "I have something to tell you."

Mom turned, her eyes narrowed. "If you're about to tell me you faked sick to get out of school, causing Dad and me to be late to our meeting with the city, I will fully, completely lose it."

The heat of Mom's impending temper spiked the whole room's temperature. Poppy sank beneath her blankets.

Mom sighed. "I'm sorry." She knelt beside the bed. "I'm just stressed about that meeting. You should see the city commissioner. He has this mustache that makes him look like the villain of a Western movie. I half expected him to pull a pistol from his cargo shorts."

Poppy gave a weak laugh.

Mom pushed Poppy's hair from her forehead. "What were you going to tell me?"

Poppy suddenly realized what a terrible idea this was. Mom wasn't going to let her keep an untamed, magic lion in the manor. She'd call animal control, or the CIA, or some other agency to take Sampson away.

"I was going to say I feel kind of dizzy," Poppy said.

"You need to get something in your stomach." Mom shed her blazer and rolled up her blouse sleeves. "I'm going to make Grandma's dumpling soup."

Poppy sat up. "Wait, you're not going back to work?"

Mom planted a kiss on her forehead. "Work can wait."

The air filled with the smell of salty soup. Poppy sat on the edge of her bed, her knees jittering. From here, she couldn't see much of the manor—just the black chimney pipes sprouting over the treetops.

She'd taken precautions to ensure Sampson wouldn't escape from that room—wedging the door shut with a balled-up pair of socks, a trick from Luca's babysitting playbook. Sampson couldn't possibly open it.

But a wandering construction worker could.

Poppy's leg jittered faster.

And had she checked the windows? What if Sampson squeezed farther into the walls and got stuck? Was he hungry? What did magic lions eat, anyway? He was so tiny, maybe he still needed milk. From a bottle? What kind of bottle? What kind of milk?

"Hey, Poppyseed." Dad came in. "I have an idea." He drew something from behind his back and grinned. "For old times' sake?" He held a picture book with a frayed spine, the edges rippled from a thousand page turns.

The Tree in Valley Blue.

All at once, Poppy was six. A box fan rattled in the window. The muggy air hummed with cicadas. Poppy was half asleep, and Dad was beside her, reading softly.

Florida had been her parents' first big job—a historic all-girls boarding school. Every morning, Dad had left before sunup. And every night, Poppy had tried to stay awake until she heard the clomp of his boots come through the door.

He'd always come straight into Poppy's room. Sometimes she'd been too sleepy to open her eyes. But he'd always sat beside her bed, opened *The Tree in Valley Blue*, and read every last word.

"Remember this?" Dad asked.

Poppy nodded. She'd missed Dad so much that year. But *The Tree in Valley Blue* had been his way of saying, *I love you. I miss you. I'm here for you.*

"Do you think this renovation is going to be like that one?" she asked.

"Could be," Dad said. "But this is Mom's dream project. When it's done, people will come from all over the country to see it. It's going to put her name on the map."

"What map?"

"It just means people will recognize Mom's talent. As they should." Dad raked a hand through his rust-colored hair. "You should have seen when she was chosen for this commission. She cried."

"No way."

Dad held up his palm. "Scout's honor. She went to our room and I heard her saying, 'We did it. We did it.' I thought she was talking to me. But when I went in, I found her holding Grandma's journal."

"Huh? Why?"

"She feels like this is a dream Grandma had for her. And"—Dad let out a long whistle—"would Grandma be proud."

Poppy smiled. Dad was her favorite parent, but if she could be like anyone in the world, it would be Mom.

Dad peeled open the cover of *The Tree in Valley Blue*. "Let's read." He lay next to Poppy, his feet sticking over the foot of the bed, and began.

> *The trees in Valley Blue*
> *all gathered at the foot of the mountain*
> *and decided*
>
> *in spring We bloom;*
> *in summer We shade;*
> *in autumn We shed;*
> *in winter We rest.*
>
> *And every seed*
> *that gripped the soil with root*
> *heard the rhythm of the seasons.*
>
> *All*
> *but one.*

Dad looked at Poppy. "Remember what you used to say here? You'd whisper—"

"Poor little tree."
"That's right."

Spring came,
and the trees in Valley Blue
stretched awake,
beckoning villagers
to climb the highest boughs
and see the sailboats sail in the sea
beyond.

Eager to join,
Little Tree twisted and strained.

"Little Tree!" the others cried.
"You are ruining our beautiful valley!
You must bloom!"
But try as she might, Little Tree could not.

So she bent to the earth,
drew her branches in,
and made herself
very

      very

            small.

The garage door slammed.

Luca appeared, backpack slung over one shoulder, wavy hair tucked behind his ears. "Poor Weasel. Oat man still got you down?"

Poppy shot him a look.

He snorted. His eyes fell on the book in Dad's hand. "Aw. Reading together. How nostalgic."

Dad frowned. "It hasn't been that long. Just last summer we read... what was it?"

To Poppy, it felt like yesterday. Stretched out on lawn chairs on the back porch, reading together until the mosquitoes chased them inside. "You don't remember?"

Dad's forehead puckered. "I guess I don't. Luca?"

Sometimes Luca would join them, scrolling on his phone and pretending not to listen. But later, he gave himself away by buying Poppy a box of Turkish delight for her birthday—one of the main character's favorite candies. Sadly, it had been disgusting, and Poppy had fed it to the ducks in the library pond.

Luca shrugged. "Can't remember." He headed for the kitchen.

Poppy groaned. "It was *The Lion, the Witch and the Wardrobe*."

"You sure?" Dad said. "I think I'd remember a title like that."

"Yes, I'm sure," Poppy said, annoyed. "It's literally my favorite book."

His brow furrowed. "That's your favorite? Why have I never heard of it?"

Poppy sat up. Dad was the kind of guy who remembered everyone and everything. *Oh, you're from Tucson? Do you know Bill? He was in my pickleball league twenty years ago! Small world!*

So why was Dad pretending to forget this? Was this some trick to force her to grow up? Poppy stared at him a beat longer, then rolled out of bed and swept into the kitchen. "Luca!"

He was arranging pizza bagels on a cookie sheet.

"Luca! Remember? Last summer we read the first book of the Narnia series."

He slid the pan into the oven. "No, it was...I don't know. But not that."

"Yes, it was! Luca! Are you kidding me?"

Luca looked at Dad, who'd followed Poppy into the kitchen. "Is she okay?"

"*The Lion, the Witch and the Wardrobe!*" Poppy said, voice rising. "We all read it together! Come on!"

Everyone stared at Poppy. Luca would never tease her like this. He wasn't that kind of brother. Besides, Dad was a terrible liar, and in his expression now, there was no glimmer of conspiracy.

Mom's spoon was stilled over the boiling soup. "Is she feverish, Spencer?"

For the first time, Poppy felt like she really was going to

retch. She scrambled into the bathroom and locked the door, pacing the tiles.

Why had her family forgotten her favorite story?

It couldn't be coincidence that she'd just *happened* to give the nymph a copy last night. What had that nymph done? What had *she*—Poppy Woodlock—done?

Poppy gripped the sink and forced herself to breathe. Maybe she was overthinking this. Maybe Luca and Dad were just distracted. It wasn't *their* favorite book. It wasn't like *they* carried around copies of the Chronicles of Narnia in their backpacks.

Poppy burst from the bathroom, nearly bowling into Luca.

"I need to use your computer," she said.

Mom hovered in the hallway. "Honey, are you feeling okay? What's going on?"

Dad called, "Soup is boiling over, Cordelia!"

Mom hurried back to the kitchen.

Luca motioned to Poppy. "Come on."

His room smelled like drugstore body spray and old pizza. His computer desk, however, was as pristine as a NASA workstation. In a blink, he input his twenty-character password and opened a search window.

"Look for the Narnia series," Poppy instructed.

Luca shook his head as he typed. "What's the deal, Weasel? Why are you freaking out?"

He hit enter.

Showing results for: ~~Narnia~~ Narcos series

Narcos. *Narcos* is an American crime drama web television series. Set and filmed in Colombia, seasons 1 and 2 are based on the story of drug kingpin Pablo Escobar.

"Whoa," Luca said. "Sounds awesome. But Mom will be ticked when she finds out you're watching that."

"What? I'm not watching that. Try again. This time write *The Lion, the Witch and the Wardrobe.*"

He did. "Nothing."

Poppy pushed Luca aside. She typed a dozen different variations, including every title from the series. Each time, Google suggested another result.

None of which had anything to do with Narnia.

Poppy raked her hands through her hair. "How is this possible?" Luca, Dad, the internet. Everyone in the world had forgotten Narnia? Had the nymph warned Poppy this would happen? Had Poppy been too excited to understand?

Luca reclined and propped his feet on the desk. "Did you accidentally invent a whole book in your head? I always knew you were special, but this is next-level."

"I'm not special! C. S. Lewis wrote the books! I think I erased them!"

"C. S. Lewis? We studied him last year in English. He wrote . . . like, a bunch of stuff. Right?"

Poppy's eyes widened. "You've heard of him? Okay, that makes sense. I didn't erase *the author* off the face of the earth. How would I erase a person? I didn't do that. Just the books." Poppy paced. Just the *books*. Plural. But she'd only given the nymph the *first* Narnia novel. There were seven more! And now they were *poof*, gone, just like that? And the movies, too? Because the first book disappeared, the rest couldn't exist? "This is crazy! Crazy! I should have known. That nymph was sneaky. But I'm going to find her and tell her this was *not* the deal. I cannot be responsible for this."

"Hey!" Luca sprang from his chair and grabbed her by the shoulders. "You have to calm down."

"Calm down? I can't! I—" The uncharacteristic concern in Luca's eyes stopped Poppy cold. "What? What is it?"

"Mom was on the phone with Aunt Deedee last week."

"So?" This wasn't the time to talk about boring relatives. Possibly *the most* boring relatives ever. Aunt Deedee brought soggy quiche to every family gathering, and Uncle Craig didn't blink enough. At last summer's reunion, he'd lurked around the lake house in a business shirt and had never even gone outside.

"Mom asked Deedee if you could live with them this summer," Luca said.

Poppy scoffed. "You're lying."

"She said you missed Virginia, and with the renovation starting, she couldn't give you the attention you need. Whatever that means."

"But... Aunt Deedee lives in a tiny apartment."

"Yeah. They made a plan for you to move into the craft room. The *craft room*. So Mom said if you don't seem settled soon, she'll fly you out for the summer. And I, personally, cannot have that. I cannot be an only child with the tyrants."

A few days ago, a summer with Aunt Deedee wouldn't have been the worst thing in the world. But Poppy had Sampson now. She couldn't abandon the lion *she'd* brought into this world.

Mom called, "Luca! Your pizza bagels are burning!"

Luca sprang for the door, then paused. "Listen, Weasel. Whatever's going on, you have to suck it up. Or shove it down. Just... hide it from Mom and Dad. Or this summer, it's going to be you, Aunt Deedee, and a wall of color-coordinated scissors."

He disappeared, leaving Poppy frozen in place.

Shove it down.

Hide it.

Luca had no idea what he was asking. *Hide* the fact that magic was real? *Hide* the fact that there was a winged lion in the manor house? Why did she always have to be the one to swallow her feelings?

But maybe Luca was right about their parents. They'd overreact and mess everything up. She could tell Luca, though, couldn't she? He was the one who got her into fantasy books in the first place. He even had his favorite graphic novels signed and framed above his bed. If he knew magic existed, he'd lose his mind.

Although—Poppy caught herself—if Luca met Sampson, she knew what would happen. Sampson would end up liking Luca more. Because everyone liked Luca more. And right now, even though Poppy had wished this magic lion cub into existence— he had no reason to love her. He had no reason to pick her.

"All right! Fine." Poppy yanked down the hem of her pajama shirt with resolve. "I'll shove it down. I'll hide it."

Chapter Eight

Mom attributed Poppy's strange behavior to a fever that didn't exist, which earned her another day home from school. As soon as her parents left for work, Poppy drove her dirt bike to the manor to find the nymph.

She clung to the hope that this was a terrible misunderstanding. The nymph would realize the mistake. She'd bring back the memory of Narnia.

But when Poppy approached the flooded room, the construction foreman's voice boomed. "Steady, Aaron! Steady! You're going to tip the machine!"

He sounded stressed. And scary.

She'd have to deal with the nymph later.

Upstairs, Poppy exhaled. Her socks were still balled up in Sampson's door, which meant no one had gone into the room. Once inside, she knelt and peered through the broken wall slats.

Sampson's eyes shone back like dark glass beads. He pursed his whiskers and bared his teeth, but no noise came out again.

Poppy gave a sharp laugh. She was flooded with relief, followed by the inexplicable urge to cry. Sampson was here. He was real.

Her worry about the nymph and Narnia books fell away. She'd messed up in trading away her favorite book. But maybe . . . maybe it was worth it.

"I brought breakfast." Poppy set out the Tupperware of milk and waited for Sampson to emerge.

The sound of leaking pipe water plinked the seconds into minutes. One. Two. Five.

Was he stuck?

Poppy untied the sweater from her waist and scrubbed the window until dull sunshine streaked through. With the added light, she got a better look at Sampson. He stared back, his head resting on his paws. Was she imagining it, or did he look . . . weak? His eyes blearier than yesterday?

He needed to eat. Maybe if she left, he'd feel safe enough to come out. But she couldn't go into the hallway and risk being spotted by a wandering construction worker. Her gaze slid to the closet.

She slipped inside, cringing at the feathery cobwebs that brushed her forehead, then drew the door shut.

The sound of whistling wind came from everywhere and nowhere. Her eyes roved across the darkness, searching for the source. And what was that smell? It was that same unfamiliar scent from yesterday: heady and thick. Like thunderstorms... and cinnamon. And... woodsmoke? It curled around her like tentacles. Her every hair stood on end.

"Can't do it!" she cried, bursting back into the room. A single inhale of fresh air cleared her head. She glared back at the closet accusingly. What was that smell? And *why* was it so creepy?

It had been no use hiding, anyway. Sampson's milk was still untouched.

Poppy paced. Maybe magic lions didn't drink milk. Maybe they only wanted fresh meat, slaughtered in a hunt. Maybe they ate something only found in the Old World and Sampson was destined to starve.

Maybe, maybe, maybe.

A metallic crash came from below. Poppy's worry spiked. It wouldn't be long before the renovation reached this room.

She bent to Sampson's hidey-hole. "Here's our problem. You can't stay here or those construction guys are going to find you. Trust me, if they weren't happy about *me* being in this place, they sure won't be happy about you."

Sampson's eyes shifted toward the sound of the machines clinking downstairs.

Poppy's eyes narrowed. "Wait. Do you understand me?"

He blinked. Not an ordinary gesture, but slow and purposeful.

No way.

Poppy motioned to the bowl. "I have milk out here for you. Don't you want it?"

He huffed and draped a floppy paw over his face.

Poppy's heart leapt. He understood her. He'd even responded.

She drummed her fingers on the floorboards. So what could she say to convince him to come out? To prove that this strange new world wasn't all that bad? Her gaze fell on her backpack.

When she was scared, one thing always soothed her nerves.

She crossed the room, then sat beneath the window and drew a book from her bag. "All right, Sampson. Since you seem to understand me, I'm going to read to you. And you're in luck because I'm right in the middle of a good one. *Night Breakers.*" She'd even dressed the part—a gray sweat suit and a neon wristwatch, or rather, a cardboard clock face taped to an electric-green scrunchie. "It's about these kids from all over the world who are fighting this virus, because for some reason they're the only ones not infected. And then they discover... well, I'll just read it. I'll even start over. Just for you."

It was really no big deal to reread the beginning. She *always* read every book twice. The first time, she sped through, eager to see how it ended. The second, she paid closer attention to details she'd missed. And she always found at least one part that made her throw her head back and say, "How did I not see the end coming?"

The second read was her favorite.

Two hours, a bag of peanut butter pretzels, and fifty-four pages later, Poppy came across a line she wanted to remember.

"Hold that thought," she told Sampson. She pulled out her fuzzy pink notebook. As she was scribbling down the passage, something moved in her peripheral vision.

Sampson slunk from the wall, creeping toward the bowl of milk.

Poppy's pen froze, her breath held.

He was even more adorable than she'd remembered—the little tufts of fur between his toes, the smattering of dark spots across his forehead, his eyes rimmed with black. As he crept, his wings dragged across the floorboards, raking feathery trails in the dust.

Slowly, careful not to spook him, Poppy slid her phone out and snapped a photo. The phone was the oldest hunk of junk imaginable, but now, it was the most priceless device in the world. Because it held real-life proof: A winged lion lived in Lark-Hayes Manor.

Sampson took one lick of milk, then looked up, pink tongue cleaning his whiskers.

Hope pushed Poppy's heart to a faster tempo. "See? I'm a friend."

Sampson's ear flicked.

She dared a crouching step forward. "It's okay."

His tail thumped against the floorboards.

A few more steps and she'd be within reach. Her fingers ached to brush his golden fur, to feel his downy wings.

The floorboard beneath Poppy creaked. Sampson scrambled back, his oversize paws scrabbling beneath him.

"Wait!" Poppy said.

To her amazement, he froze.

Poppy wasn't sure what to do next. The only thing she had was the copy of *Night Breakers*. She extended it. "You want to see this book? It's got a cool cover."

Sampson cocked his head, little ears flicking.

"Come on."

He crept forward and sniffed the cover, too focused on it to see Poppy's hand extend toward him.

His coat was coarse and thick. The sprays of fur where his wings joined his back were soft and white, and his feathers were as velvety as they looked, though a little dusty. Poppy smiled as she touched the black tufts sprouting up between his toes.

He looked up.

"What'd I tell you? I'm nothing to be scared of."

A careful hope grew in his eyes—then quickly disappeared. Approaching footsteps sent a cold rush through Poppy's veins.

The jangling of Mom's keys.

CHAPTER NINE

S pencer, look here." Mom's voice echoed down the hall. "Is this salvageable?"

Poppy crouched beside Sampson, her heart hammering. She checked the time on her phone. Three thirty. Her parents must have finished their meetings and come to check on the manor.

A thumping echoed through the corridor, probably five doors down. "Can't tell how bad the water damage in this wall is," Dad said. "Let's check from the other side." Their voices grew distant as they went into one of the rooms.

Poppy frantically searched for some way to hide Sampson. Her parents would never let her keep him. And if they were checking for water damage, they'd definitely look inside that hole in the wall.

She wished she'd brought a box or rope or *anything*.

Her eyes fell on her backpack.

She snagged it, then ran to the window, leveraging her entire body weight to push the glass pane open. It ground against the dirty treads, opening just wide enough for Poppy to shove out everything from her backpack. She almost dumped her poncho, then caught herself. *This* she could use.

Poppy tucked the poncho into her belt loop, then yanked the backpack wide, holding it like an open mouth.

"We've got to hide you," she whispered. "Hurry, into my backpack."

Sampson stepped back, eyes flicking to the hidey-hole, as though calculating whether he could make it past Poppy.

"They'll check in there, too, trust me!"

Footsteps carried through the hallway again. Mom said, "We should check every room."

Poppy shook the backpack, not daring to speak, her eyes pleading with Sampson.

"Look at these water spots," Dad said, just outside the room. *Bang, bang!* "All this drywall has to go." *Bang, bang—*

Whop! The sound of Dad punching through the wall reverberated throughout the manor.

It startled Sampson. He darted into the backpack, burying his face in the fabric. Poppy rotated his haunches, turning him face-up. His entire front half hung out.

Poppy folded his wings and slid him deeper into the bag.

She drew both zippers closed until they met on either side of his neck. The rest of his body took up every inch, his wings bulging against the sides.

His dark eyes brimmed with fear.

"Don't worry," Poppy whispered. "I'll get you out of here."

She looped her arms through the straps, then stood, nearly toppling backward. He was heavier than he looked. She threw the blue poncho over both of them.

Sampson squirmed, his paws scraping the leather bottom of the backpack.

Poppy hissed over her shoulder, "Sampson! Stay still!"

"Poppy?"

She whirled around. Her parents hovered in the doorway.

"Mom! Dad!" Her voice came out a little too high. "I was looking for you!"

"Why?" Mom asked, too confused to be angry. "What's going on?"

"Penelope Quinn," Dad said, "I specifically told you never to come here alone."

"I'm not alone. *You're* here."

"Why are you wearing a poncho?" Mom asked.

Any other day in Oregon, it wouldn't be a question. But today, of all days, the sun had decided to appear.

"I'm...reading a book about this girl who is...allergic to the sun." It was a good lie. Poppy had justified a hundred strange outfits this way.

"I see," Mom said. She exchanged a look with Dad. A look Poppy understood now. *See why no one takes her seriously? See how silly our daughter is?* Except she wasn't. And she had a winged lion in her backpack to prove it. But now was not the time for that revelation.

"I thought you were sick." Dad turned to Mom. "Isn't she sick?"

"That's what I was told," Mom said, eyes narrowed on Poppy.

Sampson wriggled. Poppy hitched up her backpack. "I feel better. And I came to tell you that—"

"Why didn't you just call?" Mom demanded.

"I didn't think your phones had service."

Mom pulled out her phone. "Dang, you're right. This cell carrier is awful. Spencer, didn't I ask you to look into that?" She turned back to Poppy. "What did you need?"

"To tell you I'm going somewhere."

"Where?"

It came to Poppy like a brilliant flash. One sure thing that would turn Mom's interrogation into a celebration. "A friend's house."

Dad frowned. "You shouldn't be going anywhere when you have a stomach bug, Pop—"

Mom elbowed him. "Who is it?"

"Annabelle, from school. To help me with the work I've missed."

Sampson wriggled again, his whiskers tickling the back of Poppy's neck. She grimaced.

"What's wrong?" Dad said. "Is your backpack too heavy?" His anxiety was running high, probably because of that hole he'd just punched into the wall. "Look at her, Cordelia. She's going to end up with a back injury. I'm going to talk with the school."

"Oh, you're going to reprimand the principal?" Mom said.

"I'm not going to reprimand him. I'm going to express concern."

"I've seen the way you express concern."

Poppy inched forward, urging her parents out of the doorway. The bickering was, for once, a welcome distraction. Her parents backed into the corridor just enough for Poppy to squeeze by.

She bumped against the doorframe and Sampson whined.

Mom and Dad went quiet.

Dad extended a palm. "Let me feel your bag. It shouldn't be over ten pounds for a girl your size."

"Dad," Poppy said firmly. "If my books were too heavy, I could talk to my teachers myself."

Mom and Dad swapped another look. This time, Mom's face said, *Well, there you have it.*

Poppy turned toward the narrow servants' staircase at the end of the hall. "I'll see you tonight!"

"Not too late!" Mom called.

Poppy descended the narrow stairs by two, one hand bracing the bottom of her backpack to steady Sampson. He bounced up and down, but stayed quiet.

She burst out the back door and stopped cold.

There was nowhere to take him. She couldn't keep him in her family's cottage. Couldn't leave him unprotected in the forest. Her gaze lifted to the roof poking through the trees at the edge of the property.

The carriage house.

Mrs. Mendoza had said it wasn't part of the renovation.

Tall grass whipped against Poppy's legs as she sprinted toward the thicket of trees. With every step, it felt like Sampson grew heavier. She made it through the meadow, then slowed, her breath staggered and shallow.

She pushed through low branches.

The carriage house came into full view: fat stones topped with a steep, rust-colored roof. A sparse gravel road led to its huge barn doors fastened with padlocks.

Sampson squirmed to get out.

"Not yet," Poppy said.

She picked her way around the back of the carriage house. Here, the forest had encroached completely, and it was hard to tell where the ivy stopped and the stone started. She went around to the other side. An archway curved over a navy blue door. It had a padlock, too, but the key was stuck in the bottom.

Poppy yanked the lock open, pocketed the key, and pushed through the door, stepping into a century of dust.

Cobwebs draped the rafters. The walls blossomed with mildew. Ivy covered the windows opposite the barn doors. It was completely empty, aside from a rusty carriage abandoned in the corner.

Sampson fidgeted, reminding her he was still crammed in her backpack.

"Okay, okay." Poppy knelt, sliding the bag from her shoulders. She wrestled with the zippers, but Sampson's wings strained at the track, and she worked carefully to not catch his feathers. "Sheesh!" she said. "It's a miracle we got you in this thing."

The bag popped open and Sampson toppled out.

Poppy could barely believe her eyes. From the time she'd put him in her backpack, he'd gone from the size of a house cat to a small beagle. Did magic lions normally grow this fast? The question was so absurd—the word *normally*—that she laughed.

She clapped her hands over her mouth.

But Sampson didn't startle. He leapt up, a cloud of dust puffing up around his paws, and peered around.

"You're safe now," Poppy said. It seemed strange that this room full of creeping vines and shadows could feel that way. And yet it did. "Go on."

Sampson ventured forward, wings tucked neatly at his sides—finally, not dragging. His ears flicked toward every new sound—the whistle of a bird, the scuff of branches on the roof. When he came to the ivy-covered windows, he lifted his face to the light and closed his eyes.

Poppy felt it, too. This little carriage house seemed like a world away from the manor. Maybe because no one had ever lived here before. There were no spirits haunting its past, no blueprints claiming its future. No one to hide from, no one to tell them to leave.

"Sampson." Poppy loved the way her voice carried, not lost in big spaces or buried beneath other voices. He sat, as though he knew just what Poppy was about to say. "I think we're home."

CHAPTER TEN

Poppy sat in math class the next day, listening to exactly zero words. A huge problem loomed overhead: The carriage house wasn't technically part of the renovation, but Mom would definitely come snooping for inspiration or materials. What would keep her away? What would keep *everyone* away?

Poppy's imagination, of course, went to the most dramatic solutions first. Dress up like Bigfoot and chase anyone who came near? Stage a murder and tape it off like a crime scene? Start a rumor that the carriage house was filled with poisonous snakes?

Wait.

Poppy's eyes widened.

She released a clap of laughter, amazed at her own brilliance.

"Penelope?" Mrs. Bartholomew asked. Every eye turned to her. "Something funny?"

"No, I . . . um . . . no." Poppy shrank in her seat. "Sorry."

"Don't be! I only thought I'd missed a good joke." Mrs. Bartholomew moved on and Poppy got back to scheming. Because there really *was* someone who could keep Mom away. Someone scarier than Bigfoot or murderers or snakes. Her parents' archnemesis:

The U.S. Fish and Wildlife Service.

After school, Poppy swung by the carriage house to check on Sampson, then hurried home for the moment her big hoax would go down. If all went as planned, she wouldn't have to worry about her parents finding Sampson anymore. If it didn't, it would lead them straight to him.

She didn't have to wait long. Luca was lounging on the couch scrolling through his phone, Poppy was doing homework at the table, and Mom was in the kitchen making minipizzas when Dad clomped in, riffling through the stack of mail.

Poppy held her breath, trying to look casual, when—

Dad's eyes narrowed on a letter. "What is this, Cordelia?"

Mom glanced through the kitchen pass-through. "Did I open that? I don't recall."

She didn't remember opening it, of course, because she hadn't.

Poppy had slipped it into the stack of mail after school,

counting on the fact that her parents were always opening each other's stuff. Because while Poppy could easily copy a heading from the internet, forge a letter, and print it out in the school library, she had no idea how to fake a postage stamp.

"It's from the U.S. Fish and Wildlife Service," Dad said gravely.

Luca's head shot up. "Oh, snap."

Mom appeared in the doorway faster than a summoned demon. "You've got to be kidding me. Not again, Spencer!"

Poppy ducked lower, trying to hide her smile. She just knew they would freak out. She knew it.

In North Carolina, halfway through construction on the Victorian house, an inspector had found a nest of tiny pink spiders in the basement. Disgusting and ugly and—unluckily for her parents—an endangered species. The Fish and Wildlife Service had swooped in and no one had been allowed within a half mile until every itty-bitty spider had been moved—costing the project like seven months and a million dollars.

Dad held up a palm. "Before we panic, let me read it."

"Aloud!" Mom yelped.

Dad cleared his throat. "To Whom It May Concern...yadda yadda...The Oregon Center for Biological Diversity has reported that the endangered Siuslaw Hairy-Necked Tiger Beetle has laid eggs inside the carriage house on the Lark-Hayes estate." Dad looked up, his glasses askew. "The carriage house? That's oddly specific. And how did they—"

"Who cares! Keep reading!"

Dad continued: "We will be sending an officer to inspect in the coming months, but until then, we insist no one goes within a hundred yards of the carriage house. The Siuslaw Hairy-Necked Tiger Beetle larvae are known to cling to passing animal fur and clothing"—this part, Poppy had completely made up, but since her parents weren't scientists, she doubted they'd question it—"and if anyone trespasses on the protected area, we will be forced to shut down the entire project for a full inspection. Warm regards, The U.S. Fish and Wildlife Service."

Dad folded up the letter.

"*Warm regards?*" Luca scoffed. "What, did Mary Poppins write that?"

Poppy shot him a look.

Mom's eyes were wide. She spoke slowly, as if trying not to spook a wild animal. "So . . . they aren't . . . shutting us down?"

"Not unless someone goes into that carriage house. Which I know you were planning to do this weekend."

"Oh, no, no, no! Not anymore. I'm not risking another endangered-bug fiasco." Mom jabbed her spoon in Dad's direction. "And tell your guys if anyone goes within a hundred yards of that carriage house, I'll fire them so fast they'll get third-degree burns. That goes for you kids, too." Mom turned her fervor on them. "Hear that? No exploring over there. None."

Luca went back to scrolling. "Roger that."

"Got it!" Poppy said.

"Good. So, we're good, Spencer? Yeah? Good?" Mom swept back into the kitchen, wooden spoon raised like a battle flag. "No one disturbs the hairy beetles!"

The next day after school, Poppy threw open the door of the carriage house. "Hello, my little hairy beetle!"

Sampson bounded over. He shimmied his wings, and a cloud of filth puffed into the air. Poppy coughed, frowning. At this rate, the carriage house would turn him into a creature so gray and grubby, he might be mistaken for a giant hairy beetle after all.

Cobwebs laced the rafters. The walls were freckled with mold. The windows were so filthy they worked better to keep the light *out*. Hooks and shelves jutted from the wall above the abandoned carriage, so rusted and useless they looked like barnacles on a ship's hull.

What had she been thinking? This was no place for a magic lion.

Her frown deepened into resolve.

"Nope," she said firmly. She was the daughter of Spencer and Cordelia. Professional fixer-uppers. "I can solve this."

Since Poppy had terrible cell service on the property, she left a note tacked to her bedroom door: *Gone to Annabelle's. Phone dead. Be home at six.*

She returned to the carriage house with a wagon full of cleaning supplies "borrowed" from the stash at the manor. She'd begin with the floors. And though her parents would have been appalled at her decision to renovate from the ground up, she was tired of seeing Sampson's underbelly covered in dust.

As she scrubbed, Sampson chased her mop, skidding and pouncing like a huge house cat. It made Poppy's heart soar to see him relaxed and playful, so different from the terrified cub she'd first met. And she couldn't help thinking of how similar they were—both dumped in a new world and expected to survive.

After a full afternoon of mopping and scraping, the floors shone. Well, maybe they didn't *shine*. But no longer packed with dirt, they revealed a black-and-white checked pattern.

It was beautiful.

The next day, Poppy attacked the windows. It took all day because the panes were made up of little diamond shapes, requiring her to scrub each section of glass individually.

As she worked, she talked.

She told Sampson about how she'd wished him into existence by making a deal with the nymph. About how none of her old "friends" had even texted her since she moved, and how in the first week here, Luca had become a class representative, so he wasn't around much.

She talked about Virginia—the fireflies and cicadas and the school librarian who always let her exceed the checkout limit.

And Florida, which was the worst, because she'd hardly ever gotten to see Dad.

Sampson listened to all of it, his yellow eyes reflecting every emotion. When she told him about Holden Cline and the Readers Club election, his eyes darkened to a muddy gray—the exact shade Poppy had felt that day.

It still amazed her that he understood everything. And he talked back, too.

One thump of his tail on the ground meant *No.*

Two thumps meant *Yes.*

Three meant *I don't understand.*

And anything else he wanted to say, he found a way—acting it out or giving Poppy a certain look. Dad always said Poppy had a *very expressive face*, but Sampson really had her beat.

Late into the afternoon, Poppy was finishing up when Sampson balanced his front paws on the sill to peer out the window. He perked up, eyes narrowing on a robin building a nest right outside.

Poppy watched, trying to gauge what he was thinking. "Wanna go out for a better look?"

Sampson pushed down from the window and shook his floppy head, looking just like Luca whenever Mom told him to cut his hair. Sampson was growing incredibly fast, but inside, he was still that scared little cub.

"Fine. We'll stay cooped up in here forever. Should be clean enough soon, anyway." Poppy tossed the empty Windex bottle and stepped down from the stool. "Let's see how we did."

The polished windows had the most incredible effect. Ivy hung like curtains outside the windows, filtering the sunshine into the dreamiest shade of green. The entire room was bathed in emerald light.

Poppy swiped the sweat from her forehead. Cobwebs still draped overhead, the walls needed paint, and she herself was covered head to toe in grime; but a hundred years of neglect wasn't going to come up in a couple of days.

And she couldn't help but feel like her parents would be proud.

Poppy and Sampson worked tirelessly the whole next week. When she entered the carriage house the following Saturday, the rafters seemed twice as high. The blue walls were scoured and cleared. And if Poppy squinted hard, the abandoned carriage in the corner almost looked ready to be used.

Poppy sat beside Sampson, gazing at their work, the warmth and light falling all around. Sampson sat up straighter, ruffling his wings.

"I agree." Poppy sighed, hooking her arm around his fleecy neck. "That nymph isn't the only one capable of a little magic."

Chapter Eleven

The Lady Day Picnic was less than a week away. Luca worked every day to build booths with the student council. Poppy's parents spent hours locked in Mom's office going over their presentation. And at school, it was all anyone could talk about.

"The prize this year is a new Jetta," Lexi said at lunch. Her dad's car dealership was sponsoring the croquet tournament, which Lexi had only mentioned about fifteen thousand times. She popped open a bag of chips and offered one to Annabelle, then Janice, then Ziva. They were barbecue-flavored, and Poppy didn't want one anyway. "He let me pick the color."

"What'd you pick?" Poppy asked.

The girls all looked at each other, then in unison said, "Orange!"

"You *love* orange," Annabelle said to Lexi.

"Just like Mercy Johnson," Poppy said, mostly to herself. Mercy was the main character from the Time Voyager series, which she'd just finished reading to Sampson.

He was still too timid to venture outside, so Poppy brought the adventure to him. Each day, they climbed into the abandoned carriage and read. Progress was slow, because every other sentence Sampson interrupted with three thumps of his tail, meaning *I don't understand*. So Poppy would have to stop reading to explain the word *hospital*, or *cucumber*, or whatever.

There was a lot Sampson had to learn.

But Poppy loved being the one to teach him. And she noticed that he liked some parts more than others. When they read action or magic, he batted at dust bunnies or lazily cleaned his wings. But anything with friendship or family—he listened intently. Maybe because that boring human stuff was *his* unknown.

Annabelle took another one of Lexi's chips. "Wait, Mercy Johnson?" she asked Poppy. "Like the book?"

"Yes!" Poppy said eagerly. "I thought you didn't like reading?"

"I read it last year in Ms. Pham's class. Oh my gosh." She turned to the other girls. "Remember Ms. Pham? And her pet, Gizmo?"

Lexi gasped. "Remember when Jason Briggs put it up in the air vent and it crawled around in the ceiling for like two days before they caught it?"

The girls cracked up.

Poppy grinned, trying to envision it. "What kind of animal was it?"

"Jason was suspended for a week!" Ziva said.

Poppy tried again. "What kind of pet was it?"

But they'd already moved on, laughing about all the pranks this kid Jason had pulled over the years.

This was where Poppy usually pulled out a book and buried herself in another world. But it didn't really bother her today. Because soon, no one would leave her out of their conversations. They'd all be talking about *her*.

What is that? they'd gasp. *A lion? A flying lion?*

Someone's riding on top! a kid would shout.

It's Poppy Woodlock!

Excitement would burst through the crowd. They'd chant her name. And she'd look down at all the people who hadn't paid her any attention and she'd know: It would never be that way again.

"An iguana." Annabelle's face came back into focus.

"What?"

"You asked what kind of pet. It was an iguana."

"Oh." Poppy smiled. "Thanks."

On Friday, Poppy left the carriage house door open, confident no one ever came up this way. Even if Mom got tempted to sneak around, she was way too busy. The manor acted like Poppy's secret ally, keeping her parents so overwhelmed that they rarely came home before dark. Each day, it revealed new problems—leaking pipes, lead paint, replacement materials Mom was going to spend forever searching for.

Still, to be safe, Poppy always left a note about being at Annabelle's taped to her bedroom door. Her parents never mentioned the note, so they'd probably never seen it, and Poppy whispered a little *thank you* to the manor every time she passed.

Some days, she swore it winked back.

Poppy had just finished reading the rest of *Mercy Johnson* to Sampson, so she was letting him play with the oversize cat toys she'd made from shed junk while she did homework. She was seriously behind in school, and if she started failing classes she'd be sent to Aunt Deedee's faster than she could say *soggy quiche*.

"Any idea what six thousand two hundred and one divided by nine is?"

Sampson gave a thump of the tail.

Poppy clicked her tongue. "Two weeks old, Sampson. You should know this by now."

In response, Sampson stole Poppy's bag of cheese crackers.

"Hey!" Poppy laughed.

Sampson shook out the bag, pouncing on the crackers as they rolled across the floor. He was never really hungry, Poppy had learned. She'd puzzled over it at first, wondering if there was something she was missing. Every living thing—magic or not—needed something to make them grow, didn't they?

Anyway, it was a relief, at the rate he was going. He was already the size of a medium dog. The smatter of dark spots had dissolved from his face; his feathers were long and white. His eye color was changing, too, warming to gold, like the night sky fading to day.

It wasn't hard to imagine how magnificent he'd be when he was fully grown. Sometimes Poppy felt a pang of guilt for wiping her favorite books off the face of the planet. And other times she'd look at Sampson and know she'd do it all over again. Because the world had a million books. But it had only one winged lion.

A shadow flashed in the doorway.

Poppy's gaze cut to it, heart skittering.

But it was just the robin from the nest outside. It landed in the rafters, fluttering from one beam to the next, its tiny wings battering the air.

Sampson spotted it, too. He crept along the floor, sleek and silent as a house cat, the bird's silhouette reflected in his dark pupils.

"No, Sampson! Don't—" Poppy started. But just when she thought he was going to pounce, he did something incredible. . . .

He opened his wings.

Poppy sat up straighter.

He wasn't hunting. He was learning.

The robin launched itself back into the air, and Sampson

followed. He lifted his wings higher, flapping in shallow bursts, but his paws didn't leave the checked floor.

With a sudden swoop, the robin found its way out of the carriage house.

Sampson gave a low growl of frustration.

"You want to fly?" Poppy asked.

He cocked his head, eyes full of timid hope.

She hitched up her backpack. "All right, then. Let's go."

But Sampson didn't follow her. He sniffed at the threshold, his wings shuddering.

"You're too scared?"

He thumped his tail once: a stubborn and unconvincing *No*.

Poppy laughed. "Then come on!"

He gave a wistful look, then curled up in the middle of the floor.

Poppy frowned. She wished she could pour courage into him. Show him how much more amazing he could be, if only he were brave.

Then she realized she could.

She rode the dirt bike home, grabbed a book from her nightstand, and rode back.

"Sit there," she told Sampson, gesturing to the doorway. "I'm going to read a story called *The Tree in Valley Blue*."

Sampson seemed very pleased with this idea. He lay on the threshold, head resting on his paws. Poppy sat cross-legged in front of him, beneath the stone archway.

As she read, she held the book upright so Sampson could see the pictures.

When she got to the part where Little Tree bent to the earth to make herself small, Sampson cocked his head, brows furrowed.

"I know, right?" Poppy said. "Wouldn't it be terrible if Little Tree gave up and never learned to bloom?"

Sampson was smart. He knew what Poppy was doing. But he was also incredibly curious—a cat, after all. He huffed, as if to say, *Stop blabbing and keep reading.*

Poppy did, and when she got to the part about the little bird, Sampson perked up.

> *Little Tree was feeling quite blue*
> *and quite alone,*
> *when a bird landed on her trunk.*
>
> *"Little Bird, you did not fly south!"*
> *she exclaimed.*
> *"Do you not hear the rhythm of the seasons*
> *like me?"*
>
> *"That rhythm is a cage," the bird replied,*
> *"and I must fly free."*
> *"For how could I miss this—*
> *the most beautiful season of all?"*

Curious,
Little Tree straightened.

Frost glittered on the mountains,
and peaceful silence fell all around:
softer than spring,
deeper than summer,
more brilliant than fall.

Indeed,
a world more wonderful
than Little Tree had ever seen.

It wasn't quite the end of the book, but apparently Sampson had heard what he needed. When Poppy looked up, he was on his feet.

CHAPTER TWELVE

Sampson stayed close to Poppy, moving in a low crouch until they reached the tree line—where the pines grew dense and boulders rose from the mossy ground. Poppy led him west, away from the manor. Away from her family's cottage. And as the scent of the salty sea grew, so did Sampson's courage. His strides lengthened and he ventured a few steps ahead, sniffing at tree stumps and wildflowers.

Against the backdrop of the woods, he looked so *alive.* Ferns shuddered in his wake. Shards of light fell over his feathers. Critters scurried from his path, and insects sounded alarms.

The whole forest seemed to say, *We see him, too.*

Poppy realized she'd been admiring Sampson too long. "All right, let's get to business." She climbed onto a boulder surrounded by a carpet of moss. "Watch me."

She stretched her arms and leapt, landing on the springy ground. "Now you."

Sampson bounded to the top of the boulder. He hesitated on the edge, his front paws kneading like a house cat's. Then he extended his wings, leapt—

And plummeted straight to the ground.

Poppy laughed as he shimmied coils of moss from his fur.

"Maybe try flapping your wings before you jump?"

Sampson tried again.

And again, and again.

They tried a dozen techniques: leaping from higher places, fluttering like a hummingbird, gliding like a bat. Poppy even cleared a runway and Sampson attempted a running start.

They slumped together on the ground, exhausted and out of ideas.

"Maybe you just need practice," Poppy said.

Sampson rested his chin on his paws. His ears drooped.

"Hey"—she nudged him—"Little Tree didn't get it on the first try, either."

Suddenly, Sampson's ears perked. He launched upright.

"What? What?" Poppy said, looking around.

The shriek of an eagle tore through the sky above. Sampson must have sensed its approach.

If anything could show him how to use his wings, it was this huge, powerful bird.

"Come on!" Poppy cried.

They ran side by side, the eagle's silhouette flashing through the canopy above. Sampson's bounding strides put distance between him and Poppy. He changed directions and leapt over a fallen trunk, his instincts kicking in.

Poppy couldn't keep up. She pumped her legs faster, raising a hand to shield her face. The sound of crashing waves came from somewhere beyond.

They were approaching the cliffs.

"Wait!" Poppy shouted.

The eagle shrieked again and Sampson bounded out of sight.

"Sampson, wait!" She ran faster, her lungs clenching.

The pine trees thinned and the ground became craggy stone. The sound of the ocean filled the air.

"Sampson!" she screamed, and broke through the trees.

He was perched on the cliff's edge, searching the sky.

Poppy pulled up next to him, hands on her knees, chest heaving. "You...can't...run...away...like...tha—"

The eagle cut through the air above them. It careened downward, toward the seething ocean, then swept back up.

Poppy hooked an arm around Sampson's fleecy neck. "Watch! Watch her."

The eagle rose higher, pounding the air.

Sampson's wings shuddered, pushing against Poppy's rib cage. She took several steps back.

Sampson threw open his wings. He brought them down, dirt and rocks kicking up around him.

"Again!" Poppy called. She crouched, a tiny storm of wind and debris swirling around her as Sampson beat the air.

But when the dirt settled, Sampson was still planted on the cliff's edge.

The eagle gave a final cry, then disappeared into the foggy distance.

Poppy stood and brushed the dirt from her clothes. Why weren't Sampson's wings working? They weren't just for show, were they?

A muted sound rose from below—brittle and echoing, like cracking ice. The nymph's cruel laughter. Another wave broke, smothering the sound, and Poppy wondered if she'd imagined it.

"You'll figure it out," she said to Sampson quietly. Uncertainly.

Sampson didn't look at her. He watched the sky, his golden eyes locked where the eagle had once been, his mouth drawn down. Then he hung his head and released a long, low moan that echoed down the sea cliff—light enough for the wind to carry, but heavy enough to break Poppy's heart.

CHAPTER THIRTEEN

Poppy stretched and rolled over in bed. Sunlight streaked through the blinds, brighter than it should have been. Her parents had warned they'd wake her at 7:00 a.m. to go over and help with preparations for the Lady Day Picnic today.

She blinked, trying to get a read on her alarm clock.

8:52 a.m.

Two hours late.

Poppy flew out of bed, swung open her door, and then froze.

The air was filled with the scent of burnt toast, so someone was awake. But it was far too calm. Too quiet.

Something felt *off*. Like she was listening to a familiar song but a single instrument was missing.

She found Dad in the kitchen, hovering over the toaster.

"Morning, Poppyseed." He was still in his plaid pajamas.

"Wait." Poppy shuffled to a stop. "What day is it?"

"Sunday."

"Sunday the fourteenth?"

"That sounds right."

"Did the picnic get canceled?"

"Picnic?" Dad dropped a charred piece of toast onto the plate. "Did we say we were doing a picnic today?"

"Yeah, Dad, the Lady Day celebration. It starts in like five minutes!"

"The Lady Day what?" Dad pinched his forehead. "I feel fuzzy. I wonder if I'm getting sick." He reached for the vitamins above the microwave and swallowed a couple.

Poppy stared. Had *Dad* fallen through the manor floor and smacked his head? Even if she'd somehow gotten the date wrong, he was acting like he'd never even heard of the Lady Day Picnic. Like he hadn't been practicing his speech in front of the mirror for the last month.

He sat at the kitchen table, chewing slowly.

"Dad, I—"

He dropped his toast and stood. "Sorry, Poppyseed. I think I need to lie down."

He went to his bedroom.

Poppy stood there for a moment, a creeping panic inching up her spine. The last time Dad had inexplicably forgotten something, it had been her favorite book.

The one she'd given to the nymph.

Poppy headed to the living room, where the Lady Lark-Hayes memoir always sat on the coffee table. Mom and Dad read it almost every night, combing it for hints about how the woman would have wanted her manor restored. Poppy's foot landed in a watery trail, where someone had dripped something all the way to the sink and not bothered to clean it up.

But she didn't have time to be annoyed.

The coffee table was empty.

Poppy turned back to the kitchen. Sometimes Dad read the memoir over breakfast. But it wasn't there, either, not between the upright collection of cooking books or behind the toaster. She even checked the sink, which smelled faintly of old fish, in case it had fallen in.

Poppy knocked on the glass doors of Mom's office. "Mom? Where's Lady Lark-Hayes's memoir?"

Mom barely glanced up from her computer. "Hm?"

"Lady Lark-Hayes's memoir. The one you and Dad read, like, every night?"

"Are you talking about the woman who built the manor? She didn't write a book, did she?"

Poppy opened her mouth, grappling for a response. She shook her head. "Forget it. But aren't we supposed to be headed to the picnic? Remember, you're giving a speech?"

Mom kept clacking away on her keyboard. "Not sure what you're talking about. Sorry, honey, can you shut the door on the way out? I'm in the middle of something."

"For the manor?"

"Yes."

"The manor built by Lady Lark-Hayes because she was tired of her royal husband and wanted a place of her own in America?"

Mom looked up. "How do you know all that? Her life was a mystery. No one knows anything about her or why she built the manor."

"I . . . ," Poppy started. "I'll . . . let you get back to work." The panes rattled as she shut Mom's office door.

Poppy slipped out the back, cranked her dirt bike, and sped down the driveway. She made it out of the gate and skidded to a stop at the graveled edge of Hesper Park.

The parking lot was empty.

The entire *park* was empty but for a few plywood booths that had been set up earlier that week.

Poppy ran to the center of the field, her helmet clutched to her chest. Rain misted down all around her, dizzying, disorienting. Where were the food trucks? The people?

Had the festival been canceled? But that didn't explain why her parents had forgotten about it *entirely*.

It was eerily like the time the world had forgotten the Chronicles of Narnia.

And just like that, Poppy knew there was only one way to figure out what was going on.

She had to go see the nymph.

Chapter Fourteen

The construction crew never worked on Sundays, so Lark-Hayes Manor was quiet, the equipment stowed on the side of the house.

The pool room was unrecognizable. The water had been drained, the ivy ripped out, leaving the walls veined with a ghostly map of where they'd once been.

Poppy ducked beneath the caution tape, jumping into the empty pool. "Nymph! Where are you? Nymph!" The floor squelched, soft beneath her feet. Dad's warning sprang to memory—

You could fall through the floor and boom! *smack your head and never wake up!*

Poppy climbed back onto the collapsed wall, searching the room. The nymph had specifically said she couldn't leave this place, hadn't she? So where had she gone? Poppy looked out to the grassy meadow that stretched into the forest.

A trickling sound came from below.

Halfway down the wall, a white pipe poked through the stone, then continued into the grassy meadow. It must have been how they'd drained the pond.

Poppy jumped down and followed the pipe. In some places, the grass grew so thick she had to crouch and feel for the smooth plastic. But when she got to the forest's edge, the pipe stopped. A trickle of water dripped from the severed lip.

The humming forest seemed to grow louder, as if laughing at her.

Poppy glared back. She was Penelope Woodlock. She'd found magic when no one believed she could. And she'd do it again.

She closed her eyes, sifting through the sounds. The chirrup of birds. The rise and fall of cicadas. The drone of croaking frogs.

Frogs.

To her right, shaggy ferns slanted away from each other. It looked like the draining pond had flowed through those plants.

Poppy leapt over the ferns and followed the muddy path. Brambly bushes clawed her shins; mud flung up the back of her legs.

The trees opened to a glade. A small pond lay at the center.

Poppy crouched on the edge. Something about this pond *did* feel similar to the last one. What was it?

A smell.

The barest trace—like cinnamon and woodsmoke and thunderstorms. The same scent from the manor! But this time, it didn't feel creepy. It felt *familiar*. She breathed it in, wondering what had changed. The scent—she realized—faintly trailed behind Sampson.

But why would the nymph and the manor and Sampson all smell the same?

Poppy's eyes widened.

It was the scent of *magic*.

"Nymph!"

Leggy insects flicked the pond's surface. A frog leapt into the water with a *plop*.

"Nymph! I . . . I demand to see you!" Poppy's voice cracked with fear. But the only thing scarier than the nymph appearing was her *not* appearing—leaving Poppy to wonder forever. "I . . . I call upon the magic of the Old World!"

The forest fell still.

The pond gurgled, like a drain had opened in the center. The nymph's riverweed hair rose from the surface, followed by angular cheeks and needle-sharp teeth. She stayed low in the pond.

"*Impudence*," she hissed. "Would I come to *your* place of refuge, disturb *your* slumber?"

Poppy swallowed. "Sorry, I—I need your help. There's a problem with my wish. A huge problem."

"You do not want the winged lion?"

"No! That's not it. Sampson is great. He's perfect," Poppy said quickly. "It's just... remember when I gave you that book? Narnia?"

The nymph lowered her chin. *"Yessss?"*

"Well, for some reason the whole series is gone now. And it's like... everyone in the world has forgotten it."

Several heartbeats passed, thumping in Poppy's ears. Had the nymph not heard? Not understood? Poppy continued: "And now I think another book has disappeared. Lady Lark-Hayes's memoir. And I'm afraid it has something to do with the wish, too."

The nymph glared back, studying Poppy for what felt like an eternity. Finally, she cocked her head. "Does your tiny mortal head hold a tiny mortal mind?"

"I... I'm not sure—"

"*Books* was the word you used, impetuous human. *Books.*"

"Yes, but... wait... does that mean... I don't understand."

"Mortal child... Do you know why the Keepers sent me here? To *this*—the Minor World?"

Poppy shook her head.

"Because they knew this was a punishment worse than all others. I *hate* the Minor World." The nymph snapped her tapered tongue. "The tediousness, the flatness, the ignorance. Most of all"—her eyes darkened to the color of steel—"I hate mortals."

Cold fear washed over Poppy. She inched back, fighting the urge to run.

"The men who crushed me beneath their machines, did they hear my cries?" The nymph drew farther out of the water, her voice rising like river rapids. "When they drained my pond, did they think of the slugs and serpents who died in their wake? *No.* You mortals take with grotesque delight. The chain of consequence, you believe, does not tether you. But you see, *sssselfish* child, you are wrong."

"You did this..." Poppy's voice trembled. "On purpose?"

The nymph smiled: a hideous, slimy grin.

"But I thought we were only trading the one book I gave you!"

"I told you, *magic costsss.*"

Poppy fell onto her hands and knees. "Please, you have to undo it."

"Magic is not a pendulum, tiny-faced mortal. It is fire. It devours and blazes forward, never back."

"H-how many? How many more books will disappear?"

"I will take one for every night the winged lion grows."

"*Every night?* Every night you're going to take another book?" Three weeks had passed since Sampson had come into this world. Twenty-one books gone. And this—Poppy realized—was the answer to her question. *Books* were the thing making Sampson grow. He didn't need food, because his power came from the thing that had brought him into existence. Books.

The nymph began to sink, her scaly waist disappearing below the pond's surface. "Goodbye, fledgling mortal. Be content with your wish."

"Wait! Stop! I'm not content! This is horrible! And why do I remember the books when no one else does? There must be something else you can take! Anything!"

The nymph's chest slid beneath the murky surface. Her shoulders. Her neck.

Poppy splashed into the shallows. "Don't leave! Please! Why do I remember? Why, nymph?"

"Cry into the depths, tiny-faced mortal. Cry until blood chafes your throat. I will not come again."

And then she was gone.

Poppy tore off her backpack and splashed shin-deep into the pond. "Nymph!" She grabbed a rock from the sludge and threw it, desperate to draw the creature back. She hurled whatever she could find, shouting, pleading.

But just as promised, the nymph did not come.

Poppy collapsed to the dry ground. It would be torture, never knowing which book the nymph would take next. She wished she could forget the books, too, so at least she wouldn't have to watch, alone, as the world changed with every loss.

She pounded a fist onto the ground.

Her hand landed in a shallow indentation. She pushed upright, suddenly alert.

It was a paw print. Clawed and twice the size of her hand.

She looked around. Her voice came out thin. "Sampson?" What had he been doing over here? Why had he left the safety of the carriage house?

Poppy wriggled out of her wet jacket and tied it around her waist. She scanned the dense forest. "Sampson?"

The underbrush shuddered. Shadows lurched.

Maybe he was lost. Or worse—maybe he'd been found.

Poppy grabbed her backpack and ran. Her sopping pants slowed her, but she didn't stop until she reached the carriage house and slammed the door behind her.

"Sampson!"

He leapt from his bed in the old carriage.

Poppy slammed the door. "You can't do that! You can't leave!" She'd thought he was content inside here, playing with the cat toys and watching the robin hatchlings outside the window.

Sampson cocked his head.

"I saw your tracks out by the nymph's pond. You can't leave unless I'm with you!"

Sampson's ears pressed back, his wings shuddering. He didn't seem to understand why it upset Poppy so much.

Guilt swept over her. She'd been too harsh. She was mad at herself, not Sampson. She'd traded away too much in her deal with the nymph. All those books. All those memories.

Sampson nudged Poppy, urging her to talk. Somehow, he knew this wasn't about him.

But she couldn't bear to tell him what she'd done. Because he loved books more than anything. Poppy couldn't tell him *he'd* cost the world those stories.

She couldn't tell anyone.

She threw her arms around Sampson's neck, buried her face in his mane, and cried.

Chapter Fifteen

On Thursday, Luca texted Poppy that he couldn't give her a ride home from school because he was staying after for a student council meeting. Poppy groaned. She'd have to take the dreaded school bus.

It was empty when Poppy got on, which was concerning. She had no idea which seats were unofficially reserved by the cool kids.

The bus driver looked up. Mr. McKee was probably about ninety years old. His hands looked like gnarled tree roots gripping the wheel.

"Go on," he said.

Poppy grimaced. "Do you know if the cool kids sit near the front or the back?"

"Never seen any cool kids on this bus until now."

Poppy laughed, then noticed she was clogging the aisle for

other kids trying to get on. She slid onto a bench in the middle, which felt like a safe choice. She pulled out her fuzzy pink quote notebook, pretending to read it, but watched out of the corner of her eye just in case anyone gave her the stink eye for taking their seat. To her relief, no one did.

Just as the bus rumbled to life, a familiar voice yelled, "Fly, Dumbo, fly!"

Holden Cline. Poppy's least favorite kid from English class.

He boarded behind Annabelle. He grabbed her wrists, raised her arms, and flapped them like a bird. Poppy's heart stopped, waiting for the moment Annabelle pushed him away and a fight broke out. But it never came. Annabelle just let him do it all the way down the aisle, her cheeks flushed and eyes on the ground.

"Nice work, Dumbo. We barely made it," Holden said, then sat with a kid a few rows up.

Annabelle plunked down in front of Poppy. "Hey." She dug through her backpack and drew out a tangerine.

Poppy leaned forward. "What was that about?"

Annabelle stayed focused on her tangerine, ripping away the peel. She shrugged.

"Is it like an inside joke? Why's he call you Dumbo?"

"My ears stick out or whatever."

Poppy scowled at Holden, who was roughhousing with his buddy, banging up against the seat in front of them. "You shouldn't let him."

Annabelle tore off another bit of peel. "I gave up a long time ago." She looked up, her eyes brightening. "How about you tell him? You could be like, *Hey! That's not nice!*"

"Me?" Poppy scoffed. "He's not going to listen to me. Have you tried telling a teacher?"

Annabelle shrugged.

Poppy wondered what *she'd* do in Annabelle's place. She knew what Luca would suggest and heard it coming from her own mouth. "How about next time, turn around and punch him in the gut."

Annabelle snorted a laugh.

Holden's voice ripped across the bus. "Punch *who* in the gut?" His eyes were laser-focused on Poppy. "What's she saying, Annabelle?"

Poppy shrank back.

She expected Annabelle to do the same. But her friend suddenly sat up straighter. "She thinks I should punch *you* if you don't stop grabbing me."

Poppy's eyes flew wide, her courage whisked out the bus window. She had *not* meant to get involved like this.

Conversations fizzled out around them. Holden scoffed. "Come on. You know I'm just messing around."

"Well, it's not funny."

"Seriously? Some loser new-girl whispers in your ear and you get all touchy?" His gaze cut to Poppy. "Why are you even talking?"

Poppy had never seen this side of Holden. Then again, she'd never been around him when he wasn't near a teacher, and the bus driver, Mr. McKee, had notoriously bad hearing. Apparently, here Holden felt safe to be as mean as he wanted.

Poppy glared back, using her *very expressive face* in place of a response.

"That's what I thought," Holden said, like her silence meant something.

Maybe it did.

Maybe she should have said, *Why am I talking? Because it's a free country.*

Or *I'm talking because I have a brain. Unlike you.*

Or *Why, is it weird for you to hear someone's voice other than your own?*

That last one was a doozy, and she kicked herself for not thinking of it sooner.

The bus rolled to a stop in front of a single-story house. The folding door snapped open. Holden stood.

Last chance to say something.

Poppy was *just* (maybe) about to shout that Holden was a bully, and if he ever touched Annabelle again, she'd let him know exactly what she thought, when he looked back and nudged his buddy.

"Look at that Penny girl," he said, just loud enough for her to hear. "She looks like she's about to cry."

"I was *not* about to cry." Poppy paced the floor of the carriage house. "But when someone says that, all of a sudden it *does* make you want to cry. It's literally a fact."

Sampson was sitting in the abandoned carriage, listening intently as Poppy paced.

"Annabelle said he's been teasing her since the second grade. And he called me *Penny*. What's that about? Was that on purpose? Or am I really that forgettable?"

Sampson gave her a stern look. He thumped his tail.

"Yeah, well. Maybe not to you. But to everyone else at school, I am." Poppy kicked a rusty screw across the floor. "That's why I need you. Once you're grown, you're going to show everyone."

Sampson bounded to the top of the abandoned carriage. He threw open his wings, leapt—

Then dropped straight to the floor, just like he did every time. He gave a low growl and shimmied his wings, frustrated.

"You'll figure it out," Poppy said, though even *she* was feeling less confident about that lately. "I just wish there was a way to teach Holden a lesson in the meantime."

This, apparently, sparked something inside Sampson. His eyes narrowed; his ears perked upright.

Then he threw open his jaws.

He didn't roar, didn't make a sound. But with saliva stringing his fangs and jaws wide enough to swallow Poppy's head, he would scare any normal person out of their wits.

And it gave Poppy the most brilliant idea.

They waited until dusk, when the sky faded to purple—light enough to see, but dark enough to provide cover. As an extra precaution, Poppy pulled a poncho over Sampson. If anyone spotted them from afar, they'd probably think Sampson was her big, lumbering dog.

They followed the main road but stayed in the trees, trudging through the moss and soggy pine needles. Sampson stalked in long, low strides beside her.

"Less prowling," Poppy whispered. "More trotting. Like a dog."

Sampson, who'd never seen a dog, began moving in a slinking, kicking motion, like a cat with shoes on.

"That's worse. Go back to prowling."

A few cars passed. Each time, Poppy held her breath as the headlights swept over them. But no one slowed, and they made it through Hesper Park, another half mile down the road, to Holden's redbrick house.

The house was ablaze with light.

"I bet his room is around back," Poppy whispered. They

crept through the woods. A chest-high tangle of shrubs separated the yard and forest. "You know the plan. Find Holden's room. I'll tap the window, then *wham!* You scare the guts out of him. And before he can make sense of it, we run awa—"

Sampson snagged the back of Poppy's shirt in his teeth, jerking her to a stop.

There was movement in the backyard.

Holden was kicking around a soccer ball, illuminated by a big floodlight. He took three running steps and punted it. It went soaring over the goal and crashed through the trees, bouncing to a stop in front of Sampson.

"The crowd goes wild!" Holden shouted. He ran a victory lap around the yard, despite the fact that he'd missed horribly.

Regret surged through Poppy. This was a *terrible* idea. Holden was the biggest bigmouth in sixth grade. If he caught Sampson, he'd tell everyone Poppy was hiding a winged lion. Sampson would get taken away.

Poppy tugged his tail. "Bad idea," she whispered. "Let's go."

Sampson, however, was not ready to give up. He shook his head vigorously, mane flopping.

"I mean it! Let's go."

Sampson looked down at the soccer ball, clearly struck with a terrible idea.

Poppy's gaze widened. "Don't . . . you . . ."

He looked her straight in the eyes and knocked the ball back out of the woods. It flew through the trees and rolled to the center of the yard. Holden jogged to a stop, his brow furrowing. His gaze lifted to exactly where Poppy and Sampson were hiding.

Poppy became nothing but a thumping heartbeat.

She pinned Sampson in place with a furious *I can't believe you did that* look. But she was sure that if lions could laugh, Sampson would be hysterical.

Holden scooped up his ball. "Is someone there?"

Poppy hooked her arm around Sampson's neck and tried to drag him away, but he was planted firmly in place.

Holden took another step forward. "Hello?"

Sampson used his giant head to nudge Poppy toward Holden. She arched and squirmed, her stiff footsteps crunching through the underbrush. She swiveled around, gesturing for him to cut it out, but he gave her another quick push.

Their scuffling drew Holden closer. "Who's there? You better come out or I'm getting my dad. He's a cop, you know."

Poppy flexed her palms at Sampson. *What are you doing!* she mouthed.

Sampson nudged her again.

"All right, you had your chance!" Holden turned toward his house.

Poppy looked back and forth between Sampson and Holden. She couldn't get this stubborn lion to leave. But she had to keep Holden from getting his cop-dad.

What to do?

What to do?

"Holden Cline, stop right there!" she bellowed. She wasn't sure where it came from, but it did the trick. Holden froze. Sampson looked triumphant.

Holden squinted. "Who—? Who's there? What do you want?"

Sampson flipped his head, demanding that Poppy speak up again. She grimaced.

"I have come . . . to deliver a message," she said in a low voice. Sampson beat his wings once, sending a gust of wind through the surrounding brush. The leaves shuddered; the branches groaned. Poppy didn't think she imagined Holden's face go a little pale.

She mouthed to Sampson, *Nice touch.*

Sampson practically glowed back, delighted with himself.

Holden drew a shaky inhale. "Derek? Riley? Come on, you guys aren't funny." He started forward.

Poppy called, "Don't take another step!"

Holden stopped at the edge of the forest. Skeptical, but obedient.

Poppy continued, "I've come to tell you that if you continue your unkindness . . . you will be punished!"

Sampson flapped again, sending another rush through the forest.

Holden shifted his soccer ball to the other hip. "How are you doing that? What is this? Some kind of prank?"

"This is no prank!" Poppy called. "And I think I am being very clear when I say that I will teach you a lesson if you do not start being nice!"

"All right." Holden dropped his soccer ball. "Here's what

I think." He punted the ball straight through the trees toward Poppy's head.

Sampson threw open his wing and stopped the ball cold. He smashed the ball with his front paw, puncturing five huge holes, then used his hind leg to kick it back.

The ball hissed through the air, flopping down at Holden's feet.

"What the ..." Holden's eyes lifted. Furious. A little terrified. "You stabbed my ball? I'm getting my dad."

Before Holden could turn, Sampson leapt to the edge of the forest, reared onto his hind legs, and threw open his wings. The floodlight cast him in sharp shadow that made him look three times bigger than he was—massive wings and glinting fangs and glowing eyes.

Holden stumbled back and fell, sprawled out on the grass. He tried to scream, but Sampson beat the air with his wings, spraying him with dirt and pine needles.

"Be nice, Holden Cline!" Poppy called. "Be nice or pay the price!"

Holden scrambled to his feet, a scream ripping from him. "Mom!" He tripped over his soccer ball and careened the rest of the way toward his house. "Mom!"

Sampson and Poppy ran faster than she'd ever run in her life, the half mile down the road, past Hesper Park, through the Lark-Hayes Manor gates, and into the carriage house.

They collapsed into a laughing heap on the floor. Poppy clutched her stomach, feeling like her lungs would burst, tears streaming down her face. They were a tangle of limbs and fur and laughter for so long, when Poppy finally caught her breath, the moon had taken its place in the sky.

She stood, still bubbling with laughter, and flipped on the battery-powered lantern she kept for dreary, dark afternoons.

During their escape, Sampson's poncho had gotten snagged and split right down the back. Poppy began to peel off the torn plastic, then realized that a snag wasn't to blame.

He'd grown again.

He was the size of a wolf now. His wings had shed the last of the fuzzy gray feathers in favor of stiff white plumes. His mane was longer and shinier.

Poppy grinned. "Well, look at you."

She pulled her cell phone out and snapped a photo. She didn't dare take his picture very often, because if her parents found the photos, it would be the worst possible way to have them discover Sampson. But a few random pics could be explained easily enough.

Her smile suddenly fell as she was struck with a thought. Sampson had grown again. Did it mean the nymph had taken another book? Had the world lost another story?

She didn't have time to dwell on it. When she closed her camera, her screen lit up with alerts. Eight missed calls. All from her parents.

A text came through from Mom:

Where are you? You didn't ask permission. Come home NOW.

CHAPTER SIXTEEN

Poppy drove her dirt bike like a madwoman, parked it in the shed, and crept toward the garage. Her parents' anxious voices drifted through the open window.

"That's the tenth call that's gone to voice mail," Dad said.

"Hold on," Mom said. "Before we involve the police, let's call the library again."

The police?

Poppy ran, bursting through the garage door. "I'm home!"

"Penelope!" Mom spun, a splatter of red sauce flying off her wooden spoon.

Dad hung up his call and rushed forward, pulling her into a hug. "You're okay!"

"Of course I'm okay!" Poppy forced a laugh, trying to sound perky and oblivious. Something garlicky was baking in the oven, and a pot of Grandma's red sauce simmered on the stove. Poppy was suddenly starving. She slipped a spoon from the drawer.

Mom caught her hand. "Where have you been?"

"I was..." She thought of Holden squealing *Mom! Mom!* as he stumbled toward his house. She swallowed a bubble of laughter. "...taking care of a problem."

Mom didn't take her eyes off Poppy. She was a hawk when she sensed mischief.

Dad said, "What problem?"

Poppy's courage dwindled under Mom's gaze. "Um...a project with this kid from school. He lives just past Hesper Park."

Dad gasped. "You can't take the dirt bike off Lark-Hayes property, Penelope! We talked about that!"

They'd noticed the dirt bike was missing. Poppy was lucky they hadn't gone searching and found it parked behind the carriage house. "Oh, right. I forgot."

"You forgot?" Dad raked a hand through his hair. "Geez, Poppy. One more incident like that and it's going away."

"One more incident, and that's not the only thing going away," Mom muttered.

She was talking about sending Poppy to Aunt Deedee's. She thought Poppy didn't know about the evil plan to send off her own daughter if she wasn't perfect and easy and invisible. Poppy scowled, nearly about to say something when the smoke alarm shrieked.

All three of them jumped.

Mom yanked open the oven, and curls of black smoke poured out. She dumped the charred garlic toast in the sink and flipped on the faucet. Water hissed as it hit the pan.

Dad used the broom handle to quiet the alarm as Mom leaned over the sink, cradling her head in her hands.

Dad drew an arm around her. "You okay?"

"As Golden as the Gate Bridge," Mom said. She obviously didn't mean it. It was just a line from Grandma's journal.

Dad said over his shoulder, "Poppy, go to your room."

But Poppy didn't move. Her mind was working at something.

The running water.

The hissing pan.

The stink of smoke. And cinnamon. And rotting fish.

She remembered the trail of water leading from the sink to the coffee table when Lady Lark-Hayes's memoir had gone missing.

The realization walloped her over the head.

The nymph had come here—had actually come *into* the house to take the book. A creature with fangs and bulbous eyes had slid through the pipes of Poppy's home, clawed her way across the carpet.

Poppy did go to her room eventually.

But that night, she didn't sleep.

"You feeling all right, Ms. Woodlock?" Mr. Thomas was cross-legged on his desk, spinning a pen that looked like a mini lava lamp. Poppy had just been to the bathroom and seen for herself why Mr. Thomas was asking—her skin was sallow, her eyes ringed with dark circles. "Didn't get much sleep last night?"

"I . . . had a headache."

"Feeling better?"

Poppy did not, in fact, feel better. She felt completely tortured—sitting in school all day while an evil magic nymph invaded her home.

The lava-lamp pen tapped her desk. "Poppy, you good?" Mr. Thomas's face was creased with concern. Behind him, the papier-mâché Scylla head stuck out the front of his desk.

Poppy couldn't believe she'd taken this long to realize—if anyone knew about mythical creatures, it was Mr. T.

"I have a weird question," she said, perking up.

"Excellent. I hate normal ones." The bell rang and Mr. Thomas held up his fingers, starting his five-second countdown to get the class settled. "See me after."

Poppy spent the entire class planning how she would bring up a book-stealing water nymph, but when the bell rang, she approached Mr. T's desk with none of the casual calm she'd intended. She tripped over Annabelle's backpack and careened forward like a bowling ball, making full-body contact with Holden.

"Geez! Next time just ask for the hug, Penny," Holden said. Sai laughed.

"It's Poppy," she said, but they were already out of earshot.

It seemed like Holden hadn't changed at all since Poppy and Sampson had confronted him. Maybe he'd convinced himself it really had been a prank. Or maybe, like the nymph, he was mean at his core and couldn't help it.

Mr. Thomas reclined in his chair. "How's the *Odyssey* assignment coming along?"

"Great. Perfect," Poppy said, hoping he couldn't tell she hadn't started.

The last of the students shuffled out as Mr. Thomas eyed her. "You know, you kids are lucky to be studying mythology in sixth grade. I didn't learn about it until high school."

"What's so lucky about that?" she asked.

"Well. These stories were how the Greeks made sense of the world. And when I read them, it was like the world made a little more sense to me."

Poppy felt like Mr. T was talking in code. Usually, she'd just smile and nod. But all the shoving it down and hiding was exhausting lately. "I don't get it."

"All right, let me give you an example. In our book *The Odyssey*...Odysseus is the hero, but he makes a lot of mistakes. *A lot* of mistakes. Even the ending isn't wrapped up in a perfect bow. So it gave me...a sort of permission. To see myself as a hero, despite my flaws." Mr. T shrugged. "And sometimes even because of them."

Poppy thought of her own massive failure: getting tricked

by the nymph and trading away the best books of all time. She hitched up her backpack. "Hey, so...going along with this mythology stuff...Do you know anything about water nymphs?"

"Water nymphs?" Mr. Thomas scanned the low shelves behind his desk. He drew out a huge book, flipped it open, then slid it across the desk. The title read: *Mythological Creatures of Greek and Mesopotamian Lore*. Below that it said, *Naiads, Nereids, and Oceanids*, followed by a drawing of a beautiful girl standing in a fountain.

Poppy shook her head. "The name is right, but that creature is too pretty. I'm talking about something terrifying. Eyes like glowing white marbles, sharp teeth and claws." Remembering the nymph's words, she added, "I think they come from the Old World?"

"Ah, okay. Well, what do you need to know?"

"Everything. What's their weakness? What are they afraid of? How can they be beaten?" These were the strangest questions Poppy had ever asked, but the thing about Mr. Thomas was he never made anyone feel silly.

"What's this for?"

"A...book...I'm writing?" It came out sounding like a question.

His brows lifted. "I like it. Let's talk it through." He began winding his pen through his fingers. "The nymphs I'm familiar with were playful and nurturing. People often prayed to them for fresh water. But this one you're describing, which you say comes from..."

"The Old World."

"This nymph sounds like she's been provoked. When they're wronged, nymphs can be extremely vengeful."

"Exactly. She was banished. And she hates mortals and wants to punish them for"—Poppy tried to remember the exact words—"for... hurting nature. And now, she's invading someone's house and taking things that don't belong to her!"

"Sounds like a part of *The Odyssey*."

"Odysseus had to deal with a monster like that?"

"Not him. But his wife. While Odysseus was away, suitors invaded her house, demanding she marry one of them. These guys were soldiers and murderers. Tough. Mean. But Odysseus's wife was clever. She promised she'd choose a suitor as soon as she finished weaving her father-in-law's burial shroud. But every night, by the light of the moon, she'd unravel the weaving she'd done that day."

"So... she never finished?"

"Nope. She outsmarted everyone. And you know what her name was?"

"What?"

Mr. Thomas leaned forward, as if he were about to divulge some great secret. "Penelope."

Poppy grinned. It felt meaningful for some reason. "All right, so I need to beat the nymph at her own game. Trick her back."

Mr. Thomas stabbed his lava-lamp pen toward her. "Exactly."

CHAPTER SEVENTEEN

That night, Poppy sat on the floor of her bedroom, thinking about Mr. Thomas's advice. Just like Penelope from *The Odyssey*, Poppy had woven this mess with the nymph. Now she had to unweave it.

But how?

She'd taken Mr. Thomas's mythological creatures book and studied it all evening. And even though the illustrator had clearly never seen a real nymph, the information made sense.

Naiads were nymphs who traveled through fresh water. Streams, rivers, rain runoff. Anywhere water went, the nymph could go. The nymph had even used the pipes to come into the house to steal Lady Lark-Hayes's memoir. Was there anywhere the books would be safe?

I cannot sssimply leave, tiny-faced mortal.

The memory surfaced. Poppy fought to remember the rest.

I am in exile. Bound within the gates of this mortal estate.

Poppy's eyes widened.

The nymph was stuck here. She couldn't leave Lark–Hayes Manor property.

But maybe . . . maybe the books *could*.

What if Poppy took the books beyond the manor gates— out of the nymph's reach? She'd use suitcases from the garage. The wagon from Dad's shed. For tonight, she'd stash the books under the picnic tables at Hesper Park. She'd find a better place in the morning. The library. Or some unused closet at school. Then, when the nymph returned to her own world, Poppy would bring the books back where they belonged.

As soon as her parents went to bed, Poppy lugged two rolling suitcases in from the garage. She began in Mom's office, packing the most important books first. Grandma's journal. Mom's beloved design books. Dad's architecture texts. A stack of fat novels that seemed weathered and well-loved.

By the time Poppy got to her shelves, there was only room for a dozen more books. She packed her favorites, filling every inch of space, and decided to come back for the rest later. On her way out, something on her nightstand caught her eye.

The Tree in Valley Blue.

She'd nearly forgotten it. She traced her fingers over the cover. The other day, reading with Sampson, she'd never gotten to her and Dad's favorite part. She thumbed through the pages to find it:

Little Tree reached farther
into the brisk, bright sky;
rooted deeper,
into the cold, cracked earth;
and for the first time,
she was glad
she did not follow the rhythm of the seasons.

Suddenly,
she felt a swell of color,
a weight in her branches,
> *and she*
>> *bloomed.*

That part. That was their favorite. And Dad had always pecked a little kiss on Poppy's head before turning to the next page.

Poppy tucked *The Tree in Valley Blue* into the suitcase, zipped it shut, and whispered, "Please let this work."

The suitcases were so heavy she could barely roll them to the porch. She closed the front door quietly and wiped the sweat from her forehead.

The gravel drive stretched longer than she'd remembered. The pines loomed taller, a sickly yellow moon hanging above them.

Poppy flexed her hands.

She just had to get beyond the property line—through the wrought iron gate a quarter mile away. Then the books would be safe.

She retrieved the wagon from Dad's shed, heaved the suitcases inside, and secured them with a rope. But when she tried to pull, the gravel drive sucked at the wheels like quicksand.

Sweat rolled down the small of Poppy's back. She wasn't strong enough.

The yellow moon rose higher.

She could tow the wagon with the dirt bike. But the buzz of the engine might wake her parents. She could beg for Luca's help. But he was the one who told Poppy to *shove it down*. Then she remembered. She had another friend—stronger than any human.

Sampson must have heard her coming because he was waiting at the carriage house door, his yellow eyes bright with curiosity. She'd never visited in the night before.

"I . . . need . . . your . . . help," Poppy panted. "It's the nymph."

Sampson's eyes darted to the darkness beyond.

"Please. She's after my books."

That was all Sampson needed to hear. He nudged Poppy out, as if to say, *Lead the way*.

Sampson stayed close, ears pressed flat to his head, scanning the forest. The crescent moon provided barely any light, and Poppy tried not to think about what he sensed out there.

They ducked beneath her parents' bedroom window and made it to the driveway.

Poppy looped the wagon rope around Sampson's neck as he eyed the suitcases.

She backed a few paces down the drive. "Come on," she whispered. "Come to me."

He started forward, the rope digging into his chest. His paws skidded over the gravel, trying to find traction.

"You can do it."

He crouched, lowering his center of gravity, then stretched out his front paw. The gravel shifted under him. He slipped and smacked his chin on the ground. Poppy gasped and started toward him, but he scrambled back up.

This time, he opened his wings. He flapped them, giving him just the momentum he needed. The wheels dragged through the gravel.

"Good, Sammy!" Poppy said, hushed. "That's it!"

The noise of the grating wheels seemed deafening, but Poppy was confident no one would hear. Mom slept with a sound machine and Dad took a sleeping pill every night.

Sampson flapped harder, picking up speed. Poppy jogged backward, coaxing him.

Halfway down the curving drive, the cottage disappeared. The night grew darker. On either side, the towering pines loomed closer, shrouding the moon. Poppy kept her focus on the books, minutes from safety.

Behind her, the gate came into view.

"Come on, Sammy! We're almost—"

Her foot sloshed into a puddle of icy water.

She stilled. Had it rained today?

Her eyes followed the water: a thin stream, trickling from the tree line. A flooded pond? Burst pipe? But there was something strange about the stream.

Poppy's blood went cold.

The water was traveling uphill.

Chapter Eighteen

Poppy's breath was suddenly visible in the midnight air. "She's here."

Sampson's paws scrabbled at the gravel. Poppy grabbed the rope and heaved. The wagon moved faster with their combined effort. But the puddle followed them, slowing the wheels.

Poppy pulled harder. "Come on!"

They were almost there. Twenty steps from the safety of the gate.

Fifteen steps.

The puddle rose to their ankles. They splashed through the water.

Ten steps.

Suddenly, the water surged in front, blocking their path.

"Tiny-faced mortal." The voice came from all around, like the gathering dew on leaves.

Poppy froze.

Sampson crouched and released a low whine.

The nymph hoisted herself from the puddle. "*Inssssolence*," she hissed. Her eyes glowed brighter than the moon. "You would steal what is mine?"

Poppy's knees threatened to buckle. She steadied herself on Sampson, who was crouched, defensive and alert.

"These aren't yours," Poppy said, her voice barely a whisper.

"We *ssssettled* this." The nymph's milky eyes darted to Sampson, her expression tightening. "So long as the winged lion grows, you owe me the promised thing."

"But the books you've been taking are important to my family! They're special!"

The nymph inched forward, the puddle gliding with her. "You mean taking *these* records punishes the mortals who destroyed my pond?" She flashed her teeth. "How *sssatisfying*." She lunged toward the wagon, water rushing with her like a wave.

Sampson sprang to meet her. The nymph lurched back, water sloshing around her. He raised his brilliant white wings. He'd never flown before, but in that moment, he looked capable of anything.

"Keep her there, Sampson!" Poppy tore the ropes from the wagon, unzipped the first suitcase, and filled her arms with as many books as she could.

"Bend to the magic of your true world!" the nymph shrieked at Sampson.

Sampson stood his ground, slowly circling the nymph.

Poppy dashed behind him, toward the property line. She stumbled and nearly dropped the books, then threw them beyond the gate and raced back for more. *The Tree in Valley Blue* hung from the suitcase. She scooped it up.

Suddenly, the nymph laughed, that sound like shattering ice.

Poppy whirled around.

Sampson teetered, fighting for balance. He buckled and collapsed.

"Sampson!" Poppy dropped the books and ran, pulling his lolling head into her lap. His golden fur had dulled. His wings splayed over the ground. "What have you done!" Poppy cried.

The nymph sneered. "Not I. But *you*."

"No! I didn't...I...How?" Poppy demanded, desperate to understand.

The nymph lifted a clawed finger, pointing to the books beyond the gate. "Our deal is bound by the magic of the Old World. It cannot be tricked. It cannot be cheated."

All at once, Poppy understood. If she broke her end of the deal, the nymph's end would be broken, too.

Sampson would stop existing.

Poppy jostled Sampson, trying to rouse him. "I won't take any more. Just please, don't let him die. Sampson! Wake up! Wake up!"

"Return the books, tiny-faced mortal."

She had no choice. She laid Sampson's head on the ground

and scrambled to gather the books. She carried them back through the gate, sobbing with relief as Sampson's wings shuddered. He blinked his eyes open, as though waking from a deep sleep.

The nymph glided toward Poppy. "Now," she said, her rotting-fish breath blowing cold over Poppy's face. "Tonight's sacrifice has yet to be taken. Which of these books wields the most power?" The scales on her cheeks reflected the light from her glowing eyes. "This one? Perhaps this?" Her claws skimmed across a green linen spine. Poppy flinched. "Ah. *Thisss.*"

Grandma's journal.

Tears pricked Poppy's eyes. "No...please..."

"Sssilence."

Poppy obeyed.

The nymph clutched the journal, her yellow claws dimpling the linen. "A book for every rising moon, tiny-faced mortal. And for this defiance, I will seek out the ones most precious. I will take those first."

Behind the nymph, Sampson had found his footing. He threw open his wings and sprang toward the creature, but his paws barely left the ground. He rolled, skidding across the gravel.

Amusement smeared across the nymph's scaly face. "Can this be? A winged lion without the power of flight?" Sampson folded his useless wings around himself, turning his face away. The nymph hummed a cruel laugh. "You are a disgrace to the

Old World." She swept her arm through the air, sending a wave of icy water over Sampson.

"Stop!" Poppy cried.

But when the water settled, the nymph was gone.

Sampson was shivering and weak, but with Poppy's help, he managed to make it back to the carriage house. He collapsed to the floor.

Poppy pulled the blanket from his bed and wrapped it around him.

After a few minutes, he settled into a shallow sleep and Poppy's worries extended beyond him. She thought of Mom and Dad waking up to find her bed empty. The books she'd left stranded on the driveway.

Grandma's journal, clutched in the nymph's evil claws.

Would Mom forget those stories? Those recipes? Would she forget Grandma entirely? Around and around, the worries churned.

Eventually, the rise and fall of Sampson's breathing must have lulled her to sleep, because she awoke to the gentle motion of Sampson licking his paws. She pushed upright.

Morning light filtered through the windows, and she could see that the glow had returned to Sampson's eyes and fur. Relief flooded her.

"You're okay?" she asked.

He thumped his tail twice. *Yes.*

"You're sure?"

Thump, thump. Yes.

"Are you weak? Stand up and...do something."

Sampson rolled his eyes.

"Come on, Sampson, I'm worr—"

He threw open his wings, knocking her over.

"Okay, that works," she said, laughing. She checked her phone.

Six a.m.

An hour before her parents' alarm went off.

She had to get those abandoned books off the driveway.

She kissed Sampson's head and promised to be back soon, then raced back to the gravel drive.

In the light of dawn, the forest lost its menace. Pale sunshine streaked through the trees. Woodpeckers drummed, warblers sang, the scent of sharp pine rode the breeze. Poppy felt her pulse fall into rhythm with the shushing leaves.

This place wasn't Old World magic, but it was *magic.*

Poppy knelt beside the suitcases. *The Tree in Valley Blue* had fallen out, and she took a moment to smooth the pages. The nymph's hissing warning came again—

I will seek out the ones most precious. I will take those first.

Poppy shook her head, clearing it. The nymph couldn't possibly know which books were most precious. She hadn't even known *any* of them were important before Poppy had told her.

At least, that was what Poppy told herself.

After four trips to and from the house—a full hour—she managed to get all the books back inside. She collapsed into bed just as Mom came shuffling out of her room.

When Mom saw the books piled into a heap in the foyer, she grounded Poppy, thinking it was some silly act of rebellion. And honestly? It was safer to let Mom believe it.

CHAPTER NINETEEN

On the third and final night of her grounding, Poppy was lying on the living room floor doing homework while Luca watched TV. She missed Sampson. She'd dropped by the carriage house every day—just to check on him—and he'd always begged her to stay, giving her the most heartbreaking pussycat eyes. But she couldn't. If her parents found out she'd broken her grounding, she'd only make it worse.

On the couch above her, Luca flipped through channels on the TV. They were probably the last family on earth without streaming services, but that was just Mom's way: everything old-school all the time.

"Nope. Nope." Luca paused on an old-timey Western. "Might come back to it." He resumed flipping.

The screen flashed with warm light and thrumming insects.

Poppy's attention snapped up just as Luca changed the channel. "Wait! Go back."

"Nah."

"Luca. I said go back," she said firmly.

He looked surprised. "Geez, okay, boss." He cut to the previous channel. "This?"

Poppy scrambled to her knees. "Yes. Stay here."

A lioness stalked across the African plains, her silhouette cast in golden light by the setting sun. A British man narrated: *"But without a kill, Sheera and her cubs won't survive much longer. Already, her energy is dwindling."*

Luca scoffed. "Come on. I don't want to watch this."

"Shh!" Poppy snapped.

"Then, a stroke of luck. An unsuspecting antelope grazing near an acacia tree..."

"Fine." Luca tossed Poppy the remote and headed for his room. "I'm going to hack the time controls on my computer. Keep the tyrants distracted if they come out of Mom's office."

"...and the chase begins."

Poppy gripped the remote in both hands, giving a yelp of relief when the lioness took down the antelope.

"Thanks to Sheera's determination, the Kovu pride will survive another day."

The lions on TV looked so *different* from Sampson—their manes matted and faces scarred. Their coats were tan and brown, not the golden-white shine of Sampson's fur. And of course, these lions had no glorious wings tucked at their sides.

But there *was* something familiar in the way they moved. And when Sheera returned to her cubs, they bounded up to her with the same look Sampson had every time Poppy came through the door.

The narrator continued: *"Bellies full, Sheera and her cubs settle down for a late-afternoon nap. It's Kovu's turn to protect the pride."*

A huge male stalked through the long grass. He opened his jaws and let out a roar so loud a cloud of birds shot out of a nearby tree.

"A lion's roar can be as loud as one hundred and fourteen decibels. That's twenty-five times louder than your household lawn mower."

"Hey!" Mom came out of her office and grabbed the remote. "No screens while you're grounded." She flipped off the TV, then disappeared back into her den.

Poppy sat there, staring at the blank screen, her mind reeling. *Lions roar.*

It wasn't like she hadn't known that. But she'd assumed Sampson would learn it in time, when the moment called for it. But the thing was . . . the moment *had* called for it. Like when he'd faced down Holden. Or protected Poppy from the nymph.

And both times, he'd reared up, opened his huge jaws . . . and hadn't made a peep.

Poppy lay in bed, listening to fat raindrops beat her window. Her family had long since gone to sleep, but she couldn't settle her mind.

Why hadn't Sampson ever roared?

It was unnatural. Tragic.

Or maybe his silence was for the best. If Sampson was out there roaring in the carriage house, Mom and Dad would discover him faster than Poppy could say *soggy quiche*. This way, he'd never call attention to himself. He'd never cause trouble.

But that didn't sit right with Poppy. Lions were *meant* to roar. And she refused to believe Sampson wasn't capable.

Distant thunder rolled, like the sky releasing a low growl.

Poppy sat up.

If Sampson was going to learn to roar, *this* was the perfect night.

Poppy snuck into Mom's office to borrow her parents' iPad, pulled a raincoat over her pajamas, and slipped out the back door. When she got to the carriage house, she slogged inside.

But Sampson didn't bound over like he usually did.

"Sammy?"

A flash of lightning illuminated the room. Unfamiliar shadows flared to life.

Poppy took a squelching step forward, fear prickling her skin. "Sampson?"

No answer.

She pulled her flashlight out and clicked it on. Golden eyes glinted beneath the old carriage.

"Sampson!" Poppy ran forward. "You scared me!"

Thunder cracked through the sky, rattling the diamond-paned windows. Sampson cowered farther into the recess, then pawed at Poppy, prodding her to come hide with him.

Poppy laughed and set her flashlight upright, spreading a hazy glow over the room. "The storm is nothing to be scared of."

Thunder cracked. Sampson retreated farther.

"Hey! This is just something you have to get used to here in Oregon. And you'll never learn to fly if you're scared of the sky."

Sampson cocked his head, as if really thinking that over.

You'll never learn to fly if you're scared of the sky.

Where had that come from? It wasn't a line from any book Poppy had read.

She gave a short laugh. "I sound like one of those motivational speakers at school assemblies." She pointed to an invisible crowd. "And remember, kids, you'll never learn to fly if you're scared of the sky." She shook her head. "Cheesy."

Sampson crept out from beneath the carriage. He stuck his whole face into Poppy's backpack, emerged with her fuzzy pink notebook, and dropped it at her feet.

Poppy scoffed. "Come on."

Sampson nudged the notebook toward her.

"No way, I only put quotes from books in there. Stuff from real writers."

Sampson sat right in front of Poppy. His gaze burned into hers.

Stubborn cat.

"All right, all right." Poppy flipped to an open page in her notebook and clicked her pen. She hesitated. What was she so nervous about? Not like anyone was ever going to read it. She wrote:

You'll never learn to fly if you're scared of the sky.
—P. Q. Woodlock

To her surprise, even on the page with all those other great writers, her own words didn't seem half bad.

She tucked her notebook away. "Okay, here's why I came. I've never heard you roar."

Sampson squinted.

"You know. Like a really loud noise when you're mad or whatever."

Sampson thumped his tail three times. *I don't understand.*

"Look." Poppy drew Mom's iPad from her bag and pulled up the video of lions she'd downloaded back at the cottage.

Sampson's ears perked straight up. He went completely still. His wide eyes glowed brighter, and all at once Poppy knew what was happening. He was realizing he wasn't alone.

She felt a pang of guilt. She should have shown him sooner. Could she take him to Africa to visit the other lions? Or the zoo? But those lions didn't have wings; they couldn't understand humans or talk back. Sampson really *was* the only one of his kind.

And he always would be.

The video ended and Sampson pawed the iPad, demanding more. Poppy laughed and played it again. And again and again. Finally, after the ninth replay, Sampson let Poppy tuck the device away. "Ready to try?"

Sampson thumped his tail twice, wings shuddering with excitement.

"All right. Just like the video. One . . . two . . ."

A flash of lightning illuminated the room.

Thunder clapped. Sampson scrambled into Poppy, nearly knocking her over. She pushed him upright. "Don't let it scare you! Roar back!"

Sampson threw his head to the sky.

But no sound escaped.

"Try again!"

Sampson crouched and opened his jaws, right in Poppy's face.

But again, no sound.

Poppy plunked down, wondering what they were doing wrong.

Lightning blazed through the sky, illuminating the room. Sampson's eyes shot upward.

"Come here," Poppy said, patting the floor. He lay down, his body wrapping her like a wreath. She stroked the soft white plumes of his wings. He could do this. He could roar, just like he could fly. She only had to teach him.

But how?

The thunder came, rattling the windows and shaking the floor; but this time, cuddled up close to Poppy, Sampson didn't flinch.

Chapter Twenty

This isn't good, is it?" Mom said, sighing. For the second time this week, they were eating soggy chicken and rice for dinner.

Dad had his architectural plans spread in front of him, drawing and redrawing lines. "Hm?" He took a bite, his eyes still glued to the plans. "It's great."

Luca dropped his fork. "Nah. It's gross."

"Yeah..." Mom rested her chin on her fist, gazing toward the kitchen. She didn't seem to understand what she was missing. But Poppy did. The nymph had taken Grandma's journal. The memories of those recipes were gone.

Poppy almost wished she could forget it, too—that delicious smell of garlic and onions and tomatoes. They'd always lived in rental houses, moving every few years. But *that* smell was home. Mom could cook it in her sleep. She definitely hadn't needed to pull out Grandma's journal every time, where the recipe was buried in the diary entries. But she always had, then sat on the counter while the sauce simmered, reading Grandma's slanting cursive, smiling at the pages and repeating her favorite lines.

Dad piped up, "Hey, Cordelia . . . come look at this."

Mom stood over him while he traced a finger over his blueprints. "If we demolished this wall, we'd get the light from the south windows. But we'd lose those original electrical fittings, which I know you're excited about."

"Oh. That would be too bad. But whatever you think is best."

The rest of the family looked up at once. Mom was not a *whatever you think is best* kind of person, especially when it came to her renovations.

Dad squinted. "You're sure?"

"I don't feel strongly about it."

"So . . . I'll have my guys start demo tomorrow?"

"Fine."

Poppy watched Mom with narrowed eyes. Mom's lost passion for cooking was understandable. But what was this all about? Was Mom just having a bad day? Poppy sawed off another piece of dry chicken. "Mom? You okay?"

Mom forced a fleeting smile. "I'm fine."

She always used to respond, *I'm as Golden as the Gate Bridge.*

But that, Poppy realized, had been a phrase from Grandma's journal, too.

Friday after school, Poppy was lacing up her boots to see Sampson when Mom burst through the door with a flurry of plastic bags. "Kids! Come see what I've got!"

"What? What is it?" Poppy asked. Mom breezed past, heading for her office.

Luca sauntered out of his bedroom, dressed in high-water slacks and a tangerine polo. He saw Poppy and stopped short. "Have you been reading *Jumanji*?"

"What?" Poppy looked down. Without realizing it, she'd dressed herself like some sort of safari guide. Tan shirt, tan leggings, hiking boots. It wasn't inspired by a book, because for the first time, her real life felt more exciting. She shrugged. "Something like that."

Poppy headed toward the office, relieved that Mom seemed back to her normal self. Mom always scoured antique stores and trade shows for *just* the right décor for her renovations, and it was one of Poppy's favorite things to watch Mom's eyes light up as she showed them off.

But when Poppy stepped into the office, the bookshelves seemed to glare down at her. They were emptier than last week.

Mom shoved Lark-Hayes architectural plans from her desk to clear space, then set down her bags. Sheets of patterned paper slid out.

Luca picked them up. "What are these? Wallpaper samples?"

"Even better." Mom drew a bin from the ground and plunked it on her desk beside the bags. "I've just been feeling a little off lately. Like I'm . . . missing something." Poppy nearly blurted out, *It's Grandma's journal!* but Mom kept talking. "And today, I realized what it is."

"You did?" Poppy asked warily.

Mom peeled the lid from the bin. It was filled with old family photographs. Mom and Dad in a canoe. Dad in a hard hat, flexing his muscles. Pregnant Mom holding up a key in front of a Victorian house.

Poppy picked up the photo. "Was this from your first renovation?"

Mom barely gave it a glance. "Yeah. Luc, look at this." A chubby toddler clung to a merry-go-round pole. "You won a cute baby contest with this pic. We won a year's supply of baby food."

"Baby beauty champ?" Luca fanned himself with the photograph. "Who's surprised?"

"Not me," Poppy said. "You totally have that child-star need for attention."

Luca whacked Poppy with the photo. Mom plucked another one from the bin, this one of Poppy wearing a princess dress and rain boots with a group of toddlers.

"Who are the other kids?" Poppy asked.

"No clue," Mom said. "Everywhere you went, you made new friends. You had this . . . infectious confidence."

Poppy stared at the photo. What had happened to that girl?

"Infectious confidence," Luca said. "Exactly how I would describe Poppy."

It was Poppy's turn to whack Luca, and then they both craned to see the next photo. It was little Luca holding a newborn. "This was the day you got your nickname, Poppy," Mom said. "For the life of him, Luca could not pronounce *Penelope*."

"Never say I gave you nothing, Weasel," Luca said.

"These are cool, Mom," Poppy said. "But I want to see the stuff you bought for the manor."

"What? Oh, these aren't for the manor." Mom began unpacking the bags, and Poppy's confusion deepened. Construction paper. Rubber stamps. Pads of stickers that said things like CUTIE PIE! and MY FIRST BIRTHDAY!

"I'm legitimately scared," Luca said, holding a package of colored scissors with serrated edges.

Mom said, "For the past few weeks, I've been feeling off. I was talking to Deedee and she hit the nail on the head. It's because you two—my babies—are getting older. I started looking at old pictures, and suddenly I realized: *This* is what I should be doing. Organizing these photographs. Connecting with our past."

"Is this what a midlife crisis looks like?" Luca said. "Seems extreme. Maybe you should just buy a convertible like a normal person."

Poppy's guilt got the better of her. "Mom. I have to tell you something. What you're really missing is . . . is Grandma."

"My mom? She died when I was six, Poppy. I know nothing about her."

Mom went back to sorting her craft supplies. Obviously, she'd forgotten the stories from inside the journal...but that didn't explain why she was acting so different.

"But, Mom...you *did* know about Grandma," Poppy pressed. "You knew her red sauce recipe and made it, like, twice a week. You knew all her cheesy catchphrases, like *Golden as the Gate Bridge*. And you knew these stories, like how Grandma used to take you to the swing set behind the grocery store."

Mom squinted, that misty, confused look falling over her again. Like she'd walked into a room and forgotten why she was there.

"Oh!" Poppy said, remembering Mom's favorite story of all. "And the time when you were five, right before Grandma died, you colored all over your favorite dollhouse, and Grandma wrote that someday you were going to..."

Poppy gasped.

"What is it?" Mom asked. "What's wrong?"

The realization walloped Poppy. Why hadn't she connected it sooner? "Grandma wrote that you'd made the old dollhouse look even better with all that crayon and tape....She wrote that you were destined to fix up old houses someday."

Was this the reason Mom had lost interest in the renovation? Had *that* story sparked Mom's passion?

"What on earth? Poppy, where are you getting all these stories?"

"From Grandma's journal."

"She didn't leave a journal. She left nothing. Literally nothing. Which is why I refuse to do the same. I'm going to document every moment from your childhoods." Mom began gathering the supplies with fierce determination. "Starting now."

"But Grandma did leave a journal!"

Mom went still, cradling the acid-free markers. "*Why* are you making this stuff up, Poppy? Are you *trying* to make me sad?"

"No! I just want you to remember! You used to read it, like, every day!"

"Enough!" The markers clattered from Mom's arms, spilling over the floor. "That's enough, Penelope. I don't remember my mom, she didn't leave a journal, and I can't stand you making these things up." Mom crouched to gather the markers.

Poppy opened her mouth to argue, but Luca nudged her. "Let it go."

"But—"

"Seriously, Poppy. Or you know what…" He opened and closed a pair of orange serrated scissors and mouthed the words, *Deedee's craft room.*

CHAPTER TWENTY-ONE

On Saturday, Poppy told Mom she was going to Annabelle's, then packed a lunch and stuffed it into her backpack beside *The Tree in Valley Blue*. She didn't let the book out of her sight, except while she was at school, when she hid it in the vent above her bed.

If the nymph wanted this one, she'd have to pry it from Poppy's cold, dead hands.

At the carriage house, Poppy drew the key from her neck and slipped it into the lock. She heard the scuff of Sampson's claws on the floorboards as he leapt up. Lately, he liked to pose in the corner like a library statue whenever Poppy arrived. She'd pretend not to see him, then shriek when he tackled her to the ground.

A branch cracked behind her.

Poppy froze, scanning the forest. Probably a rabbit or falling pinecone.

But the sound came again— rhythmic and deliberate.

Footsteps, moving through the forest on the other side of the carriage house.

Who would come up here?

Whoever—whatever—it was, Poppy had to shoo them away. But she couldn't be caught this close to the carriage house, either, or Mom would ground her for life. She ducked into the trees, moving quickly. Her foot caught on a root and she stumbled, then froze, breath held.

The trespasser stalled. They'd heard her.

The heavy footfalls began again. But the person was moving toward Poppy now. She crept on all fours—slowly, carefully. The strides of her stalker suddenly quickened, barreling toward her.

She saw a flash of dark through the trees. Poppy broke into a run.

A gunshot rang out; shrieking birds launched from the underbrush.

Poppy fell to the ground, throwing her hands over her head. "Stop! Stop!"

"What the devil?" A man rushed forward, his shadow falling over Poppy.

"Am I shot?" She felt no particular pain, probably because of the adrenaline coursing through her. Her heart was hurtling to make up for the blood loss. She needed a hospital.

She was dying.

"No, you're not shot. That was a warning shot, aimed to the sky. Hold on...." A hand clamped down on Poppy's shoulder and rolled her over. The construction foreman loomed over her. "The Woodlock girl? What are you doing out here? And why are you running around on all fours?"

"Wh—what am *I* doing?" She clambered to her feet. "This is where I live!"

He jabbed his hunting rifle toward the carriage house. "Telling me you live in that building?"

"No. I meant I live *here*. On the property. You know that." She turned the accusatory finger back on him. "What are you doing here on a Saturday? And with a *gun*!"

The foreman's nostrils flared, his jaw tightening. "Look here." He slung his rifle beneath his arm and marched back toward the manor, where the trees gave way to meadow. Poppy followed, guarded but intent on making sure he stayed away from the carriage house.

He jammed a finger downward. "See this?"

Three huge animal tracks were stamped into the mud. Poppy crouched and spread her hand, gauging the size. Immediately, she knew.

Sampson.

Her pulse picked up again. She'd never brought Sampson over here. Which meant he'd been exploring without her. *Again*. "What...what do you think it is?"

"Bear."

"Oh, right, of course," she said, grateful the foreman hadn't said *lion*.

As if he'd heard her thoughts, he added, "But that's no black bear."

She looked up. "What?"

"Long time ago, grizzlies roamed these woods. Most people think they disappeared, run out by hunters. But these tracks tell me different." The foreman's gaze raked the forest beyond.

It was a ridiculous theory. Everyone knew grizzlies didn't come this far south. But the foreman couldn't possibly know these prints belonged to a magic lion.

Poppy brushed the dirt from her knees and stood. "Well, good thing I have my bear spray. And it's their woods, anyway. You can't just hunt here because you see a track."

The foreman looked down at her. "I can't what now?"

Poppy's confidence wavered. But she'd never be able to sleep again if she was worried about this man shooting Sampson dead. "You . . . you heard me. You can't hunt here."

The foreman tromped toward the forest. "Go home."

Poppy called after him, "Maybe I *will* go home! And then tell my dad about you almost killing me! And then I'll tell my mom about you snooping around near the carriage house!"

The foreman stopped. Every muscle in his back tensed. "Pretty sure neither of us was supposed to be up there."

"Yeah, but only one of us can get fired for it."

Poppy didn't know if she'd regret bossing around a grown

man like this. She didn't know if he'd even believe her threats. All she knew was that in this moment, fear for Sampson gave her courage. "Or...," she began slowly. "You can leave. Never bring your guns back. Never go near that carriage house again. And I won't say anything."

A heartbeat passed. Two.

The foreman stared at Poppy, as if wondering how this was the same scared girl from the manor only weeks ago. Finally, he turned. Poppy followed him across the meadow, half expecting more trouble. But he didn't even look back until he'd loaded up his truck and thrown open the door. He paused on the footboard.

"Thanks," Poppy called. For what? She didn't know. But he'd lost, they both knew it, and she didn't want to be a sore winner.

He scoffed, his annoyance cracking just enough to reveal a trace of amusement. Then he slammed the door, cranked his ignition, and disappeared down the gravel drive.

Back in the carriage house, Poppy scolded Sampson.

"Was this what you were doing while I was grounded? Wandering the forest by yourself? You nearly led that guy straight to us!" She checked the windows, rattled the locks on the doors. She threw her hands up. "How are you getting out, anyway?"

Sampson paced, his tail tucked between his legs. He was nearly full grown, all muscle and round edges, his mane a coarse wreath of gold and white. He ruffled his wings and let out a low, frustrated growl.

"I know. I know. But if you do it again, I'm...I'm..." For some reason, the words *I'm going to send you to Aunt Deedee's* nearly came out. Poppy sighed. "I'm just trying to keep you safe."

Sampson slumped down in the corner, his back to Poppy.

He looked too big for this place lately, like a teenager in a toddler bed. But what was she supposed to do? Let him go out and get shot? Or taken away?

"I'm sorry." She wrapped her arms around him. They only circled half his body. "I'm just grumpy because I didn't sleep last night."

He looked back, still mad, but concerned.

Poppy had wanted to pretend everything was fine. But as usual, she couldn't keep anything from Sampson. "The nymph took more books...out of my *room.*"

Last night, she'd reached for a story, then stopped cold.

Some were missing. She knew because she kept them color-coordinated, and suddenly the blues jumped straight to magenta. Then she'd smelled it. Seen it. The faint whiff of magic and fish. The trail of water across the carpet, leading from the hall bathroom.

The nymph had been there.

Poppy had stayed awake for hours, eyes peeled and ears straining. She'd heard the distant crash of the sea. Dad snoring. The clack of Luca's keyboard. The familiar sounds had eventually soothed her to sleep; but she'd clutched *The Tree in Valley Blue* so tightly, she'd woken up in knots.

Sampson pushed to his feet, his eyes big and worried.

"Don't worry. She isn't after me. She's after my books." The nymph was doing exactly as she'd promised—trying to take the books most precious to Poppy. And it was only a matter of time before all her favorite stories were gone forever.

Poppy dropped her head into her hands.

Sampson pawed at the floor.

She looked up.

He tossed his head in the direction of the cottage, then pawed at the floor again.

"No way. No chance."

Sampson thumped his tail twice. *Yes.*

"No."

Thump, thump. Yes.

"I won't bring my books here, Sampson! I won't put you in danger!"

Sampson's gaze narrowed, his eyes darkening a shade. He reared up on his hind legs and threw open his wings. They nearly spanned the entire length of the carriage house. He was twice Poppy's height. His paws were as big as her head.

The sight stole Poppy's breath.

He landed back on all fours, looking like he'd just made a very good point. And maybe he had. If there was anyone the nymph would think twice about crossing, it was him. And with Poppy's favorite stories under Sampson's protection, she could fill her shelves with cookbooks and textbooks. Trick the nymph into taking those instead.

Another thought occurred to her—even more convincing than the rest. If Sampson had to protect the books, maybe he'd stay in the carriage house and stop roaming around. He'd think he was protecting the books... but the books would be protecting him.

"Fine, Sampson. You win. But only—only!—if you make a promise."

Sampson dropped his head into a single nod.

"If the nymph comes for the books, you give them up. You got it? You are *not* allowed to fight her."

Sampson started dodging and pouncing around the room, battling an invisible opponent.

Poppy was not amused. "I'm not laughing, Sampson! I couldn't live with myself if anything happened to you."

Sampson's expression sobered. He nuzzled Poppy with his giant head.

"You're worth more to me than all the books in the world," Poppy said. Which felt all wrong to say.

But it was true.

Hours later, Poppy had successfully brought every good book from her room over to the carriage house. Surrounded by a moat of books, Sampson was a sight. Like a king on his throne of paperbacks.

Poppy plucked one from a stack. "Shall we, Your Highness?"

She and Sampson climbed into the abandoned carriage together.

She opened to the first page and began: "It was not quite summer, nor fall, when the Darby family moved to Winslow, but those strange few days right between..."

But before she'd finished the first sentence, Sampson laid his head in Poppy's lap, closed his eyes, and fell asleep.

CHAPTER TWENTY-TWO

The night before her *Odyssey* project was due, Poppy stayed up late working on her poster. She'd put it off until the very last minute, since she spent all her time with Sampson. But she didn't want to let Mr. Thomas down.

Dad shuffled into the kitchen in his flannel pajamas. "Poppyseed. Time to call it a night." His voice was hoarse, his eyes bleary. Mom had clearly woken him up to drag Poppy to bed.

Poppy's own eyes had gotten heavy around 9:00 p.m., so she'd snuck one of Luca's sodas, and the caffeine had done its job a little too well. "I know. I just have to glue these feathers onto the shroud."

The poster was some of her best work, despite her procrastination. She'd decided to compare herself to Penelope from *The Odyssey,* the story Mr. Thomas had told her about. She'd made a long, fleecy burial shroud—the kind Penelope had unraveled to trick the suitors—using tiny feathers she'd collected from the carriage house.

Dad craned his neck. "Where did you get these feathers?" He moved in for a closer look. "What class is this for?"

"English."

Dad blinked hard, as if trying to chase off sleep. "Is this a book report?"

"Yep. *The Odyssey*." Poppy capped the glue stick and looked up.

"The *what*?" Dad had that same puzzled, out-of-focus expression as when the Narnia books disappeared. The same look Mom got whenever Poppy brought up Grandma's journal.

The glue dropped from Poppy's hand and rolled across her poster. "Dad ... you've heard of *The Odyssey*. Right? We own it." She distinctly remembered packing it up on the night she'd tried to take the books to Hesper Park. But she hadn't thought to put it in the carriage house with Sampson. She'd only taken her own books over there.

"*The Odyssey*? What's it about?" Dad asked. "You said it was a book?"

The glue stick plunged off the table. "It ... was."

"Hm. Well. We've got to get some sleep." Dad shuffled toward his room and switched off the lights, leaving Poppy in near darkness. "If you stay up any later, tell Mom I threatened grave punishment."

Poppy wove through the chaos at school, her poster tucked beneath one arm. She still clung to a sliver of hope. It was possible Dad had never read *The Odyssey*. Or he'd been too sleepy to remember. Or Luca had borrowed it from Mom's shelf for his own schoolwork.

This would be the moment of truth.

In the hallway ahead, the class president, Chase Parker, and his gang took up so much space that everyone else had to squeeze past by smashing up against the lockers.

Poppy stopped. "Excuse me."

None of them acknowledged her, so she groaned and joined the other kids sliding past. Her poster wrinkled up against the lockers, making the burial shroud lose some of its feathers.

In English, a bunch of students were already in their seats.

None of them had posters.

Poppy stopped in front of Mr. Thomas, who was doing a Sudoku puzzle and chewing the end of a black pen. Which was strange. He never sat behind his desk—only on it. And he never used regular old pens.

Not only that, but the classroom looked completely different. The faux ivy was gone. The Greek columns, gone. The papier-mâché monster Scylla, gone. Now you could actually see the chalkboard, and on it, Mr. Thomas had written *Lesson 11.1: Subject and Object Pronouns*.

"Where did all your decorations go?" Poppy asked.

"I took them down."

"Why?"

Mr. Thomas closed his Sudoku book. "Because...to be honest, I don't know why I put them up in the first place. I came in this morning and couldn't even remember what purpose they served. It was...very bizarre, to say the least. But we're moving on." He pointed to the chalkboard over his shoulder. "Pronouns."

Poppy held up her poster. "Do you know what this is?"

"A...very original art project?"

"It's the assignment due today. Remember? *The Odyssey*?"

"Ah...that. Yes, I fielded about fifty emails from concerned parents over this. Apparently, I'd assigned a book no one could track down. Must have been a typo. Anyway, I canceled the project. Did your mom not get my email?"

So that was it. *The Odyssey* no longer existed. What did that mean for the world? For art? How about for historians and professors? Did they miss *The Odyssey*? Did they even *know* they missed it?

Poppy had done this. She'd only taken the books important to *her* to the carriage house. But she'd left the rest to be picked off by the nymph, one by one.

Mr. Thomas ruffled the poster's feathers with his pen. "Brownie points for imagining up whatever this is, though."

"It's Penelope's burial shroud."

"Your what?"

"No. Not *me*. The lady from the book." Strong, faithful, clever Penelope. Forgotten forever. Who else was lost? "Circe, Odysseus, Scylla." Poppy watched Mr. Thomas for any sign of recognition. "Telemachus, Calypso—"

"Poppy, I have no idea what you're getting at."

Poppy's guilt boiled over. "*The Odyssey* wasn't a typo; it was a real book! Your favorite book! And now you've forgotten it! Everyone has! And it's all my fault!"

Mr. Thomas started to say something and then stopped, squinting at the poster. As if he was actually trying to remember.

Yes! Maybe this was the answer. If Poppy forced people to confront the books they'd forgotten, maybe she could bring the memories back. Maybe all the knowledge was buried deep inside, and they just needed a good shake.

But then Mr. Thomas looked up, no glimmer of remembrance in his eyes. "Listen, if you want to go to the nurse, just say so. No need for theatrics."

It was the first time he'd ever made Poppy feel silly. Where was the cool Mr. Thomas, almighty god of grammar, collector of stories and bow ties, enthusiast of ancient Greece?

He sighed. "I'm sorry. I didn't get my coffee this morning. I apologize."

"Oh. Yeah. Coffee is a big deal with my mom, too," Poppy said, eager to accept that excuse. *Coffee* was the reason Mr. Thomas was acting so different. But how could she ignore the fact that he'd specifically said *The Odyssey* had helped him make sense of the world? And now that it was gone, he seemed... different?

Poppy rolled up her poster, stuffed it in the bin, and took her seat.

The bell rang, followed by the sound of Holden's sneakers skidding through the door.

"You're late, Mr. President," Mr. Thomas said.

"My bad," Holden replied, sweeping past Poppy.

Mr. President.

Readers Club.

Why hadn't Poppy thought of it sooner? At Readers Club, she could be around other kids who loved books. Watch to see if—and *how*—anyone else changed.

Even better...maybe she could help them remember. She could have sworn Mr. Thomas had almost recalled *The Odyssey* when he'd looked at her poster. She could start with Narnia: Rewrite the story and read it aloud. It wouldn't be word for word, but maybe it could jog their brains enough to bring it back.

She whirled around. "Holden! When is Readers Club?"

He made a face. "Why do *you* want to know?"

"What do you mean *why*? Don't you know when your own club is?"

Holden scoffed. "Duh, I know. I just don't want to tell *you*, Penny."

Poppy glared. It was, unfortunately for him, not the time to mess with her. "You know what, Holden? I've been here for two months now. You should know my name. And I know it's five whole letters, but try *really* hard to remember: *P-O-P-P-Y.*"

Annabelle let out a clap of laughter. Holden glared. Everyone else seemed to be holding their collective breath.

"Like I'm going to tell you now," he muttered.

"It's Wednesday," Grace Jennings said without looking up from her phone. "Readers Club is Wednesday in the band room."

"That was so funny with Holden."

Poppy looked up, surprised to see Annabelle waiting after the bell rang. She usually hurried off to walk with Lexi to lunch.

"*P-O-P-P-Y,*" Annabelle imitated.

Poppy stood, sliding her backpack onto her shoulder. "He's the worst. Does he still call you Dumbo?"

Annabelle's eyes brightened. "*No.* Last week, he saw me running toward the bus, and I swear he was going to do it. And then all of a sudden he got this scared look on his face and didn't say anything. He just, like . . . walked away."

Poppy grinned. So her and Sampson's prank hadn't been for nothing after all.

Ahead, Lexi was waiting in the empty hallway. She threw

her hands up. "What took so long? I want to check out the science fair showcase."

"Oh yeah, I forgot," Annabelle said, then turned to Poppy. "Want to come? Or wait, you probably want to read or whatever."

Poppy frowned. Why would Annabelle think she was planning to read at lunch? She'd only done that when she was being left out. She'd never *wanted* to sit there with no one to talk to.

"No, I'll come," Poppy said.

The three started toward the multipurpose room, and Annabelle retold the story of Poppy standing up to Holden. Lexi's eyes peeled wide. "I don't think anyone has ever told him off."

Poppy shrugged, feeling brave. "Yeah, well, no one gets between me and Readers Club. You guys want to go with me?"

Lexi said, "No, thanks."

"I can't, either. I have tutoring," Annabelle said.

Poppy wished she hadn't asked.

Then Annabelle said, "But maybe I'll ask my mom to change it. I think you and I need to keep Holden in line."

CHAPTER TWENTY-THREE

Annabelle's mom wouldn't change her tutoring schedule, so Poppy was on her own for Readers Club. When she got to the band room Wednesday, abandoned chairs and instruments scattered the floor, but there was no sign of anyone.

A huge trash can rolled into the room, pushed by the custodian, Doc Mimi.

"You looking for someone, baby?" she asked.

Doc Mimi ended every sentence the same way. *Say hi to your mom for me, baby. Throw that gum away, baby. That's a lunch detention, baby.* She was a big lady with blond hair and a raspy laugh that carried across the whole cafeteria. And she wore blue doctor's scrubs every day, which had earned her the nickname Doc Mimi.

"Do you know if Readers Club meets here?" Poppy asked.

The custodian snagged a few pieces of trash with her grabber. "Readers Club? You mean Holden Cline and them?"

"Yes, ma'am."

"They call themselves the Readers Club? Seemed to me they were just messing with the instruments and spilling soda on my carpet. I came Wednesdays to keep an eye on them, but they stopped coming."

Poppy slumped into one of the blue plastic chairs.

Holden *knew* Poppy was coming to Readers Club and still hadn't bothered to show up. He'd probably told everyone the new girl was trying to join, and how *hilarious* was that—didn't she know no one wanted her around?

Doc Mimi sat beside Poppy. She tapped her foot in a funny rhythm, as if listening to some secret music. "You know... I always see you with your nose stuck in a book. Why don't you be in charge of Readers Club?"

Poppy dropped her head. "I had a chance. I blew it."

Doc Mimi shrugged. "Sometimes you don't get it right the first time. You have to grow a bit, then try again."

"But Holden's already president. What am I supposed to do? Stage a mutiny?"

It was a complete joke. But Doc Mimi said, "Maybe. Because he's doing a terrible job with the responsibility. So"—she leaned forward, the scent of peppermint and coffee on her breath—"maybe it's time to take it."

A fire burned in Doc Mimi's expression that Poppy's heart

recognized. For some reason, she thought of Sampson. That night by the manor gates, he'd faced off with the nymph even though he couldn't fly or roar. Even though he'd barely stood a chance, Sampson had fought back.

He'd protected the books.

Poppy barely heard herself saying goodbye, barely heard the squeak of her boots down the hallway. But she definitely heard herself stop in Mr. Thomas's doorway and say, "I should be Readers Club president."

Mr. Thomas slid some papers into his leather briefcase. "Unfortunately, Holden holds the position."

"But he isn't doing meetings."

"Who told you that?"

"Doc Mimi. I just went to the band room and no one was there."

Mr. Thomas looked up, his eyes sharp and amused. "You went to Readers Club?"

"Yes."

"All right. Here's what we can do. We'll bring this information to your classmates and put it to a vote on Friday."

Maybe it was time to bring Sampson out of hiding. She'd have no problem getting people to vote for her with a magic lion by her side. But he was *so* far from ready. Couldn't fly, couldn't roar. Poppy couldn't blow his chance to amaze the world just because she wanted to lead some school club.

Poppy groaned. "No one will vote for me."

"Well, Poppy. If you want people to vote for you, first you have to vote for yourself." Mr. Thomas zipped his bag, then flipped off the lights. "Speak up this time and see what happens."

Poppy followed him out. "And say what? Just tell me, and I'll say it."

"Telling you what to say is one thing I will never do." He made it halfway down the hallway then said, "And you're wrong, by the way."

"About what?"

"About no one voting for you. One person has been voting for you this entire time."

"What? Who?"

Without turning, Mr. Thomas called back, "Me."

"Here's what I've got so far...." A salty breeze ruffled Poppy's paper. She sat cross-legged on the sand and smoothed her speech-in-progress over a low, flat boulder.

She and Sampson had found this little beach yesterday. It was completely secluded by cliffs, so they'd climbed down, lain in the sand, and watched the swooping gulls. "That'll be you up there, someday," she'd told him. "Can't you see it?"

Sampson hadn't responded, just watched, his honey-colored eyes blinking upward. Longing. And kind of sad.

Today, the gulls were elsewhere, but golden shafts of light filled the sky. The weather was perfect to splash around in the waves with Sampson, but first, Poppy had to plan for Friday's Readers Club election. Mr. Thomas had specifically said to "speak up," and she wasn't about to show up unprepared again.

Poppy cleared her throat. "Okay so, I'm Penelope Woodlock, but everyone calls me Poppy. I moved here two months ago, when my parents took a job...."

Ahead, Sampson exhaled a sharp breath through his nose. He'd been lounging in the shallow water, raking the sand with his giant paw in search of tiny crabs, but now he was staring at Poppy with a very clear look of exasperation. She wondered if lions in the Old World rolled their eyes as much as he did.

"What?" she asked. "You don't think I should talk about my parents?"

He slapped his tail down. *No.*

"Fine." She bit the cap off her pen. "No talk of parents. So. I'm Poppy Woodlock. I moved here *for no apparent reason*, and I think I'd be a great—"

Sampson shook his mane, spraying seawater everywhere.

Poppy shielded her paper. "Hey!" She scanned her speech for the phrase that had apparently bugged him again. "Cut *I think*?"

He thumped his tail twice. *Yes.*

"Okay. Fine. I *would* be a great president because I love

reading. And even though I've never been a president, I have some good ideas. And if I got a chance, I—"

A wet paw slapped her paper.

Sampson's golden eyes bored into hers. His huge face took up the whole of her vision, mane whipping in the wind. They spent so much time together, sometimes Poppy forgot just how magnificent he was.

He nudged her to stand up on the boulder, like it was a stage, then sat in front of her.

What did he want to hear? Or more importantly...

What did Poppy want to say?

She cleared her throat. "All right, so... I'm Poppy Woodlock, and I'm here to tell you..." Her voice was dwarfed by the waves. Sampson stuck his head beneath her face, lifting her chin.

"I'm here to say Readers Club is important," she continued. The wind swirled around her and rushed toward the sea, carrying her voice farther. "Which is why the president must be someone dedicated. And I think I could be that leader."

Sampson stamped a paw.

"I... *am* that leader?"

His eyes glowed.

"I'm creative. And passionate. And I'll make sure everyone feels included." Before, she'd been trying not to sound too confident. But these words felt good and true. And for the first time, she understood what Mr. Thomas meant by *you have to vote for yourself.* "So, let's make Readers Club into the best club ever! Vote for me! Poppy Quinn Wood—"

Sampson crouched, his attention cutting to the cliffs at the end of the beach. Poppy dropped next to him.

"Is someone over there?" she whispered.

Sampson's tail swished three times. *I don't know.* He took a creeping step forward.

Poppy scooped up her backpack and inched alongside him.

When they reached the edge of the beach, where the sand gave way to a rugged jetty, Sampson sniffed the air, leading Poppy's gaze to a narrow cave in the cliff. Trickles of water bled down the dark rock.

A sharp sob echoed within.

Someone was hurt.

Or trapped.

"Come on!" Poppy scrambled over the jetty and into the cave, Sampson close behind.

They ran, splashing through shallow puddles. The air cooled. The cave took a sharp turn, and hazy blue light flickered on the walls. All at once, Poppy smelled it, stronger than ever before—

Thunderstorms. Cinnamon. And woodsmoke.

Poppy reached out for Sampson, but he already knew. His head was ducked low, his eyes narrowed on the blue light beyond.

"Please!" the nymph's voice came. "Surely my penance has been paid!"

Sampson nudged Poppy, signaling to leave. But she couldn't contain her curiosity. She peered around the bend.

The nymph bobbed in a wide pool, her back to Poppy, riverweed hair falling in tangles down her scaly back. In front of her, a veil of water cascaded from the cave's ceiling. A blurry image shimmered in the center—

The apparition of a creature.

Poppy's breath caught, fear shooting up her spine.

The thing in the waterfall was tall and thin and cloaked in blue. Dozens of gold horns sprouted from its head like a crown. But it had no eyes or nose, its pale skin broken only by a gaping mouth.

Sampson crouched beside Poppy, opening a protective wing in front of her.

The creature peered down at the nymph, its featureless face cold as stone. "The Old World does not grieve your absence." Each word sounded like a hundred beings, a chorus of voices from a single mouth.

"It cannot be, great Keeper!" the nymph cried. Poppy wondered at that word, *Keeper*. What exactly did this terrifying creature keep? Secrets? Enchantments? "My sisters have surely—"

"Your sisters do not claim you."

The cave fell so quiet Poppy could hear her own heartbeat.

The nymph's voice came as thin as mist. "They've not sought mercy for me?"

"You cost them sacred magic, a crime not soon forgotten."

The nymph's resolve seemed to grow. "I shall restore their confidence. Replace the magic. Look into my remembrance. . . . *Ssssee* for yourself." She bowed her head.

The Keeper lowered its chin. Pricks of blue appeared where its eyes should have been, growing bigger, brighter, so bright Poppy nearly had to look away. As quick as it happened, they faded back into taut, white skin.

"You gather records from the Minor World?" the Keeper asked.

Poppy's eyes widened. This faceless creature was a mind reader? How much could it see? What other magic was it capable of?

Beside her, Sampson was incredibly still, his breathing slow and deep. He seemed entranced. As if something in him recognized this ancient magic.

The nymph looked up. "These books are not merely records, but *magic*. A mortal told me this. If you allow my return, I will bring the books with me."

A wave of understanding fell over Poppy. The nymph wasn't stealing just to spite mortals. She thought it would fix whatever terrible thing she'd done back in the Old World. She was trying to earn back her place.

The faceless creature lifted its chin, gold horns glinting. "The Keepers are intrigued with your offering."

The nymph clasped her hands. "Yes! Please . . ."

"You return when the mortal moon burns."

The nymph gave a sob of relief. "Thank you, noble Keeper! Tell my sisters of my return. Tell them I beg forgiveness. Tell them—"

The Keeper disappeared and the waterfall surged, spilling over the cave floor. Poppy's feet lost traction. Sampson snagged her backpack in his teeth, narrowly saving her from slamming into the ground.

She dangled there for a moment, staring down at the jagged rocks. "Close one," she whispered to Sampson.

But she'd spoken too soon. Because when she looked up, the nymph's wild orb eyes were on them.

CHAPTER TWENTY-FOUR

The nymph gripped the cave floor, her long claws bending under the pressure. "Tiny-faced mortal. Winged lion." Her voice echoed off the walls. "You dare watch me in secret?"

Poppy scrabbled upright. "We—we heard crying...then we saw..."

"Ah." The nymph's expression ripened to amusement. "You glimpsed the Old World? Lion, did you as well?" She cocked her head, her voice suddenly cold as an arctic sea. "Winged lions of the Old World walk alongside the Keepers, powerful companions to the oldest magic. But I wonder.... What would the Keepers think of this one? A winged lion without the power of flight? Without the voice of thunder?"

Sampson returned a steady gaze, but Poppy saw the faint wilt in his wings. The droop in his ears. The shame.

The nymph turned her cruelty on Poppy. "And you. Did your weak mortal heart cower at the sight of the world beyond?"

"N-no."

"You tremble even now."

Poppy clenched her fists. But her curiosity burned brighter than her fear. "How did that creature know you were taking books?"

"The Keepers see the past mind."

The past mind. "You mean it can read memories?"

The nymph looked disgusted by Poppy's ignorance. "*Yesss,* witless child."

"So it saw you taking the books?" Poppy's wonder grew. "But if the books aren't here . . . and you haven't sent them back to the Old World yet . . . where are they?"

The nymph hummed a low, cruel laugh, as if she knew exactly what Poppy was hoping. She drew a single claw down a crack in the cave wall. "They await me, in the place between worlds. An infinite space, without time or light. No one will ever find them but me. And now my name, once ruined, will be restored." The nymph lifted her webbed palms. "For I return with the magic of the Minor World."

"But books aren't actual magic! I just said that to convince you! They're just . . . they're just paper and ink!"

The nymph cackled. "You think me a fool?" She inhaled through her slitted nostrils. "Ahh . . . perhaps so. Because I sense there is magic you carry with you even now . . ."

Little Tree. In Poppy's backpack. What would happen if this book disappeared? Would Dad change like Mom? Treat Poppy differently, like Mr. Thomas?

Poppy stumbled back. "You can't have it!"

Sampson released a low growl, opening a wing to shield Poppy. The nymph moved toward them, undeterred. The water around her began to swirl. "The deal was sworn."

"I don't care! Take something else!"

The nymph looked briefly struck by Poppy's defiance. Her leathery lips curled. "No."

The nymph's pool erupted like a geyser, propelling her toward Poppy. Sampson leapt to meet her. But midair, the wave changed course, pitching the nymph out of Sampson's path. He smashed into the cave wall and crumpled into a heap.

"Give me that book!" The nymph whirled back toward Poppy. "You will see the deal through!" She lunged again—a terrifying bullet of glowing eyes and razor teeth.

"No!" Poppy swiveled to protect her backpack, catching the creature's needle-sharp claws across her arm. They tore through her flesh.

The nymph's white-orb eyes flew wide. For a moment, she looked as stunned as Poppy. Then her expression steeled. "You brought it on yourself, *recklessss* mortal," she hissed, then plunged into the pool and disappeared.

Poppy gripped her arm, trying to stop the blood surging through her fingers.

Sampson bounded toward her, his eyes big with fear.

"It's okay ...," Poppy said, voice trembling. "I'm okay." She lifted her hand. Four slashes cut diagonally across her arm, each so deep she glimpsed the white of bone.

She gasped, knees buckling. Sampson caught her in the crook of his wing.

Poppy fumbled for a clear thought. She had to get home. Mom would take her to the hospital. But could doctors even help her? These wounds felt deeper than they looked—as if infused with some horrible magic. Poppy could feel it surging through her veins even now—burning and evil and hungry.

Her shallow breath quickened. Sampson jostled her with his wing, trying to keep her awake.

Home was forever away. She was bleeding too fast. She'd never make it.

The world shifted. Tilted.

Then went black.

Glinting fractured light.

The scent of old wood and a piney breeze.

Something warm and rough, running over her arm.

Poppy blinked awake, her surroundings slowly coming into focus. She was in the carriage house, nestled in the curve of Sampson's body. A ruddy sunset streaked through the diamond windows.

It took Poppy a moment to remember the nymph's attack. The blood.

She closed her eyes again, bracing for the pain.

But nothing came.

She sat up, confused. Had she dreamt the attack? The carriage house door swung wide, the jamb splintered, like it had been forced open. Crimson spots bloomed across the floor, forming a bloody trail to where she sat.

Poppy shook her head. "What happened?" she asked.

Sampson licked her arm.

She nudged his huge head aside. Sure enough, four raised pink lines striped her skin. But they looked months old, not like the gaping, gushing wounds from only hours ago. Could Poppy really have healed so fast? Was nymph magic so weak?

Sampson licked her again, and this time, she saw it: The wounds faded before her eyes. They thinned. Lightened. It even felt like Sampson was somehow drawing the pain from her.

Poppy's voice came slow and full of wonder. "Sampson... you healed me?"

He looked up.

It was like seeing him for the first time all over again, like a best friend revealing a secret identity. It hadn't even occurred to Poppy that Sampson was capable of magic. Was there more she'd discover about him a month, two months, two years from now?

She sat up straighter, excitement quickening her pulse. "What else can you do?"

Sampson gave three thumps of his tail. *I don't know.*

The response was so honest and innocent, a laugh burst from Poppy.

But the sad thought followed: What if Sampson had powers he *never* discovered? What if he lived his whole life without reaching his potential? There were no other winged lions on earth. No one to show him the way. All he had was Poppy.

And, really, what did she know?

Poppy snuck through her bedroom window, changed out of her bloodstained clothes, and reentered through the back door. The kitchen was deserted, takeout boxes from a place called Wendy's Fish Grill scattered over the table.

Poppy followed the sound of her parents' voices into the living room.

Mom was cross-legged on the floor, surrounded by a moat of crafting supplies. Every night, she called Poppy into her office to show off her scrapbooking progress. Poppy always tried to seem interested, or at least undisturbed. But what if Mom never got over this? What if she spent her whole life trying to fill the hole left by Grandma's journal?

Dad stood over Mom, hands stuck in his overalls. "Cordelia, for heaven's sake—"

"Back up," Mom said. "You're tracking dirt on my stencils."

"I'm home!" Poppy said.

Mom swiveled. "Penelope! I told you to be home an hour ago!"

"Why do we even pay for your phone if you never use it?" Dad demanded. "Where were you?"

Poppy gripped her arm where the nymph had attacked her. *I was with a winged lion exploring a sea cave, where we saw magic from another world and I was almost killed by a water nymph.*

Mom's hawk vision narrowed. "What's wrong?"

Shove it down, Poppy. "Nothing."

"Talk to me."

Hide it. "I am talking to you."

"Then where were you?"

"I was at Annabelle's. Didn't you see the note on my door?" Her parents exchanged a glance.

"It'd be nice to meet this new friend," Mom said.

"Why don't you have her over?" Dad suggested.

"Yeah, okay," Poppy said, sure she wouldn't. She didn't need another friend to take up her time. She had Sampson.

Dad gestured toward the hallway. "Go to your room and finish up your homework," he said, clearly trying to get rid of her. "I'll be there in a minute."

Poppy lingered in the hallway, listening.

"Sophia Mendoza stopped by the manor," Dad told Mom. "Checking on the status of the entrance gate design."

"Oh. Right," Mom said. Poppy heard the *pop* of a glue stick opening. "I'll get to it."

"If we don't decide by Monday, we'll lose our priority with the ironworker."

"Goodness gracious, Spencer, you act like I'm not doing my best."

"You didn't even show up to the manor today. If you spent less energy on *this* nonsense, maybe you'd have the time to get it done."

"So, our children are nonsense now?"

"Our *children* are back there. Living and breathing and alive in their rooms. This? *This* is . . . I don't know what this is. An obsession with the past? Where did this idea even come from? Your sister Deedee?"

An obsession with the past.

The words coiled around Poppy like a snake. There was something there. Something true, demanding to be unraveled.

Mom had always loved the past. But maybe fixing up old buildings had been Mom's way of connecting with Grandma. And now, without that connection, her passion was . . . displaced. She was spending all her time scrapbooking instead of going to the manor. Missing renovation deadlines in favor of old photos and stamps.

The rooster clock above Poppy's head ticked a full twelve seconds before Mom said, "Look at this one. Luca's first taste of ice cream."

Dad sighed. "I *need* you, Cordelia. I can't get this renovation done unless you get your head back in the game."

"My head is fine where it is." The rooster ticked another four seconds. "I'll be to bed in a minute."

Even Poppy knew what that meant. Dad was dismissed. Poppy hurried to her room and clicked the door shut, jumping onto her bed just as Dad gave a curt knock.

"Come in," Poppy called.

The mattress springs whined as Dad sat on the edge of the bed. "So, you were at Annabelle's tonight?"

Poppy shrugged. She hated lying to Dad. "And you were at the manor chasing raccoons?"

The crinkles around Dad's eyes deepened. "That's definitely one way to put it."

"How's everything going?" Poppy asked tentatively.

"A few hiccups, but nothing the dream team can't conquer." The laugh in his eyes disappeared. Even Poppy knew *the dream team* wasn't conquering. It was floundering. It was usually Mom who was the first to arrive and last to leave. Mom, poring over research and blueprints late into the night. Mom, demanding Dad work faster.

"I think she'll snap out of it," Poppy blurted.

"What?" Dad looked puzzled, probably unsure *how* and *how much* she knew.

But sadly, Poppy understood the change in Mom better than anyone. "I think Mom will get back to her normal self soon."

She wanted so badly for it to be a promise.

But for now, it was just a hope.

CHAPTER TWENTY-FIVE

Mom and Dad seemed to think they'd stumbled upon a brilliant idea, having Annabelle over for dinner. Poppy tried about every excuse, but Mom put her foot down. "You're not allowed to go to her house again until we meet her."

In other words, Poppy would have no alibi to see Sampson until Annabelle came over.

To her relief, Annabelle accepted the invitation and said she'd been dying to see inside the Lark-Hayes cottage. Poppy warned that it wasn't as exciting as advertised, but Annabelle still had that familiar look of vague disappointment as she sat at the dinner table, surveying the wood paneling and linoleum floors.

The evening was warm, and the screened back door was propped open, filling the house with cricket song and the smell of jasmine blooming behind the shed. Somewhere in the distance, a storm was brewing, thickening the air.

Dad plunked three pizza boxes on the table. "We've got pepperoni, cheese, and the Spencer special: mushroom and hot pepper."

Poppy pushed back her chair. "We'll just take our food to my room."

Annabelle had only been there a few minutes, and already Poppy had deflected about a dozen weird comments from her parents about *how much time you two have been spending together* and *Mr. Thomas sure gives a lot of group projects* and *Thanks for being so welcoming to our Poppy.* Luckily, Annabelle was so chatty that the conversation kept on rolling, but it was only a matter of time before Mom's hawk senses alerted her that something was off.

"I'll take pepperoni," Luca said, not looking up from his phone.

"Luca! No Spencer special?" Dad sounded deeply hurt.

"I'll have the special," Annabelle offered.

"Now we're talking! And Poppy? Two specials coming right up." He offered a plate to Annabelle, then drew back. "If it's too spicy, just say the word. You want to try it first and let me know? It's probably too spicy. Sorry, I should have—"

Poppy snagged both flimsy plates. "Thanks, Dad."

"Poppy, don't rush off." Mom appeared from the kitchen. She set a frosty can of soda in front of Luca and gestured to his cell phone. "Trade?"

Luca weighed his options, then slid his phone to Mom

and cracked the soda. "I need it back after dinner. The student council thread is blowing up about the new prom theme."

Annabelle took a backward step toward Luca. "Wait.... Are you the Luca who won the student council debate?"

Luca lifted his soda and bowed his head. "I am he."

"No way!" Annabelle whirled to Poppy. "You didn't tell me your older brother was Luca!"

And just like that, Poppy knew she'd lost any chance of peeling Annabelle out of there.

Poppy sat and braced herself for more awkward—and possibly disastrous—conversation. She was tired of staving off disaster. *Exhausted*. She was ready to give up. And why not? Why shouldn't she sneak off and return with Sampson? Smack everyone with the glorious truth. Family dinner with a side of magical lion.

But something whispered, *Not yet*. Sampson was so close to the grand entrance he deserved. He was full-grown and getting closer to flying every day. Just yesterday, he'd taken a running leap and hovered over the ground for a full three seconds.

Annabelle swung her braids over her shoulder. "My sister is Jasmin Ingraham."

"Oh, for real?" Luca said. "I love Jazzy. Yeah, she's in my bio class. Ridiculously smart."

"I know," Annabelle said. "It's impossible to be her sister. This pizza is super good."

Mom nudged Dad. "Give her another slice, Spencer."

He slapped one onto a plate and Poppy passed it. "What do you mean it's impossible?" Poppy asked. "You're super smart, too."

"No, I just study a lot."

"Hey, now," Dad said. "Don't be modest. We celebrate our strengths in the Woodlock house. Poppy is a voracious reader. Cordelia is a *brilliant* historic preservation planner." Dad glanced at Mom, but she pretended not to notice, suddenly very intent on gathering used napkins from the table. Sadness flashed across Dad's face, but he continued, "I'm the guy who came up with mushroom and hot pepper pizza. And Luca, here, is our trendsetter."

Luca muttered, "Was."

Mom stopped collecting trash. "What, Luc?"

Outside, the storm made a gentle entrance. Sheets of rain knocked the screen door in a steady rhythm.

Luca tore the crust off his pizza. "I don't know. Chatlain High got weird real quick. It's just...different than I thought it would be."

"Well, maybe if you got a nice haircut like we've been telling you...," Mom said.

Luca raked a hand through his curls. "Maybe."

The response was so unlike him that Poppy let out a clap of laughter. "Don't you mean, *I like my hair and I am an independent human, not an extension of my parents?*" It was a phrase from his favorite graphic novel, *The Lie Keeper*, and Mom never had a good response for it, so Luca said it all the time.

Luca snorted. "Good one, Weasel."

Poppy stopped chewing. Was she imagining it—or had Luca just given her credit for something she definitely did not make up? She stared at him a beat longer, then decided she was over-thinking and now was *not* the time to get weird.

Annabelle said, "Jazzy told me about how you crushed the other kids in the debate and they didn't even know it. I was dying laughing."

Luca gave a halfhearted smirk. "Yeah."

Poppy polished off her pizza. There was no better combination, she decided, than pizza and a rainstorm. And if Sampson were here, it would complete *everything*.

Mom snagged a slice of Dad's special. "We ordered way too much. Annabelle, you'll have to take some home."

"Oh, my parents don't like gluten in the house. Thanks, anyway."

Mom's brow furrowed. "Oh. Really? I thought Poppy said your parents made sandwiches last—"

"Hey, Luca!" Poppy said abruptly. "I don't think I've ever heard the whole story about the debate! You should tell it."

Annabelle clapped. "Yes!"

Even though Luca seemed grumpier than usual, Poppy knew he couldn't resist a chance to be the center of attention. And after a minute of everyone pleading, he gave in.

"There were nine kids debating," he began. "But the moderator was Vice Principal Hicks, who couldn't control a room of sedated kittens. Everyone was yelling over each other. When he asked a question about the dress code, it got so loud there were people in the audience covering their ears. I was about to walk offstage. Actually, I did."

Dad gaped. "You what?"

Mom squinted. "You walked out of the debate and still won?"

Annabelle said, "He became the moderator! Oh, sorry." She looked bashfully at Luca. "You tell it."

"I snagged the moderator's mic and announced that the next person who interrupted was getting disqualified."

Poppy's eyes widened. "You had the power to do that?"

"Of course not. But it shut everyone up, so Hicks let it go."

"Geez, son." Dad rubbed his beard. "I'm surprised you didn't get in huge trouble for that. Rules are rules for a reason." Mom gently patted Dad's hand, a thing she did when he was worrying too much.

Luca swigged the last of his soda and crushed the can. "*Please.* Before I came along, Hicks was using his tie to wipe the sweat off his face. So I got out my phone and began timing everyone's responses while he asked the questions."

Annabelle asked, "And then what was the thing you said at the end?"

Luca leaned back in his chair and Poppy knew this was going to be good. "Everyone thought I'd bowed out of the election, since I was helping moderate. But after the closing statements, I stood up and said, 'Now, you tell me who deserves to win. The ones up there raging at each other, or the one already in charge.'"

"Everyone went nuts!" Annabelle said.

Mom smiled proudly. "Luca, you are one of a kind."

Dad chuckled. "It's like that part from our book, huh, Pops?"

"What?"

"From *The Tree in Valley Blue*, remember?" He turned to the rest of the table. "There's this tree who isn't blooming with the others. And in winter, when the forest goes to sleep, she gets some advice from a bird who lands in her branches."

Poppy remembered. Every time they came to that part, Dad would pause, and it felt like all the world hushed to hear his low, gravelly voice say—

"Sometimes the softest voice is the one worth listening to," Dad said.

Mom's expression warmed.

Annabelle gave a short "Hm!"

"Wow." Luca clasped his hands over his heart. "Wow. That was so...so...incredibly corny."

"Luca Shane," Mom scolded.

Luca balled up his napkin and tossed it to his plate. "It's not that deep. I just think everyone was tired of the noise." He stood and stretched out his palm. "Can I get my phone back?"

Poppy sat straight-backed at her desk, surrounded by the chaos of kids shuffling into English. But her focus didn't waver. The forgotten books depended on her. And she wasn't the same Poppy Woodlock who'd bowed out of the first election. She'd found magic. Become best friends with a winged lion. Defied a water nymph.

Holden was the one who should be scared.

The bell rang and Holden came skidding in. As he passed, Poppy's *very expressive face* was stone-cold and deadly, a warrior greeting her opponent. He didn't notice.

But Annabelle did. "You got this," she whispered. After dinner, Annabelle had found Poppy's speech in her bedroom. They'd rehearsed it together, and afterward, Annabelle had said it was obvious Poppy was Luca Woodlock's little sister, which was the best compliment of all time.

"An order of business." Mr. Thomas swiveled in his chair. "It's come to my attention that Readers Club hasn't been holding regular meetings."

Poppy waited for a murmur of outrage that didn't come.

"I mean, yeah," Holden said. "Doc Mimi kicked us out of the band room."

Poppy whirled around. "She did not kick you out. She asked you to stop messing with the instruments."

"That was Sai!"

"Come on, dude!" Sai yelped.

Mr. Thomas pinched the bridge of his nose. "Here's what we're going to do. Since we have another eager volunteer—"

"Wait up," Holden cut in. "Will I still get the extra credit?"

"No."

"Then I want to stay president! I'll do better!"

"As I was saying, Mr. Cline, since I believe in the ideals of democracy, we are going to have another vote. Think of it as a second-term election."

Holden rubbed his palms together. "Who's my opponent?"

"Poppy Woodlock."

"Wait. Didn't she already say no?"

Mr. Thomas ignored him. "Poppy, Holden, come up here." He arranged them side by side, then moved behind his desk. "You each have thirty seconds to tell us why you deserve to be president. Then we'll vote."

"I'll go first," Holden said, without even waiting for permission. He paced, the heels of his sneakers scuffing the tile. "I deserve to be president because I know all about being a leader. I'm the soccer team captain. Last year, my club team went all the way to State. *And* I'll buy anyone who votes for me a can of Mountain Dew."

Everyone cheered and Mr. Thomas called out that bribery in an election was not acceptable, but the damage was done.

"Beat that, Penny," Holden whispered.

Poppy glared back. He'd called her *Penny* again to rattle her. But it wouldn't work. Because he might be louder and more popular, but she actually deserved this.

"Do you have anything to say, Poppy?" Mr. Thomas asked.

"Yes, I do." Poppy stepped forward, ready to deliver the speech she'd written with Sampson and practiced with Annabelle. "I'll be a good president because I'm dedicated. And passionate. And I'll make sure everyone feels included. And unlike Holden, I understand that books are . . . are . . ." *Books are important*, she was supposed to say.

But everyone stared back with bored eyes. *Hurry up*, they seemed to say, *so we can all vote for Holden*. Grace Jennings wasn't even pretending to listen, staring at the phone in her lap.

No one cared about Poppy's speech—or this election— because they didn't *care* about Readers Club. Even when Holden was president, none of these kids attended club meetings. But what could Poppy say to convince them otherwise?

She looked at Annabelle for encouragement. But even *she'd* only accepted Poppy's invitation to dinner because she'd been dying to see inside the cottage.

It hit her.

"Hey—you all know that place Lark-Hayes Manor?" Poppy said.

Grace Jennings looked up. "That old mansion in the woods?"

"What about it?" someone called.

"My family and I live on that property."

Holden crossed his arms. "So? I've got a soccer field in my backyard. And a hot tub."

Poppy ignored him. "If I'm president, we can hold our meetings inside the old manor."

A murmur of interest rippled through the class.

Holden seemed to sense the mounting threat. "That's not even cool. That place is freaky. Like, haunted."

It backfired. The interest grew.

Holden called, "Not the good kind of haunted! My dad said someone died there! Like murdered!" His voice cracked. "He knows because he's a cop!"

The noise. Luca was right: Poppy was tired of the noise— and she was tired of the *same* kids always making it.

Poppy held up her hands in surrender. "Holden's right."

The room went immediately quiet. Even Holden looked surprised enough to stop yammering.

Poppy shrugged. "He's right." Then her expression filled with mischief. "Maybe it *is* haunted. Elect me and find out."

The room erupted. Girls squealed. The guys in the back row drummed on their desks. Annabelle cheered.

The only people who didn't appear thrilled were Holden and, strangely, Mr. Thomas. He frowned at Poppy, which was the opposite of the reaction she'd expected. Wasn't he proud she'd spoken up? Didn't he see how excited everyone was?

"Hold on!" Holden called over the clamor. "I'll have meetings at Sai's house. It's haunted, too! Once I saw a dead body in his pool!"

"What the heck, dude?" Sai balked.

But it didn't matter. This time, no one was listening.

"Let's vote!" someone called.

But Poppy knew before they even counted the hands.

She—Penelope Quinn Woodlock—was the new Readers Club president.

CHAPTER TWENTY-SIX

"No," Mom and Dad said at dinner that night.

Poppy dropped her fork with a clatter. "But I already promised we'd have meetings at the manor!"

"Un-promise it." Dad crumpled his napkin. "It's a construction zone. Completely unsafe."

"But!" Mom said. "We are *so* proud of you." She kissed Poppy on the top of the head and started closing takeout boxes.

Poppy looked to Luca for backup. But he didn't meet her eyes. "Can I be excused?" he asked.

"Dish in the sink," Mom said.

Poppy spent another ten minutes failing to convince Mom and Dad, but they closed the conversation and began bickering about the renovation again. Mom had apparently never gotten her design plan over to the ironworker, and now they were officially set back. But, Poppy noticed, Mom's scrapbook was finished—set up on a tiny gold easel in her office. Poppy had the terrible hope the nymph would mistake it for an important book and snatch it next.

She cleared her plate and knocked on Luca's door. "It's me."

"Okay."

That seemed like invitation enough. She flopped across his bed. "What am I going to do about the tyrants not letting me use the manor for my club?"

Luca jabbed at his computer keyboard. "I don't know. They're probably right."

Poppy launched onto her elbows. "You're on their side?"

"Safety first or whatever."

"Safety first? Since when? I thought it was gaming first, then pizza bagels, then fashion, then a hundred other things, *then* safety."

Luca didn't laugh. He kept furiously typing.

He looked different. His clothes were more boring than usual—a black shirt and jeans, plain white socks. And his hair—

"Luca! You got a haircut?" She leapt up. It looked too neat—short and combed into a clean part.

"Got sick of Mom bugging me, I guess."

"Why'd you give in?" Poppy asked. The images of his computer battle scene reflected in his pupils. Poppy nudged him. "Hey. What's up?"

He jabbed a key a few times. "I don't know. I just realized... like... what's it all for?"

"What's *what* all for?"

"Fighting with Mom and Dad. I'm over it. It's just easier to be what they want."

"No way. Remember? You are an independent human and not an extension of them."

Luca gave a dry half smile. "That's what you said the other night. Where'd you get that?"

Poppy's smile faded. He wasn't kidding. He'd forgotten. Which meant only one thing. Her gaze cut to the frames above Luca's headboard, where he kept *The Lie Keeper* and two other graphic novels he'd gotten signed at a convention.

The frames were empty.

"Luc...," Poppy said, hopeful for a different explanation. "What happened to the graphic novels above your bed?"

He shrugged. "Don't know."

"Well... where's the rest of your collection?"

"Under my bed."

Poppy knelt and pulled out the crate of novels. She sifted through them, her panic mounting. She didn't find *The Lie Keeper*.

Poppy closed her eyes and knocked her forehead against the bed frame. This change in Luca was no coincidence. The nymph had taken his favorite story. And now he was different.

Those stories had helped shape him. Of course they had. Poppy lived for those little glimpses into what she was, or was not, or what she could become. The characters of her favorite books changed her, sometimes in a big way—like when she'd read *Charlotte Doyle* and sworn off dresses—or in a tiny way, so small she'd never realize it.

Who was she—or anyone, really—without the stories she loved?

Poppy looked at Luca, his dad haircut and white socks and defeated eyes.

I am an independent human and not an extension of anyone.

Maybe that phrase had first given Luca the courage to be himself. Like a seed planted in his soul. Maybe then it had grown little by little, branching into the quirky, confident Luca Poppy knew and loved.

And now, without that seed, the entire tree had disappeared.

Poppy thought of the new Mr. Thomas: uninspired and grumpy, twirling his boring pen in his boring classroom.

Of Mom: ignoring the Lark-Hayes manor in favor of some old pictures and cardboard pages.

Poppy could no longer pretend these things weren't connected. She could no longer pretend the lost books were just forgotten words on paper.

The seeds had been ripped from the souls of the people she loved.

And it was Poppy's fault.

CHAPTER TWENTY-SEVEN

The streetlamp above Hesper Park flickered on, emitting a low buzzing sound. Poppy drew her hood lower to shield herself from the misting rain. She glanced at her phone. It was only quarter to five, but the clouds had darkened the sky enough to trigger the streetlamps.

It felt like a bad omen.

A car pulled up and unloaded two kids. As they started toward her, the boy shouted, "Readers Club!"—drawing out the words like a basketball announcer.

Poppy didn't recognize them. A boy and a girl, both wearing all black.

"Are you the girl in charge?" the boy asked. He looked like stretched taffy, everything about him long and thin.

Poppy nodded.

"Wow. You're, like, a baby," the girl said. Her dyed-pink hair sprouted from beneath her beanie. "You sure we're allowed to do this?"

Poppy was about to answer when Taffy Boy said, "Of course we're allowed. Her parents own it. Right, what's-your-name?"

"Poppy Woodlock. And my parents don't own it, they're just—"

The boy laughed. "Wow. Full name. Like James Bond."

"Woodlock," Pink Hair said in a low voice. "Poppy Woodlock."

Poppy felt her expression sour. But before she could say anything, three more cars looped the parking lot, dropped kids off, and left. Poppy scanned them for familiar faces. A girl from science class. Grace Jennings. Six other kids from English. Chase Parker, the class president.

Finally, Annabelle arrived in her signature puffer jacket. Poppy had switched meetings to Fridays just so Annabelle could come.

"Okay, this is a big group," Annabelle said.

Poppy counted twenty-two kids. "Has to be a record, right?"

"For sure."

An SUV with tinted windows squealed to a stop at the roundabout.

"See you never!" the driver called—a brother, judging from the way he peeled out. Holden jogged toward the group. He clapped hands with Taffy Boy, but it barely made a sound, since for some reason, Holden was wearing snow gloves.

Poppy felt the sky darken.

Holden turned to her. "What? You have a problem?"

Poppy glared back. But, realizing there was no good way to get rid of him, she decided to pretend he wasn't there at all. "We should get going," she announced. "Everyone stay close."

They started down the gravel path and through the gates. Poppy stepped carefully to avoid the puddles, traumatized by that horrible night with the nymph. But behind her, the kids splashed along, oblivious. Poppy winced with every step, wondering if she should warn them, but she couldn't think of a way to do it without sounding completely unhinged.

"What's down that way?" someone called, gesturing to the small driveway that split off from the main one.

"The cottage where my family lives," Poppy said. The house was dark and quiet—her parents at a dinner meeting that would keep them out until late.

Ahead, the manor peeked through the trees.

Everyone rustled with excitement. Someone howled like a wolf, prompting the other kids into a chorus of creepy noises.

Poppy walked backward. "Stay quiet until we pass the manor."

"Pass it? I thought we were going inside!" Holden called. "That's what you promised!"

"We *are*," Poppy said. "We're going in through the back." The front entrance would be locked. But the small servants' door, the one Poppy had used when she'd snuck Sampson out in her backpack, was open. She'd made sure of it.

"Okay, you heard Penny," Holden called. "Shut up!"

The kids quieted, but Poppy was absolutely not grateful for the help. He'd called her Penny again. Why was he here, anyway? To cause trouble? To try to reclaim his position as president?

Maybe she was overthinking it.

But as the narrow servants' door came into view, dread hit Poppy like a brick. This group was way too big to control. All it would take was one kid—probably Holden—to wreck something irreplaceable.

This manor had been her secret ally these past few months. It had given her magic. And what had she done in return? She'd erased the memory of Lady Lark-Hayes. She'd brought a bunch of kids to trash its insides.

The group stumbled to a stop behind her, knocking into each other.

"What's going on?" someone called.

"I just . . . ," Poppy said, breathless. "I need a moment to think."

"Hey," Holden said. "What's that up there?"

Traitorous clouds parted above the carriage house—sending a shaft of light across its roof.

"Nothing," Poppy said quickly.

"It's totally something." Holden started toward it. "Hannah, P. J., come on. That's the perfect place."

"Stop!" Poppy threw her hands up like a crossing guard. "Get back here!"

Holden swiveled, his cheeks ruddy. "What's your problem? You said we could explore."

Poppy marched between him and the carriage house. "I never said you could explore without me. And I *didn't* say you could go over there."

"Why? What are you hiding up there? Dead bodies?"

A winged lion. A winged lion who couldn't fly or roar. And this dark, rainy night with a bunch of strange kids was definitely *not* Sampson's glorious moment. "Endangered beetles laid eggs in that house. The U.S. Fish and Wildlife Service will sue you if you go in."

Holden scoffed. "Who's going to sue a kid?"

Poppy grappled for a better lie. "Also, there was a bear sniffing around up there last week."

The whole group tensed, shuffling into a tighter knit of bodies.

Pink Hair yanked Taffy Boy's hand. "Let's get out of here. My mom will kill me if I die."

Holden groaned. "Come on, Hannah. It's the perfect night for our séance. Tell her, P. J." He gestured for backup, but Taffy Boy looked nervous.

The only person who seemed unfazed was Annabelle. "You guys shouldn't even be here."

Pink Hair turned. "You talking to us?"

"Yeah. You don't even go to Chatlain Middle." Annabelle turned to Poppy. "Pretty sure they're freshmen."

"They're my guests," Holden said.

Annabelle made a face at the high schoolers. "You guys hang out with a sixth grader?" Taffy and Pink Hair looked a little embarrassed.

Poppy said, "Why are you here in the first place, Holden?"

"Same reason everyone came to your dumb club. To see some ghosts."

"That's not the only reason people came," Poppy said sharply.

"Oh, really? You think anyone wanted to spend their Friday night here because they care about stupid books?"

"Y-yes," Poppy said. But her confidence faltered.

"Let's take a poll. Who came tonight because it's haunted?"

Eyes traveled nervously between Holden and Poppy. Rain misted down around them.

Pink Hair's hand shot up. "Here for the ghosts."

Her admission gave others courage. One. Five. Ten. Nearly everyone.

"Okay. And who cares about books?" Holden demanded.

Only a few hands went up.

This was why Mr. Thomas had looked so disappointed during the election. Poppy had become president by promising kids a haunted mansion—not by inviting anyone who actually loved reading.

Poppy flexed her fingers, trying to ease the tension in her hands. "You know what?" Her goal was to get people to remember the Narnia books. She could still do that, even if everyone was here for the wrong reasons. "It doesn't matter *why* you're here, only that you are." She turned to Holden. "Except you."

Holden's blond hair was plastered to his head by the rain. He threw his arm around Poppy. "Come on. You don't mean it."

She shoved him off. "Don't touch me."

He looked briefly shocked; then his expression darkened. "How about this? How about I'm going up there and you can't stop me." He drove his shoulder into hers.

Poppy's foot slipped and she fell back. Her backpack saved her from hitting her head, but the contents jabbed her spine with such force she lost her breath.

A few kids gasped.

"Holden!" said Pink Hair.

He ignored her and trudged toward the carriage house, fists swinging at his sides.

Shock weighted Poppy in place. And guilt. She'd messed up big. She'd betrayed the manor by bringing people here. And if she didn't do something quickly, she would have betrayed Sampson, too.

She scrambled to her feet and yelled, "Holden Cline! Stop right there!"

He froze in his tracks, turning. His eyes narrowed, a memory working.

He'd recognized Poppy's voice, she felt sure. She'd called his name that same exact way the night she and Sampson had sent him crying for his mom.

Uncertainty crept into Holden's expression. As if he was thinking, *No way it was this girl who scared me.*

Poppy decided to snuff that little spark of doubt.

She glowered. "Be nice or pay the price."

Holden's eyes widened. "*You,*" he said, no longer a question. "It was you. How did you do that? The other night with the monster. How?"

Poppy let the question hang in the air a moment. It was good to see him questioning *himself* for once. "I don't know what you're talking about."

Holden scoffed and said, not too convincingly, "Forget it. You don't scare me." He pivoted back toward the carriage house.

"If you don't listen to Poppy," another voice cut in—Annabelle's—"I'll tell the principal about how you call me Dumbo. Bullying is zero tolerance, Holden. So say goodbye to your precious soccer team."

Holden looked over his shoulder, furious. Two against one now. Every breath in the group seemed to be held.

He made a sound of disgust and gestured to his friends. "This isn't even worth it. Let's go."

Holden trudged away, back toward Hesper Park, Taffy Boy beside him.

"We should all go," Pink Hair said.

Every gaze fell on Poppy.

Poppy could probably get them to stay. But her adrenaline was cooling into a heavy pit in her stomach. Her first meeting as president had been a disaster. She wanted a redo. A clean slate. And she wouldn't get it tonight. "Everyone should walk back to the park together."

To her relief, they seemed eager to obey. No one wanted to see the haunted manor after all. Maybe that showdown with Holden had been scary enough.

Annabelle lingered. She looked at Poppy, wide-eyed. "I can't believe we beat Holden Cline."

"I can," Poppy said.

Grace Jennings trotted toward them. "Hey, Poppy," she panted. "Holden is really mad. I just thought you should know...." She glanced back toward the departing group. "He's already talking about coming back."

Poppy looked toward the carriage house. She'd have to secure the building. Board up the windows. Triple-lock the doors.

Annabelle saw her staring. "What's up there, anyway? Is it really beetles?"

Poppy was tired of lying. And Annabelle was the closest thing she had to a friend. She *was* a friend. What if Poppy took Annabelle to meet Sampson right now?

But before she could say anything, Annabelle said, "Crap, I gotta go. Don't want to walk back to the park alone." She jogged off to catch the rest of the group. "See you back at school!"

Poppy locked the front door and nailed tarps over the windows. The battery-powered lantern cast a pale, eerie glow over the room.

Sampson paced, his tail flicking. He was already looking too big for this place, and now she was cooping him up even more. "At least you have lots of books to read?" She gestured to the stacks around the abandoned carriage.

Sampson huffed. He'd probably flipped through each of those a hundred times already.

"I'm sorry. This is just for a little while, until I can take you home."

She imagined it: Sampson lounging in the middle of their cottage like some overgrown house cat. His body would take up the entire rug. His wings would span from one wall to the other. The whole thing seemed suddenly ridiculous.

Impossible.

Then again, Poppy had lived the impossible before. That first month in middle school, it had seemed impossible she'd be a club president. Impossible she'd find a magic nymph and make a wish and become best friends with a winged lion.

Poppy wrapped her arms around his neck. "We'll show the world you belong here. Things always seem impossible until they're done."

Then, like words freed from Sampson, or some sort of magic on the wind, came the thought, *The impossible is not far off.*

CHAPTER TWENTY-EIGHT

Poppy was reading aloud when Sampson pawed at the door. It wasn't like him to interrupt a story. But ever since she'd covered the windows, he seemed desperate for space and fresh air. To make matters worse, the robin chicks had flown the nest, and now Sampson had one less thing to keep him occupied.

"I don't know...."

Sampson reared onto his hind legs and pushed the door, juddering it against the padlock. If she didn't let him out soon, he might break down the door himself.

"All right, all right!" She peered outside to make sure no one was around.

Sampson bounded out and Poppy jogged to catch up. He was even bigger than a full-grown lion now—his mane a mop of fur that caught the breeze, his wings probably twelve feet wide. It wasn't just his size, but his growing courage that worried Poppy.

Every day, he wanted to venture a little deeper into the woods, a little farther down the coast. When would they go too far? Wander into some unsuspecting person's path? How much longer could she keep him cooped up in the carriage house?

Sampson leapt onto a fallen tree and vaulted off, his wings extended. He landed with a graceful thud and kept running. He used to flap furiously, get frustrated, then look to Poppy for advice. But now, his failure didn't even seem to faze him. Like, he didn't really expect to fly anyway.

Poppy shook the frown off her face, hurrying to catch up. "I have to find somewhere cool to hold Readers Club next week. Since last time was such a disaster, you almost getting discovered and all that."

Sampson turned, his furry brow lowered. At first, Poppy thought he was saying, *You should have known better*. But there was something else in his expression. Like he was disappointed.

"Someday you'll meet everyone. My family first. Then we'll make a grand entrance for everyone else."

Invigorated by the thought, Sampson bounded around the forest. It was kind of amazing how he could carve through the trees without hitting a thing, his huge wings angling this way and that.

Suddenly, he stopped. He sniffed at the ground, the ropy muscles in his back tensed.

"What is it?" Poppy picked through the huckleberry bushes. She nudged him aside to get a look.

Animal tracks.

The same ones Poppy had seen near the pond; the same ones the foreman had shown her.

She had been sure they were Sampson's. But side-by-side inspection showed this print had an extra toe and deep indentations on the ends.

"Sampson . . . these aren't yours?"

Sampson's tail thumped the mossy ground.

"I've been blaming you for sneaking out . . . but all this time, it wasn't you? Why didn't you tell me?"

He couldn't exactly have said the words, but they had other ways to communicate. Poppy almost always understood him.

But then again . . . maybe he *had* tried. Maybe Poppy had been so stuck thinking she knew what was best, she hadn't been listening.

The forest darkened.

Sampson sniffed the air.

His eyes were fixed on something beyond the thicket of trees. He took a step, shoulder blades cutting upward. He'd never killed anything—not even a bug. And this could be the grizzly bear the foreman had warned about. Or worse—the nymph. She still hadn't gotten her slimy green hands on *The Tree in Valley Blue*, and Poppy felt sure she was still after it.

Poppy whispered, "Let's go."

Something dark flashed in the shadows. The heartbeat of the forest seemed to slow, every creature watching.

Poppy said again, low and deliberate, "Let's go now, Sampson."

The seriousness in her voice seemed to snap him out of it. He swept toward her, crouching. It took Poppy a moment to understand.

He wanted her to get on his back.

She swung her leg over and climbed on, gripping his mane. They charged toward the carriage house. Poppy ducked, clinging tighter to Sampson as branches and trees whirred past. He leapt over a fallen log, and she braced herself for the impact of landing. But it barely came, his gait so graceful it nearly felt like flying.

Poppy closed her eyes and imagined how it would be if he opened his wings and lifted off the ground. The wind in her hair. The sky all around. Sampson's infinite potential stretching before them.

He shifted beneath her. She opened her eyes and found him craned back, searching for whatever lurked in the shadows. But Poppy didn't turn.

She didn't need to look to know something was watching.

"Poppy! Come here, please," Mom called that night after dinner.

Poppy found her in the bathroom, bundled in a robe. Mom

flipped on the bath spout, and water rushed into the claw-footed tub. "You've been home for two hours, my girl. Take off your backpack and stay awhile."

"I will." She wouldn't. The backpack, which held *The Tree in Valley Blue*, never came off while she was on Lark-Hayes property.

Mom leaned toward the mirror, wiping off her makeup. Her hair hung long and loose around her shoulders. "What'd you do today?"

"The usual. You know."

Poppy's hair used to be long, too. But right before they'd moved here, Mom had dragged everyone to the salon for "first-impression makeovers." Luca and Mom had caused a huge scene, arguing about how much of his hair to cut.

When it had been Poppy's turn, the stylist had raked her fingers through Poppy's ends. "I know girls who'd kill for this length. And you know what they say. A girl's mood is only as good as her hair."

Poppy had looked back at Mom, who'd given her a mischievous smile that felt like permission. It was one of those rare, perfect moments when they were a team—the two of them against the world.

"Should I really do it?" Poppy had asked.

Mom had said, "It's your hair."

Poppy had turned to the stylist. "Chop it."

Mom's voice came quiet but sharp, pulling Poppy back into

the present. "You have anything to tell me?" The rushing bath-water warmed the room with wispy curls of steam.

"Huh?"

"I'm giving you a chance to come clean, Penelope. Final warning."

What was Mom getting at? There was no way she'd be this calm if she'd discovered Sampson. Had she found out Poppy took the Readers Club to the manor? Noticed all the missing books?

There were a dozen lies Mom could have uncovered. Poppy felt the weight of each of them. But maybe even heavier was the silence. The *shoving it down*. The *hiding it*.

"Come clean?" Poppy said. "Why would I *come clean* when I know about your secret plan to send me off to Aunt Deedee's if I do?"

"Wha— Who told you that?"

"Doesn't matter."

"Your brother." Mom tossed her washcloth into the hamper. "Honey, that was a passing conversation with my sister. I was just exploring options I thought would make you happy."

"You... aren't planning to send me away if I don't like it here?"

"Oh, heavens, Poppy. If I were going to send you to Deedee's because you weren't adjusting, I would have done it already."

"Good. Wait, what?"

"Oh yes. You had me fooled for a while. But guess who I ran into at the pharmacy today? Latoya Ingraham."

Poppy couldn't connect the dots fast enough. "Who?"

"I wouldn't expect you to know. Because you've never been to her house. Not once, in the dozens of times you told me you had."

Latoya Ingraham.

Annabelle's mom.

Poppy's heart stopped. She grappled for an excuse. "I . . ."

"Where have you been going all this time?"

"I've been . . . um, exploring around. I didn't want you to worry."

"Well, now I *am* worried. Very worried."

"Why? Because you want me to have a million friends? Sorry I'm not Luca."

"I don't care about that. I care about the lying."

"Really? Because that's not what you told Dad. You said I didn't have any friends because I was silly. Remember? You don't like my outfits. You don't like my books."

Mom opened her mouth but nothing came out.

"I know," Poppy continued. "I know you want me to be the easy one. The one that blends into the background. But I can't do it anymore. I'm not good at being a nobody."

Mom took Poppy's face in her hands. "You listen to me. You have never been a nobody. Never. You are my everything—my *everything*, you understand?"

Poppy wasn't sure why, but she started to cry.

Mom wiped her tears. "I'm sorry for saying you're my easy

child. I guess I thought it was a compliment. But you're so right. It's not your job to be easy. It's not your job to be anything but yourself. So be as hard as your little heart desires. I'm ready." Mom gave one of those conspiring smiles Poppy loved. "Your brother's given me good practice."

Poppy gave a sniffly laugh.

"And what I said to Dad... I didn't mean it. I just couldn't understand why kids weren't lined up outside, begging to be your friend."

"You forgot no one in middle school begs to be *anyone's* friend."

"Yeah. Well. It feels like I've forgotten a lot of things lately," Mom said, looking wistfully away. The guilt could have made Poppy cry all over again, but Mom snapped out of it. "I'm sorry." She pecked a kiss on Poppy's forehead, then one for every apology. "I'm sorry, I'm sorry, I'm sorry."

Poppy laughed and squirmed away. She wiped her face with her sleeve. "I shouldn't have to change to get other kids to like me."

"You"—Mom tapped Poppy on the nose—"are wise beyond your years. And look how wrong I was, Ms. Readers Club President. Obviously, you should never listen to me again."

"Really?"

"No, not really. I'm still your mother. But from now on... I promise to listen, too." She gave a small smile, stroking Poppy's cheek. "Anyway, I don't get *everything* wrong. The dirt bike?"

"What about it?"

"You hated it when we first gave it to you! But it's been getting plenty of use, after all."

Poppy looked at Mom, puzzled. "How'd you know I hated it?"

Mom's smile warmed. "Because I know you, my girl. A lot better than you think."

Poppy hadn't planned to tell Mom about Sampson. But this felt like the exact moment she'd been waiting for. She took a deep breath. "Mom...I...There's something I've been doing, whenever you thought I was at Annabelle's. Something I want to show—"

The air shifted, like a sharp inhale. The bath faucet sputtered and choked.

Poppy's eyes cut to the tub. A tiny whirlpool began to form, and beneath it, the color of the water distorted, flashing iridescent. *No*. Poppy was imagining it. She had to be. She squinted through the steamy haze.

Two glowing orb eyes lurked beneath the surface.

Mom moved in front of the tub, oblivious. "Something to show me? I'm excited to see. Right after—"

"Stop!"

Mom jumped. "What! What?"

Behind Mom, the nymph's scaly green hand broke the bath's surface. Needle-sharp claws and webbed fingers stretched toward a book set on the edge of the tub.

Poppy's voice dropped. "Don't . . . move."

"What is it? Spider?" Mom swiveled around, looking at the floor.

The nymph's empty hand slipped beneath the water, leaving only a ripple in her wake.

"Shoot, this is too high." Mom flipped off the faucet. "But I think that was a bit of an overreaction, don't you?" Poppy snatched the book and tried to hide it behind her back. Mom turned, her eyes narrowed. "What are you doing?"

"I—I've been meaning to read this."

"You've been meaning to read *A Woman's Purpose*?"

Poppy pulled the book from behind her. The edges were wrinkled and worn, like it had been read a dozen times. "Well . . . I am a woman—going to be a woman—so . . . it would be good for me to know."

Mom jerked her bathrobe closed. "Very funny. Give it."

"No, really. I . . ." Another lie perched on the tip of Poppy's tongue. But she couldn't do it. Not right after the talk they'd just had.

Mom snatched the book, then steered Poppy out by the shoulders. "I love you. But I need to unwind. You go finish your homework and—"

Poppy spun around in the doorway. "I know it seems ridiculous! I know. But I need that book. And you *just* said from now on you'd listen to me. You said that."

Mom scoffed. "Okay, so what is this? A test?"

"If I say yes, will you give me the book?"

It was hard to pinpoint the look in Mom's eyes as the door shut between them. Poppy pressed her ear to the door, breath held. On the other side, Mom was shuffling around. Kicking off her slippers. Hanging her robe.

Then came a long pause. A sigh.

"Okay, Penelope Quinn." The book slid under the door. "You win."

CHAPTER TWENTY-NINE

Poppy went to school early Monday morning to fix her Readers Club mistake. She would *not* be taking anyone back to Lark-Hayes manor. In doing that, Poppy had managed to become the worst president in Readers Club history—quite an achievement, given that her predecessors were bully Holden Cline and do-nothing Greyson Jager.

But unlike those guys, Poppy actually cared. She'd spent all weekend rewriting the story of Narnia. It was eighteen and a half pages in total, and she was pretty sure she'd gotten some parts word for word. Now all she needed was a new spot for meetings.

And she knew the perfect place.

Poppy found Mr. Thomas in the teachers' lounge, hunched over a stack of essays.

Another teacher filling her coffee cup spotted her. "Excuse me, young lady! You can't be—"

"—in here. I know," Poppy finished. She gestured to Mr. Thomas. "I'm with him."

"What do you need, Poppy?" Mr. Thomas asked without looking up.

"Can Readers Club meet in your room on Wednesdays?"

Mr. T marked a big red *B* on the paper and flipped it into another pile. "I host Yo-Yo Club."

"Thursday?"

"Debate Team."

"Friday? Monday? Tuesday?"

"Photography Club, Gay-Straight Alliance, and parent conferences..." He scrawled another *B* on a paper and slapped it onto the pile. "Respectively."

Poppy did not try to hide her irritation. "Seriously? Yo-Yo Club?"

"Are your interests more important than theirs?"

"I mean, I would say no ... but ..."

Mr. Thomas waited for her to finish.

"Actually, yes, books are more important than yo-yos. Because if yo-yos disappeared, it wouldn't change the way people acted. Not in the way these disappearing books are changing everything." Poppy felt herself unraveling, saying too much, but she couldn't stop. "Have you ever thought about that? About what would happen if you'd never read that *one* book that changed your life?"

Mr. Thomas squinted at Poppy. Then he did something he hadn't done since the nymph had stolen *The Odyssey*: He began twirling his pen. "Not exactly sure where this is coming from, but you make an interesting argument. Explore it a little further. Can books—do books—ever alter the course of someone's life?"

Poppy thought of Mom and Luca, both so different since their favorite books had disappeared. "Of course. That's the point."

"Let's flip it around. If a book fails to change someone, is it still of value?"

Poppy considered this. "Yes. Because you know what? Fun books are just as important."

"*Just* as important?"

"Yes. Because for us kids, life is all *rules*. Can't stay up late. Can't go into the teachers' lounge. Can't be president. But books never tell us that. Books only tell us what we can do."

"Ah, so. Books are permission."

Poppy liked that phrase. "Yeah."

"What kind of permission have books given Poppy Woodlock?"

She got the feeling Mr. Thomas was looking for a specific example, but no single one came to mind. She saw stacks of books. Mountains. She saw every costume she'd ever worn as tribute to them. Even today, she was wearing overalls—an outfit inspired by the novel she'd read with Sampson, *The Winds of Winslow County*.

"The permission I get is to be someone else for a little bit. I'm the main character. I'm all of the characters. I'm everything in the story. And it feels good to be big when everything else is trying to keep me small."

For the first time, Poppy was able to put words to the thing happening all around her. With every book that went missing, people were becoming smaller.

Mr. Thomas asked, "So, what would you tell someone who doesn't like to read?"

"I'd give them my favorite book and dare them not to like it."

"Nice. Remember that."

Poppy grinned. "So you'll let us meet in your room instead of Yo-Yo Club?"

"No. But you should ask Mrs. Bartholomew. I believe her classroom is free most afternoons."

"What! But Mrs. Bartholomew is so...so..." Boring, uptight, old. *You know.*"

"No, I don't," Mr. T said. "Now leave the teachers' lounge, or you owe me cookies."

"Can you believe I have to ask Mrs. Bartholomew?" Poppy paced the checked floor of the carriage house. Rain pattered on the roof. She'd pulled a tarp from the window to let in some light, and Sampson was perched in front of the diamond panes, staring at the empty robins' nest. Maybe he didn't know that once babies flew the nest, they never came back. But Poppy didn't have the heart to tell him.

He wasn't himself lately. His eyes were a little dim. His whiskers drooped. He was cooped up. But there was no other way to keep him safe, so Poppy did her best to cheer him with extra stories and longer walks.

"Mrs. B is the *opposite* of what I promised everyone. Not exciting. Not fun. Not cool."

Sampson looked back at Poppy, his whole expression flattened out.

"What? She isn't!"

Sampson crossed the room. Poppy loved watching him move, lazy and strong and fully grown. She loved listening to his paws clack against the floorboards. But her smile fell when he picked up her backpack and turned it over. Books and pens spilled everywhere.

"Hey!"

Sampson rifled through the mess with his nose. He walked over to Poppy and dropped *The Winds of Winslow County* at her feet.

They'd finished reading it last week, and Poppy had ended up loving it. She'd even added a new quote to her notebook. "You want to read it again?"

He thumped his tail. *No.*

"Then what?"

Sampson padded back to the scattered contents of Poppy's backpack, then picked up her fuzzy pink notebook and dropped it at her feet. He nudged it open to the line she'd copied down:

> *He'd judged them. And the rest of Winslow had convicted them. But in the end, he was the real criminal. Because he'd killed his chance to ever understand the Darby family.*

"Sampson . . . are you saying I shouldn't judge Mrs. B?"

Thump, thump. *Yes.*

He turned away and went back to watching the empty nest while Poppy stood there, feeling slightly scolded and a lot amazed.

With all the reading they were doing, Sampson was getting too smart for his own good.

After school the next day, Poppy found Mrs. Bartholomew trimming her potted bonsai tree. Rumor was, at the beginning of the year, someone had knocked it off the windowsill, and Mrs. Bartholomew had cried in front of her whole class. Some kids called her *Mrs. Bartholo-mess* behind her back.

"Hi, Mrs. B," Poppy called from the doorway.

The teacher startled. She pushed up her glasses. "Oh! Penelope. To what do I owe this pleasure?"

Poppy inched forward. "I was wondering if the Readers

Club could meet here after school on Wednesdays." She said it quickly and without enthusiasm, half hoping Mrs. Bartholomew would say no.

The teacher straightened. Her skirt brushed her ankles, revealing bulbous black shoes. "You . . . want me to host?"

Poppy nodded.

Mrs. Bartholomew clasped her hands. "I would be honored." It seemed like an overstatement.

But apparently Mrs. Bartholomew meant every bit of enthusiasm, because on Wednesday, a banner spanned the width of her classroom—WELCOME, READERS!—and she'd brought enough homemade brownies to feed the entire sixth grade.

Poppy sat cross-legged on a desk, her handwritten story of Narnia in her lap. This had seemed like such a brilliant idea at first.

But lately, it felt like shoveling the sidewalk in a snowstorm. Every day, another book went missing. And every day, her family felt less familiar. Her parents had stopped reading together at night. They never talked about the renovation unless it was a fight: Dad begging Mom to show up, Mom snapping that he didn't understand what she was going through.

Luca rarely came out of his room. He'd gotten into a fight with some kids who were teasing him and had been suspended for two days. They didn't even have family dinners anymore, just takeout containers spread across the table each night.

Mrs. Bartholomew swept a pile of bonsai tree clippings into her trash.

"Do you do that every day?" Poppy asked.

"Once a week or so." The teacher made a final snip, then stowed the scissors in her desk. "What time does Readers Club start?"

"Three."

Mrs. Bartholomew glanced at the clock. Her expression registered with the worry Poppy felt. It was 3:20. Annabelle had gotten a B on her math test, so her mom was making her do extra days with her tutor this week. But where was everyone else?

"Ah. So . . ." Mrs. Bartholomew forced a smile. "Maybe it's just us. What luck! Grab a brownie and tell me what you've got there."

Poppy ate a brownie to make Mrs. Bartholomew happy. Then she read the entire Narnia story aloud, glancing up every so often to see if there were any signs of remembering. And though Mrs. B applauded enthusiastically at the end, she'd clearly never heard the story before.

The full hour passed and no one else came.

Afterward, Poppy sat on the curb, waiting for Luca to pick her up. A rowdy group came out of the school building behind her.

Holden broke from the pack. "How was Readers Club?"

Poppy gathered every bit of pride she still had left. "Great, thanks for asking."

"Really? Because I walked past. Literally no one was in there except you and Mrs. Bartholo-mess."

Poppy's face warmed.

Holden scoffed. "Seriously? You thought anyone would come to a club led by *you*? What a joke."

On the drive home, Luca didn't feel like talking, either.

Whatever was bothering him, Poppy couldn't muster the energy to pry it out. It felt like a fist was clenching her lungs, and it didn't stop squeezing until she got home and swung open the carriage house door.

Poppy threw her arms around Sampson and buried her face in his mane.

When she pushed upright, he nudged her, urging her to explain. But she couldn't do it. Because no one loved books more than Sampson. And she couldn't bear any more disappointment today.

She turned and ran, racing along the path she and Sampson had carved a dozen times.

Sampson stayed by her side. Every few strides, he'd open his wings and clap them back, and his paws would lift off the ground for a single beat; then he'd find his footing again.

Tears whisked into Poppy's hairline. She should have known she couldn't do it. She'd failed. And she was failing Sampson, too. After two months of trying, he still couldn't fly. Couldn't roar. Couldn't do anything he wanted to.

The two of them were made for each other after all.

The pines thinned, and the ground became packed soil beneath Poppy's sneakers. The horizon appeared, leaden clouds above the restless sea. Poppy skidded to a stop at the cliff's edge, kicking dirt and pebbles toward the water below.

She clenched her fists and screamed. Her voice joined the wind and crashing waves. It was a song. The saddest, angriest song.

But for once, it felt good to be loud. To be huge.

She didn't stop until her lungs gave out.

Beside her, Sampson watched, head cocked, like he was trying to understand. Then he turned to the ocean . . . and *roared*.

Poppy threw her hands over her ears. A cloud of shrieking birds erupted from the canopy. Sampson's jaws hinged wider, baring every massive tooth. His roar grew until the sound of the waves fell away. The air filled with all the things he'd been shoving down, too—his failures, his frustration. Everything he couldn't do because he was hiding in the carriage house.

He clapped his jaws shut.

Poppy's ears rang, the air still vibrating around her. Sampson looked at her, his gaze fierce and conspiring.

Then, in unison, they turned to the sea and roared together.

A second rush of birds soared from the trees, heading out to the ocean. Poppy stepped toward the edge of the cliff and screamed louder. But now it was a cry of triumph.

He'd done it.

They'd done it.

That was the last thought she had before the cliff collapsed and she plunged toward the sea.

CHAPTER THIRTY

Poppy screamed, sliding down the steep cliffside, shielding her face from rocks and sticks. She rotated, clawing at the ground slipping away beneath her. Her fingers found a root and she closed her fist.

The world jolted to a stop.

She pressed her cheek to the cliff, her eyes peeled wide, trying to make sense of her surroundings. One hand gripped the fraying root above her head. Her right foot balanced on a ledge only six inches wide; her left dangled in the empty air.

Poppy's breath came ragged and shallow.

Fifty feet down, jagged boulders broke the foaming sea like black teeth.

"Sampson?" Her voice was a croaking whisper. She stifled a sob, then tried again, louder. "Sampson?"

He moaned from somewhere above. A helpless, haunting sound that echoed all around.

Her cell phone vibrated in her pocket, loosening the earth near her hip. The dead root that had stopped her fall peeled an inch from the cliff.

Poppy whimpered, praying whoever was calling would hang up.

Bzzz. Bzzz.

The root split another inch.

Poppy's throat strangled. "Samp—"

The root snapped.

This time, there was no earth to break her fall. There was only air, sharp and cold and hissing past. She threw up her hands to protect her skull.

She hit something—the sea or the rocks. The force stole her breath.

But she wasn't dead. She wasn't wet.

And how, she thought, was she suddenly falling upward?

Her eyes flew open. She swept up past the cliff, the gray sky stretching toward her.

Beneath her, Sampson roared, his great wings carving through the sky.

"Sampson!" Poppy cried. His roar was so deep it shook the earth, sending shards of the cliffside into the sea.

Poppy twisted to straddle him. She wrapped herself around

him, gripping his mane. His chest bobbed with every beat of his wings; his golden fur whipped in the wind.

He seemed to fill the whole sky, drawing light from the sun itself. As graceful as he was powerful.

Sampson stopped beating the air and soared. Poppy lifted her face skyward. If the wind had not been so sharp and cold against her skin, if Sampson's body had not been so warm and real beneath her, if the rush of her own blood had not been so exhilarating, she would have thought this was a dream.

Poppy spread her arms. The sky embraced her. "We're flying!"

Sampson veered from the ocean, heading for land. Poppy wrapped her arms around his neck.

The world darkened as they entered the forest. Sampson maneuvered through the trees as if he'd done it a thousand times before, his wings snapping twigs and leaves, everything passing in a blur of green.

He pressed his wings back and spiraled up and up. Poppy hugged him with every muscle in her body until they broke through the canopy. A wave of rustling pines shuddered in their wake.

"Head back to sea!" Poppy called. They were safe from being spotted there.

He tilted and made a wide arc.

Poppy rested her chin on Sampson's head, watching their

approach to the ocean. Before them, the clouds broke on the horizon, edged by the setting sun. The sunset reflected on the sea: a pink and gold mirror fractured by white froth.

Sampson swooped down, cutting the ocean with the tip of his wing, sending a spray of salt water over Poppy. She laughed and followed suit—stretching her toes to skim the sea that had terrified her only moments before.

He ascended again, heading straight into the cotton clouds. Poppy hugged him, tears streaking her cheeks.

He nuzzled her back, so proud and powerful, but still her little lion after all.

"Sampson," she called over the rushing wind. He'd found his roar. He'd found his wings. And it was time for the world to see. "We're ready!"

All evening, the confession danced on Poppy's tongue. *There's a flying lion in the carriage house.* She waited for the right time—a break in conversation, a moment of eye contact, the question *Why are you in such a good mood, Poppy?* But it never came. Her parents spent the entire evening arguing in the office, and Luca didn't get home until after Poppy had fallen asleep.

In the morning, her family was a whirlwind of late starts and missing items, and Mom herded Poppy into the car and dropped her at school without getting off her phone once.

Poppy stood on the school curb, her patchwork skirt flapping around her shins. She'd made it last week—a tribute to *The Sound of Lonely*, a book about a treasure-hunting orphan who makes a family from the people she meets along the way. It was the twelfth book Poppy had read with Sampson, and maybe his favorite so far. But she had a feeling it would also be the last one for a while.

Now that Sampson could fly—they'd never stay on the ground again.

She looked up at the dull building in front of her. How was she supposed to survive a boring school day when she could be soaring through the clouds? She closed her eyes, remembering the whip of the wind, the crash of the sea, the gentle roll of Sampson's body as his wings beat the air.

"Hello, Penelope!" Mrs. Bartholomew called. Poppy found the teacher shuffling toward her. "I...I want to apologize for Readers Club yesterday."

Poppy felt she'd missed something. "Apologize?"

"Yes. I'm very sorry...about...about how it turned out. But I have some exciting news. I found out Mr. Wilder has an open classroom on Thursday afternoons."

"Wait. You don't want to host anymore?"

"Of course I want to. But...you know, I think Readers Club is very important. And I think you're a great president." She gave a sad smile and leaned close. "You'll have more success with Mr. Wilder as the host."

Poppy understood. Mrs. Bartholomew thought no one had shown up because of *her*. It was sad that Mrs. B was no one's favorite teacher. But it was even sadder that Mrs. B knew it.

Poppy shook her head. "If it's okay, I want to keep meeting in your classroom. I had fun yesterday."

A match strike of hope lit Mrs. B's eyes. "But... are you sure? I've already spoken with Mr. Wilder."

The first bell rang, warning Poppy she had one minute to get to class. One minute until the intercoms screeched to life for morning announcements.

An idea began to form.

"I'm sure," Poppy said, then, before she could think better of her idea, said goodbye and swept into the school office.

The intercom microphone was already on the counter for Ms. Spiducci, who was scribbling something on a yellow legal pad.

"I'd like to make an announcement about Readers Club," Poppy said. "I'm the president."

Ms. Spiducci waved. "Go ahead and write it down; I'm about to start."

"I'd like to say it."

Ms. Spiducci glanced over her shoulder to the school secretary, who gave a little nod, as if to say, *She's a good kid.* "All right. Just a sentence or two. Understood?"

"Got it," Poppy said.

The second bell rang, and Ms. Spiducci flipped the button

on the base of the intercom. The speakers throughout the school came to life with a long, low *beeeep*. Ms. Spiducci led the Pledge, then said, "And now, a quick announcement from our Readers Club president...Ms...."

Poppy wiped her sweaty palms on her pants. One little announcement. If Sampson could leap off a cliff and fly, she could do this tiny thing.

"Ms....um...," Ms. Spiducci faltered.

Poppy leaned over the microphone. "Penelope Quinn Woodlock." She wasn't sure why her full name had spilled out, but it felt good. "I'd like to announce that Readers Club meets Wednesdays after school in Mrs. Bartholomew's class, room two-forty."

Ms. Spiducci reached for the microphone, but Poppy gripped the base with two hands. This next part was important. "And if you don't know Mrs. Bartholomew, she's awesome, and she makes the best fudge brownies you've ever had."

Poppy hoped that somewhere in the school, Mrs. B was smiling.

"Very nice," Ms. Spiducci whispered, reaching for the intercom with far less patience.

But Poppy wasn't done. She pulled the intercom off the desk, yanking the cord taut. "And if you don't want to come because you think you don't like reading, I'll make you a deal. I'll lend you my favorite book. And I bet a plate of brownies you like it."

Ms. Spiducci was now trying to pin Poppy in place with her eyes. She flipped up the countertop, gesturing for Poppy to surrender the intercom.

But that couldn't be all Poppy said. She'd made the mistake of inviting people to the club for the wrong reason last time. She needed kids to come for books, not just brownies.

Ms. Spiducci grabbed the base of the intercom as Poppy pulled the other way.

The microphone popped free from the stand.

Ms. Spiducci gasped. Poppy gaped. The microphone gave a high-pitched whine.

It was wireless.

Poppy swept out of the office, mic in hand.

Stragglers hurrying to class froze in their tracks to watch the spectacle: Poppy, a bandit on the run, and Ms. Spiducci, struggling to catch up in her pencil skirt and heels.

"Go, girl, go!" someone called.

The cry was picked up by the mic, echoing through the whole school.

Poppy stayed laser-focused on her message. "Most important of all, I want to say that everyone is welcome at Readers Club." She picked up speed and rounded the corner, leaving Ms. Spiducci in the dust. "And everyone needs more reading in their life, because books are like . . . are like . . ."

She searched for a comparison. A map? A compass? No.

Reading never told her where to go. But, like she'd told Mr. T, every time she finished a book, she felt . . . bigger.

Reading was *building*.

It came to her in a flash: Dad's Lark-Hayes manor plans spread across the table. "Books are like blueprints. If you build your house without blueprints, sure, you might end up with four walls and a roof. But with books . . . you can have a castle."

There. She was done.

Poppy turned, ready to surrender the mic.

Her smile faded. Ms. Spiducci had thrown off her heels and was running full-speed, her pantyhosed feet slipping over the tile. She slid to a stop and ripped the microphone away, covering it with her palm. "That's a week's lunch detention. A week!" She uncovered the mic and switched to a honey-sweet voice. "Wow, thank you for that rousing speech, Penelope. That wraps up our announcements. Have a brilliant day, Road Racers."

Across the hall, Annabelle slammed her locker shut. As soon as their eyes met, their smiles spread into laughter. They passed Mr. Thomas, who leaned in the doorway to his classroom, twirling a pen.

"*There* she is," he said, winking at Poppy.

She wasn't sure exactly what he meant.

But *this*, she thought, was how Sampson must have felt when he'd flown.

Poppy paced the hallway in front of Luca's closed door, rehearsing the conversation. "Luca, I have a magical lion in the carriage house." No. She had to ease him into it. Start from the beginning. "You remember that time I freaked out about the Narnia books? Well...it's a long story, and it involves an evil nymph." Much worse. She had to lead with the good part.

The door swung open and Luca bowled into Poppy. He stumbled and caught her, but his backpack went flying.

"Sorry." Poppy scooped up his bag. "I...I need to talk to you."

"About what?"

"About..." She glanced down the hall to make sure her parents were out of earshot. The blue light of the TV flashed on the living room walls. "I—wait. Where are you going?"

Luca took the bag and slung it over his shoulder. "Library."

"Since when do you go to the library?"

"Since I want to get out of the house before Mom and Dad try to cheer me up with another bad CGI movie. If they notice I'm gone, tell them I'm at a friend's."

Why wouldn't he want their parents to know he was going to the library? They always *begged* him to study more. And why would they be trying to cheer him up?

Suddenly, Poppy realized. It was prom night. The marquee board in front of Chatlain High had been announcing it for months. Poppy ran in front of him. "Hey, why didn't you go to prom?"

"Why are you bugging me, Poppy? Seriously, you're so annoying lately."

The hurt must have registered on her face immediately, because Luca groaned. "I don't know. People are being...you know. I didn't want to put up with it."

A sinking feeling dragged Poppy's insides. "Are people bullying you?"

"I'm not five years old. I don't get bullied."

She didn't buy it. Kids didn't stop bullying. They just got better at it.

An explosion came from whatever show Mom and Dad were watching.

"I'm leaving," Luca said impatiently. "Did you need to tell me something?"

"No." Poppy met his eyes. "I need to show you."

"We're going to the manor?" Luca called over Poppy's shoulder. His voice barely carried over the buzz of the dirt bike. Poppy had made him ride on the back, and then refused to tell him where they were going. She didn't want to give him the chance to say no.

"Just hang on," Poppy called back. "It's bumpy here." The bike moved slower under the weight of two people.

"Where did you learn to drive it like this?" Luca sounded impressed. Poppy's smile widened behind the helmet. If he was impressed now, just wait.

Just wait.

"You smell that?" Luca called.

"Smell what?"

Her answer came.

The trees parted and the manor came into view. Poppy clenched the brake. The back tire skidded, propelling the bike into a half turn. They lurched to a stop.

Poppy ripped off her helmet and ran forward a few steps.

Behind her, Luca yelled, "The forest is on fire!"

"No...," Poppy said. Behind Lark-Hayes Manor, black tendrils curled into the sky. Distant flames painted a red halo around the mansion. "That's the carriage house."

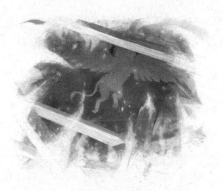

CHAPTER THIRTY-ONE

Plumes of black smoke billowed up behind Lark-Hayes Manor.

Luca cursed. "Is this what you wanted to show me? Poppy!"

"Of course not!" Poppy cried. "Call 911!"

Luca jabbed at his phone. "No service!" He vaulted onto the seat of the dirt bike and twisted the throttle, revving the engine. "We've got to tell Mom and Dad! Get on!"

"You'll go faster without me!" Poppy shouted. "I'll wait here!"

Luca grimaced, but they didn't have time to argue. "Poppy, do *not* move!"

The dirt bike buzzed out of sight.

Poppy sprinted toward the carriage house. She dared to hope it was a small fire. Just in the surrounding woods.

But as she rounded the manor, hope fell like ashes at her feet.

Smoke billowed through cracks in the barn doors. Flames engulfed the entire back wall.

"Sampson!" The scream ripped from her.

Her feet did not touch the ground as she flew toward the burning carriage house.

She tore the key from her neck, jammed it into the door, then gripped the handle to yank it open. The scalding metal seared the soft skin of her palm. She tore away. A white, angry blister bubbled up immediately. She shed her jacket, wrapped it around her hand, and yanked the handle again, but it was melted shut.

"Sampson!"

A low moan rose from the crackling fire.

Poppy ran around the back, searching for a way in. But the windows were shattered, spewing flames.

She ran back to the door and kicked at it. Each kick rattled the padlock, weakening the old wood around the mount.

The shock of her burned palm began to wear off. Poppy gasped, clutching it as she ran and kicked the door with her entire weight. It burst open, raining shards of wood.

Inside, flames danced along the walls. Huge sheaths of plaster collapsed to the floor. Poppy unwound the jacket from her hand and held it over her mouth, squinting against the sharp sting of smoke.

Sampson's low moan came beneath the roar of the fire. He crept out from behind the carriage, soot and sparks powdering his mane.

Poppy ran to him and stumbled over a hard round object, turning her ankle, barely catching her balance. A small glass rolled out from beneath her. There were others. Dozens of candles, still burning.

She had no time to make sense of it. The fire was inching toward the open doorway. Poppy hooked her arm around Sampson's neck. "Straight through there!"

Poppy tried to steer him out, but he was a thousand pounds of dead weight. His knees buckled and he collapsed. His bleary eyes moved to the stacks of books stranded near the flames.

The books.

If they were destroyed, Poppy's deal with the nymph was broken. Sampson would no longer exist.

Poppy ran to the piles of books, beating the flames back with her jacket. A few covers were scorched, but they hadn't been burned yet. "Hang on!" she choked.

She gathered as many as she could and ran through the door, throwing them to safety. She gulped the fresh air, clearing the wooziness from her head, then raced back for more.

The ceiling beams spat sparks down on Poppy, threatening to give way. The flames inched closer.

Finally, she tossed out the last of the books. Sampson pushed to his feet.

Poppy grabbed his face, forcing him to focus. "You okay?" He blinked, his eyes still a little dim. "Okay, let's get out of here!" She hooked an arm around his front leg. She'd drag him out if she had to. "Through the door! One ... two ..."

The overhead beams cracked and gave way. Sampson yanked Poppy back as the beams crashed in front of them, a flaming mass of wood. It barricaded the door.

There was no way out.

Voices came from outside. Shouting.

"I'm in here!" Poppy screamed, her voice thin. She coughed into her jacket. "I'm in here! Help!"

"She's inside!" Dad shouted. "Poppy, hold on! I have an ax!"

Dad was going to burst in here, terrified and swinging a weapon. He'd see Sampson and panic.

Poppy grabbed Sampson's face as smoke thickened around them. "Sampson. As soon as my dad ..." She wavered on her feet, light-headed. She grounded herself in his eyes—perfect circles of gold against the black smoke. "When the door opens ... you have to get away. Understand?"

Something slammed against the barn door.

"Harder, Spencer!" Mom screamed.

The ceiling crumbled, crashing down in hunks of flaming wood. Sampson threw a wing over Poppy as debris and sparks rained down over him.

"Poppy!" Mom shouted. "Poppy! Are you okay?"

"I'm okay!" Poppy choked out.

Sampson shimmied the sparks from his wings. Above, the collapsed roof revealed a fissure of sky.

"Go, Sampson!" Poppy pushed him. "Fly!"

He nudged her to climb on.

"I can't!" She had to be here when Dad got inside. He wouldn't leave the barn unless he found her. He'd die searching.

Another crack of the ax rattled the barn doors.

"Sampson, go!" The scream shredded the flesh of Poppy's throat.

Sampson looked between the ceiling and Poppy, his wings shuddering, his eyes pleading. *I can't leave you*, they said.

The ax struck again, and the barn door crashed open. Thick plumes of smoke poured out, sweeping past them.

"Poppy!" Dad cried.

Sampson retreated, out of Poppy's reach. She inhaled to scream, but her lungs filled with smoke. The world spun.

The floor swung up to meet her.

Dad's arms lifted her from the rubble. Poppy forced her eyes open, fighting for consciousness.

"Sampson . . . ," she murmured.

Sirens wailed. Ashes fell like black snow.

Above, the smoking roof gaped like an open mouth; and in it—Poppy caught a flash of white, a tuft of golden tail.

"One more time, breathe in," the doctor said.

An air-conditioning vent above the bed blew a steady

stream of arctic air. Poppy's thin hospital gown did nothing to shield her from the cold. She shivered, arms clutched to her chest.

The doctor draped her stethoscope around her neck. "Her lungs sound good. I'd still like to order X-rays and blood tests. And in the meantime, we're going to keep this pulse oximeter on to monitor her oxygen levels." She adjusted the clamp around Poppy's index finger.

Poppy's knee bounced, her bandaged palm resting limply in her lap. She squeezed her eyes shut and saw the flash of Sampson's wings against the black smoke. She'd been so near passing out, she wondered if she'd imagined it.

Dad paced the floor, rubbing his beard, squinting at the beeping machines like he understood them. "Is there a chance some symptoms don't show up for a couple of days?"

The doctor nodded. "It's possible. Keep your eyes open for coughing, shortness of breath, nausea. Confusion or muddled thinking. If any of that occurs, come back in."

Poppy felt certain the firefighters hadn't found Sampson— or else it would be all over the news, which was playing on low volume on the little TV across the room. That meant Sampson *had* escaped through the roof. He was somewhere out there. Hiding in the forest. Alone. "How much longer until I can go?"

The doctor typed something on the computer. "We need to take a blood sample; then we have to wait for the results from the lab. X-rays may take a little longer. Plan on several hours."

"What?" Poppy launched from the hospital bed. The pulse oximeter ripped off and toppled to the ground. "I—I've got to get back home."

The doctor's eyes shifted to Mom and Dad.

Mom slid her arm around Poppy's shoulders, gently pulling her back into bed. "We'll stay as long as she needs."

The doctor reattached the monitor, then left with a murmur of gratitude from Poppy's parents. Dad slid off his jacket and draped it over Poppy's shoulders. It was heavy and warm from his body heat.

"Mr. and Mrs. Woodlock?" A policeman hovered in the doorway. "Do you have a minute?"

Mom looked to Dad. "Can you handle that?"

Dad went out to talk with the officers in the hallway, and Mom sat at the foot of Poppy's bed. She looked out the window. "There's supposed to be an eclipse tomorrow," she said. "Super Blood Moon."

Poppy didn't know what that meant. But right now, it didn't feel important. "I'm sorry, Mom. I'm really sorry."

Mom gave a brittle smile. She tucked a lock of hair behind Poppy's ear. "I'm just happy you're all right. But what on earth were you thinking?"

"I thought...I thought I could save the carriage house."

"But that wasn't your responsibility. Help me understand."

Poppy drew Dad's jacket tighter around herself. She didn't have to bring Sampson into it. She could just tell Mom about how she'd spent every afternoon fixing up the carriage house. How the light came through the windows in a dreamy shade of green. How the air smelled like rot and damp soil. How she would curl up and read there for hours on end.

But then she'd have to admit she'd forged the letter from the Fish and Wildlife Service. And right now, she couldn't muster the energy for that conversation.

Mom wiped the tears from Poppy's cheeks. "They found candles all over the floor. Be honest. Did you take those in there?"

"No. I would never do that."

"But the books? The ones scattered all over outside? Those were from your room, right?"

"I—yes. But the fire wasn't me. I swear. This kid from Readers Club. His name is Holden Cline. I think he started it."

Mom leaned back, putting space between them. "You brought people onto the property after we specifically told you not to?"

"Yes, but . . . but I didn't even let those kids inside the manor. Holden was being a jerk, so we got into a fight. . . ." Mom's eyes widened, but she didn't say anything, so Poppy continued, "And after that, everyone went home. I bet Holden came back. He kept saying something about a séance."

Had Holden discovered Sampson? Maybe that was why the candles were left burning—before he could start his séance, maybe he'd come face-to-face with a magic lion. Maybe he'd gotten the scare he deserved.

"But that doesn't explain why you were taking Luca to the manor tonight."

Poppy remembered the look on her brother's face when he'd said he wasn't going to prom. "I wanted to cheer him up."

"Oh. Yeah. I know. Oh, Luca." Mom looked away—her expression tight and teary again. "You know, if I ever meet the kids bullying Luca...Well, they don't call us mama bears for nothing."

Poppy launched upright. "What happened to my books outside the carriage house?"

"They're safe. Back home."

Poppy slumped back into the bed, relieved. "And my backpack?"

"Luca took it to the house, too." Mom pulled out her phone. "Do you need it? I can call him and have him bring it—"

"No! No. I just wanted to be sure it was safe."

"What's so important in there?"

"Just a book. You remember that little tree one I used to read with Dad?"

Mom laughed softly. "Of course I remember. I thought for sure Dad would make you sick of it."

Poppy thought *she'd* been the one who wanted to read it every night, but all at once, she was unsure. "Did Dad really love it or something?"

Mom's expression softened. "You know why he calls you Poppyseed, right?"

Poppy shook her head.

"He says because someday you'll realize *you're* Little Tree."

Poppy looked over Mom's shoulder. Dad stood beneath the fluorescent lights, his voice carrying over the waxed floor tiles. But Poppy couldn't hear him, her ears filled with the final words from *The Tree in Valley Blue*.

> *One day,*
> *a child looked up in wonder.*
> *"This tree knows a secret," she said.*
>
> *"What's that?"*
> *the mother asked.*
>
> *Little Tree bent to hear the reply,*
> *which came as a whisper,*
> *small and true:*
>
> *"She knows*
> *she makes the world beautiful*
> *when she blooms in her own time."*
>
> *Then they filled their baskets*
> *and wove through the sleepy forest*
> *as the tree in Valley Blue*
> > *bloomed*
> > > *taller.*

CHAPTER THIRTY-TWO

They didn't get home from the hospital until 4:00 a.m. By the time Poppy had showered and changed into pajamas, the sky was woolly and gray with the promise of morning. Mom tucked Poppy into bed as Dad hung a blanket over her window, darkening the room. They gave her a pill for the throbbing in her burned hand.

"Get some rest," Dad said, kissing her forehead.

"We love you," Mom said, tears in her voice.

The door clicked shut.

Poppy's eyes were dry as tissue paper. She glanced at her clock. A few hours of sleep. That was all she needed. Then she'd sneak out and find Sampson.

She slept fitfully, tortured by the scent of fire clinging to her skin and hair. She dreamt of smoke monsters. Of Sampson, alone in the woods. Worst of all, she dreamt of her lost carriage house.

The diamond-paned windows.

The checked floors.

The safety within those pale blue walls.

In that dream, Poppy lay in the crook of Sampson's wing, reading. The book was one she didn't recognize—a dark cover with a gold-embossed title. Suddenly it changed, the way things can change only in dreams. The cover became wings. The book flew into the rafters, swooping around like that little bird who'd shown Sampson how to fly.

The bird split and multiplied, became two, ten, a hundred, a thousand. They shrieked and flapped, sending down a furious gust of wind. Poppy cowered in the corner. "Help me, Sammy! Help me!"

Somewhere out of sight, he roared.

Poppy woke with a start, her mind floating in that space between dream and reality. What had awoken her?

Her parents' voices.

Even through the walls, Poppy could hear the tension. She rolled to her side, checking her clock. Seven p.m.

She'd slept for an entire day.

Sampson.

She launched out of bed and swung open her door, squinting into the hallway lights. Across the way, Luca's door was shut, but loud music thumped from inside. She stepped out, nearly tripping over the sagging backpack where Luca must have left it. She held her breath and checked inside. Little Tree was still there. Relief flooded her, but not for long.

Dad's voice came from the living room. "We made a commitment!"

"We made a mistake," Mom said.

Poppy slung the bag around her shoulders. She cradled her throbbing palm as she crept down the hall. Mom stood in the center of the room, her back to Poppy, and Dad leaned against the fireplace mantel. "I cannot believe I'm hearing this. Twenty years of work in the making. Your dream project. And you want to walk away?"

"Things change," Mom said.

"Are you overwhelmed? We can scale back, ask for an extension."

"I'm tired of going in circles on this."

"You aren't thinking clearly! Our reputation will be shot! Walking away from a project like this? No one will ever hire us again!"

"Our reputation? That's what you're worried about?"

A pain worse than the one in Poppy's hand began to form in her chest. Mom wanted to quit the renovation? She'd seemed distracted lately. Uninterested, even. But never in a million years did Poppy think she'd quit.

"I won't do it," Dad said. "I won't follow you into self-ruin."

They stared at each other for a moment, unspoken words

passing between them. Something was happening they didn't want to say aloud.

"And Luca?" Dad asked sharply.

Mom responded carefully, "This has been hard for him, too. And that fight at school? It was so out of character. He agrees this move was a mistake."

"You already talked to him about this?"

A pause. "Yes. He wants to come with Poppy and me."

"So you're splitting up the family"—Dad's voice cracked—"just like that."

Poppy stepped into the dull yellow light of the living room. "Mom? Dad? What's going on?"

Mom swept her into her arms. "That was a nice long sleep, my girl. How are you feeling?"

Dad slid a hand beneath Poppy's backpack, pressing his palm to her spine. "Can you do a deep breath?"

Poppy inhaled, exhaled.

"Good. Good." He sounded relieved, but the worry didn't leave his eyes.

Poppy stepped out of their reach. "What's going on?"

"Go ahead, Cordelia," Dad said quietly.

Mom tried to relax her expression, but her voice came out strained. "Your father and I have been talking a lot these past few weeks. About the decision to move here."

"I heard that part," Poppy said. "I heard you say you were leaving."

Mom pressed her lips together. Dad leaned against the mantel, his head in his hands.

"Next Sunday," Mom said, "we're going back to Virginia."

"What? We can't move! What about the renovation?"

"That's not for you to worry about, honey."

Poppy turned to Dad. "And...and you're not coming with us?"

His expression was familiar. She'd seen it in Mom's eyes when she'd forgotten Grandma. In Luca's when he'd forgotten himself. Dad's heart was broken. "I've got to finish what we started."

Poppy looked back and forth between her parents, hoping for a break in someone's resolve. "But...but the dream team..."

Why were *these* the only words she could manage? This wasn't just about Mom leaving. Or losing her passion for renovations. It was about Mom forgetting a part of her that bound her to Dad. A stitch in their family beginning to unravel.

Poppy buried her face in Dad's chest. "This is all my fault."

"No." Dad held her. "Your mother—"

"Don't blame Mom," Poppy said. "This is my fault, because I'm the one who wished all the books away. Nothing has been okay since then!" She pushed upright. "Mom, you have to remember! Remember Grandma and that story about fixing up the old dollhouse! Remember how much you love renovations! Just try!"

Mom opened her mouth to respond when a curt knock came at the front door.

Her parents locked eyes. Poppy swiped a sleeve beneath her nose.

The knock came again louder. "Mr. Woodlock? Mrs. Woodlock?"

Mom checked her face in the hall mirror, then swung open the door.

A construction worker stood on the porch, panting and red-faced like he'd run here, though his car rumbled in the driveway. "We tried to get ahold of you. You weren't answering your phones."

"We're dealing with a family issue," Mom said. "What's going on?"

"There was an attack at the manor. We need permission to bring more men onto the grounds for a search party."

Dad strode forward. "An attack?"

"An animal," the man panted, "dragged one of our men into the woods."

"What? Who?" Mom gasped.

"Aaron Kemp. Young guy who worked the digger."

Poppy's heart skittered. She rushed to the door and pulled it wider. "What kind of animal attacked him?"

Dad said, "Permission granted. We're right behind you."

Mom headed for the mudroom. Dad raced toward the back door for his boots.

"What kind of animal?" Poppy called. But the man slid into his car and skidded out of the driveway.

Mom reappeared in her trench coat, her purse jangling.

Dad clomped his boots onto his feet, then jabbed a finger toward Poppy. "You and Luca are not to leave this house. Do you understand?"

The door slammed behind them.

Poppy didn't wait to hear the car start. She grabbed Luca's windbreaker and threw it over her pajamas. Her hands shook so badly she could barely do the zipper.

Sampson would never have attacked someone. This had to be something else. Maybe the nymph. Or that bear who'd been leaving tracks all over the forest. Either way, in minutes, there would be armed men all over these woods. And if Sampson was caught . . . he'd be blamed.

He'd be killed.

Chapter Thirty-Three

The trees whipped by as clawed black shapes. Beyond the high-pitched buzz of her dirt bike, the forest seemed unsettled. Unbalanced.

"Sampson," Poppy pleaded, "please be okay. Please be okay."

She was distracted. A sharp turn took her by surprise. She yanked the handlebars, overcorrected, and skidded, hitting the ground. She tucked her arms to her chest and rolled. Dirt kicked up around her as the bike spun on its side and smashed into a tree.

Poppy rolled to a stop on her back in the center of the path.

The full moon hovered above the tree line. Bigger than she'd ever seen. Glowing a strange, ruddy color.

A man's shout from the woods jolted through her.

Poppy scrambled to her feet and heaved her bike upright. She kicked the throttle. It revved, then died.

"No!"

She ripped off her helmet.

It was only a quarter mile to the manor.

Her feet had never moved faster. They beat the ground to the tempo of a single word: *Sampson. Sampson. Sampson.*

Finally, the manor came into view. Flashlights roved the darkness, and a crowd gathered near the front doors. The construction foreman stood on the manor steps, addressing them.

Mom and Dad were farther down the driveway, their backs to Poppy, locked in conversation with Mrs. Mendoza. Poppy ducked into the crowd for cover.

"We can't wait for the park ranger," the foreman announced. "I have three guns in the back of my truck, and Matty has two. If you don't have a firearm, pair up with someone who does."

Poppy's heart stopped. She asked the man beside her, "What kind of animal are they searching for?"

He didn't answer, too focused on the foreman, who continued, "Matty is passing out whistles. If you see any sign of Aaron, blow like you're trying to wake the dead."

Poppy pushed deeper into the crowd, stopping near two men crouched on the ground, sliding bullets into hunting rifles. She leaned close to hear.

"—stopped answering the walkie, so the foreman went out to find him. Found the walkie and huge tracks leading straight that way." The man hitched his head back. He slid the last shell into his rifle, then snapped it shut. "Ranger hasn't shown up to identify the tracks yet. Foreman thinks bear. Maybe wolf. Something big."

The men stood and the crowd began to disperse, heading for the woods. Poppy had no doubt now: If they found Sampson, they'd kill him.

She raced up the steps, turned to face the crowd, and threw open her arms. "Everyone stop!" Her shout came raspy and ragged, still hoarse from the carriage house fire.

A couple of men glanced over their shoulders. Mom and Dad trailed off mid-conversation, their eyes widening with shock, then fury.

Poppy tried again. "Everyone, wait!" She cleared her throat, forcing the words louder, despite the pain. "Wait for the ranger to identify the tracks! There are other animals out there!"

No one even seemed to notice her but Mom and Dad. They pushed toward her.

The foreman, two steps above Poppy, bellowed, "Comb the forest closest to the manor, east to west, then ten paces outward, spreading deeper into the woods."

Poppy climbed to the highest step.

"Listen to me!" The words ripped from her, different this time. Bigger, as if the manor had amplified them; her voice rebounded against the trees, echoed and multiplied.

The scattering men froze. They peered back at her, crags in their faces filled with shadow.

"You can't go shooting at every moving thing out there!" she yelled.

The foreman spun around. "You again? What the devil do you think—"

"Don't talk to her like that," Mom snapped. She marched up the manor steps, Dad behind her.

The watching crowd fell quiet, edged with tension.

The foreman looked between Mom and Poppy.

"She's not wrong, is she?" Mom said. "You can't go out there, guns blazing. We don't need anyone else getting hurt."

The foreman swiped sweat from his temple. He turned back to the search party. "No one shoots unless you're in danger. Otherwise, use your whistle."

The crowd murmured, breaking into hushed conversations. The foreman bounded down the steps and joined them.

Mom yanked Poppy aside. "Have you lost your mind? How did you get here?"

"I told you not to leave the house!" Dad barked. "There's a wild animal out there!"

"I know! I'm trying to tell you that. There's . . . there's a lion out there! A magical lion I got from a wish and there's no time to explain but he's harmless and alone and—"

"Oh, Poppy." Mom covered her mouth.

Dad's lips pressed into a thin, straight line. "This is what the doctors warned us about—the confusion and nonsense talk."

"You have to believe me! On the night of the carriage house

fire, that's why I ran inside. I was trying to save him. Sampson's been living in there. I've gone there every day to see him."

The admission stoked Mom's anger. "You've been going inside the carriage house *every day*? Even though the Fish and Wildlife Service sent that letter?"

"There is no letter, don't you get it? I made that up!"

Lights flashed in the trees; a whistle shrieked through the night.

Someone had found something.

Dad caught Poppy's arm. "Where do you think you're going?"

"To find Sampson!"

"Oh no, you're not," Dad said.

Mom's eyes searched Poppy, anger and confusion warring in her expression. "Did you just say you forged that letter from the Fish and Wildlife Service?"

Poppy ripped her arm away. "Yes. I did it for Sampson. He exists. And I'll prove it."

Their shock gave her the moment she needed.

She leapt down the staircase and sprinted toward the forest. Mom screamed her name, but it only pressed Poppy faster. Dad tried to catch her, but she wove through the crowd, slipping through the spaces between them. She ducked behind the line of cars in the gravel drive, losing Dad, and curved around the back of the manor.

The long grass whipped against her legs; dewy fog rose all around. In the eerie moonlight, the carriage house was a ghost of itself, its charred rafters like a half-eaten carcass. The roof was collapsed inward, the beautiful diamond-paned windows shattered. Heaps of rubble surrounded it like a moat.

Poppy swallowed a sob and ran faster.

According to the foreman, the search extended away from the manor in a spiral pattern. That meant if Poppy ran straight into the woods, she was ahead of them.

But not by much.

The drone of voices fell away and she slowed to a stop. Her breath came ragged. She wished she'd grabbed a flashlight. But the huge, red moon shone through the pines in pale shafts.

"Sampson!" Her burned hand throbbed with every pounding heartbeat. She gripped her wrist, trying to ease the pain. "Sampson!"

A bush rustled. A bird flew into the night.

Poppy couldn't stop her imagination. It became a movie reel, sliding through scenes of Sampson—trapped or cornered. Shots ringing out. His beautiful wings splayed over the ground, his golden eyes glassy and wide.

Poppy squeezed her eyes until white spots dotted her vision. "Sampson!"

A branch cracked.

Her eyes flew open. She heard the low huff of his breathing. Felt the tension of the surrounding forest.

She took a step, hope driving her heart to a faster tempo. "Sampson?"

A form lumbered from the shadows.

Matted, dark fur. Fatty haunches and bowed legs. Eyes like colorless glass beads. The same size as her beloved lion, the same length claws and teeth, but—the horrible realization came—*not* Sampson.

CHAPTER THIRTY-FOUR

The creature huffed through its nose and advanced. Everything Poppy had learned about bears ricocheted in her head. What was she supposed to do? Run? Climb a tree? Be small? Be loud?

She staggered back, but the bear closed the distance in one stride. She reached behind herself, groping over the ground for a weapon. Her fingers closed around a branch, and she swung it with a guttural scream. The bear flinched.

"Get back! Get away!"

The bear reared onto its hind legs, and for the first time, Poppy grasped its immensity. Its weight alone would crush her. Its knife-length claws would rip through her like butter.

Poppy was suddenly on the ground, sprawled on her back, unsure if she'd slipped or collapsed. The bear towered over her.

Another heartbeat was all she had left. She thought of her

parents, living separate lives on opposite coasts. Of Luca, hiding in his bedroom. The thinning bookshelves. The confused teachers. The lost history.

All of it—Poppy's fault.

A shadow flashed overhead, darkening the sky. The bear suddenly careened backward, crashing to the forest floor.

Sampson pinned the bear, his snow-white wings spread.

"Sampson!" Poppy screamed. The bear bellowed and slapped Sampson across the cheek.

He staggered back and the bear rolled upright.

They circled each other, heads low. The bear snapped its jaws, and Sampson whipped his tail, growling in short, staccato barks.

The bear rose to its hind legs, claws glinting in the moonlight. Sampson matched its height and threw open his wings, beating the air. He rose off the ground, making him taller still.

The bear dropped to its feet, sensing it was outmatched. But Sampson closed his wings and advanced.

Something rustled in the forest behind the bear. Poppy's eyes cut to it, praying the hunters hadn't found them.

Four tiny gleaming eyes flashed in the underbrush.

Cubs.

"Sampson, stop! Let her go!"

He let out a long, low growl, warning the bear off. She trudged back a few steps, then turned and galloped into the dark woods, her cubs close behind.

Sampson trotted toward Poppy. He looked her over frantically, trying to see if she was hurt.

"I'm okay. I'm all right." Poppy said. "Are you?"

He thumped his tail twice, then nudged the bandage on her burned hand.

Poppy winced. "It's from the fire." She unwound the dressing, grimacing as the gauze pulled away from her blisters.

Sampson ducked his head and licked her hand. The bubbling gray blister tightened into pink skin. Poppy marveled at it, turning her palm to catch the moonlight. It looked as if nothing had ever happened. The pain had even disappeared.

But the ache in her chest— that, Sampson couldn't take away. "My mom is moving back to Virginia," she said. "Luca, too. They want me to go with them."

Sampson squinted. He looked toward the manor.

"She doesn't want to do the renovation anymore. It's my fault. When I wished away those books, it changed everything."

He gave a soft, low moan.

"No." Poppy took his face in her hands. "This is my fault. It's mine."

Sampson shuddered his wings. Poppy noticed they were bathed in a strange light, his snowy feathers glowing pink.

She lifted her gaze to the sky. The moon shone a red so deep the clouds looked like flames. A memory swept through her: the Keeper's silky, warbling voice—

You return when the mortal moon burns.

Poppy gasped. "Sampson... I think this is it. The nymph is leaving. Going back to her world."

Their eyes connected. There might only be moments left. It might even be too late. But if there was any chance they could save those books—her *family*—they had to try. One last time.

Sampson hitched his head, as if to say, *What are you waiting for?*

Poppy scrambled onto his back. "Head toward the manor! She was living in the pond nearby!"

He sprang from the ground and they erupted through the trees.

"Fly along the coast! Stay high so no one sees us!"

Sampson veered left, soaring west until the ground dropped away.

The sea thundered below, throwing itself against the cliffs, illuminated by a single streak of eerie red light. A bitter cold wind rushed off the water, lifting Poppy's backpack as if trying to tear it from her shoulders.

She held tighter to Sampson, finding a pocket of warmth between his wings, and turned her focus to the land. To the task ahead. Convincing the nymph wouldn't be easy. They'd already tried begging. Tried reasoning. Now it was time for a different approach.

The trees thinned in the distance, ablaze with searchlights.

"There's the manor!" Poppy shouted, her voice dwarfed by the waves. "The pond is just south!"

Sampson angled inland, soaring over the treetops.

Poppy scanned the forest. Any minute. Any minute.

Ruddy moonlight reflected off a mirror of water. "There!"

Sampson tucked his wings and dove. Poppy hugged him tighter as branches snapped against her thighs. At the last moment, he reared up, and the ground came softly to meet them.

"Wait," Poppy whispered. She held her breath, scanning the woods for any sign of people. Nothing came—no lights or voices in the darkness. The search party hadn't made it out this far yet.

Poppy dismounted and ran to the edge of the pond, Sampson by her side. "Nymph! I know you're in there! Show yourself!"

The forest hummed. Sampson sniffed the air. Poppy tried again: "I call upon the Old World!"

Nothing happened. Sampson released a low huff and nudged Poppy.

Poppy shook her head. "Did you hear me? I said I call upon the Old World!" Why wasn't it working? She thought there had been power behind those words before. But maybe she'd been fooling herself.

Sampson nudged Poppy's backpack again, harder. Suddenly, she understood.

The Tree in Valley Blue.

If the nymph was still anywhere in this world, she'd come for it. Poppy tore off her bag. "Sampson, you're brilliant."

She hesitated, the risk settling over her. The nymph could snatch the book before Poppy reasoned with her. Dad would never remember this piece of their relationship again. Just one more loss Poppy would have to live with forever.

But she saw no other way.

Poppy knelt at the edge of the pond, the book in her lap. She drew a deep breath. Her voice carried over the water. "Well, nymph. I won."

Sampson crouched beside her, eyes narrowed.

"You didn't get the most magical book of all. And now you have to go back to your Old World knowing you missed it. I hope you think of this book every day. I know I will. I'll look at it and remember how I kept it from you."

Wind shimmered through the pines, carrying the scent of thunderstorms and cinnamon and woodsmoke. Yes. *Yes!*

Poppy's voice grew stronger. "You thought you'd fix your mistakes by taking our books back to the Old World? Well, guess what else you're taking with you? The knowledge that you were outsmarted by a mortal."

The song of night creatures quieted to a hum.

The nymph was coming.

Poppy held her breath as she slid the book back into her bag, eyes fixed on the pond. It rippled, something moving far below the surface.

Sampson tensed; his pupils dilated. Poppy touched his back, telling him to stay calm.

All at once, the rippling stopped.

The water became glass. Everything too quiet. Too still.

"No..." Poppy straightened, her eyes narrowed. It was as if the nymph had turned back, decided Poppy wasn't worth the trouble. "Don't you leave without facing me, nymph!"

Sampson sprang into the air. He tucked his wings and spiraled downward, plunging beneath the pond's surface. Water sloshed over Poppy's knees.

"Sampson!" she cried. The forest shrieked. Frogs, crickets, birds. Poppy scrambled forward. What was he thinking? The nymph had needle-sharp claws and teeth. She could kill him. Drag him back to the Old World. "Sampson!"

The pond split and a thrashing form emerged—Sampson with the nymph in his jaws.

Poppy fell back, gasping.

He dropped the nymph to the shore, her scaly body slapping the mud. She writhed—her lower half like a pinched, slippery eel's tail—but Sampson pinned her with a huge paw.

The nymph wasn't injured, but her fury was explosive. She thrashed and shrieked, trying to throw Sampson off. But he was four times her size, fierce and unflinching as he glared down at her.

He shimmied, drying his coat.

Poppy scrambled to his side. "Be quiet, nymph! Stop! There are people with guns in the woods!"

The nymph froze, her gaze narrowed. "*Insssolent* child." Her scaly chest heaved beneath Sampson's paw. "What is the meaning of *thisss*?" Her rotting-fish breath nearly robbed Poppy of courage.

Nearly.

"Return the books you took," Poppy said.

"I have told you, I cannot—"

"You can. You're lying. You're one of the most power-ful creatures in the Old World. If you weren't, the Keepers wouldn't have had to send you to a whole different world for punishment."

The nymph sneered, spit stringing her barracuda teeth. "Ah. So, you believe yourself clever?"

The nymph hadn't admitted it, but she hadn't denied it, either. Poppy pressed on. "The Keeper said you lost sacred knowledge; that's why you were punished. But now you're stealing *our* knowledge. Don't you see? You're making the same mistake all over again!"

"What do I care for the things of the Minor World?"

"Do you want every world to hate you, not just your own?"

"My world does not hate—"

"I heard the Keeper. They don't want you back."

For once, the nymph had no response. Anger boiled in her eyes.

"I heard you say you had no choice when you destroyed the Old World magic," Poppy said. "But in this world you *do* have a choice. You can stop this."

The nymph spat, "I would choose death before helping mortals."

"What have I ever done to you!" Poppy cried. "Why do

you *hate* me so much? I saved you because I loved magic! I still do! And I can't even force myself to hate you back, because *you* gave me Sampson!"

The nymph's fury faltered, her riverweed hair wilting. She squinted her white-orb eyes. "If you care so much for books, tiny-faced mortal, you should have been content in their company, not seeking the magic of other worlds."

Poppy dropped her head. "Maybe you're right."

Sampson gave a soft, low moan, aching to comfort Poppy but unable to leave the nymph unguarded.

The nymph's voice came like the sudden quiet of a river after rapids. "I do not hate you, tiny-faced mortal. Else I would not have left you the memory of your books."

Poppy looked up. *That* was why she could remember the books? The nymph had *let* her keep the memories, some sort of attempt at kindness?

But it wasn't a gift. It was a curse. Because Poppy, alone, would have to live with the guilt of those lost books forever. "But I don't want to remember. I—"

The *crack* of a gunshot exploded through the air.

Poppy dropped to the ground, covering her head. She held her breath, waiting for the pain. But nothing came.

She looked up and screamed, the reality far worse than her fear.

She hadn't been shot.

Sampson had.

CHAPTER THIRTY-FIVE

A smatter of dark blood stained the fur on Sampson's chest, but he was crouched, searching the woods for the hunter.

"Sampson!" Poppy fell onto him, patting his bleeding chest, feeling for the bullet wound. She dug through his mane with her fingers. But there was no gushing source, his fur only flecked with blood. "Wait..." The realization first came as a hope. "You...you're okay?"

Sampson's tail thumped, his eyes still locked on the woods.

The crunch of a footstep gave the hunter's position away. Sampson bounded toward him and threw open his wings. The man stumbled back and fled.

A gurgling sound came from the pond's edge.

Poppy turned and gasped.

The nymph lay on her back, chest heaving. Blood bubbled from her shoulder and spilled over the ground. The air thickened with the scent of thunderstorms, as though the very magic was leaching from her veins.

The nymph's claws twitched, her orb eyes wild and searching. "What mortal magic...struck me?"

Poppy approached, Sampson at her side. "You...you've been shot," she said quietly.

The nymph's gaze cut to her, pained but fierce. "Leave, tiny-faced mortal!"

"But—"

The nymph let out a ragged cry. "Leave!"

Poppy stepped back but couldn't look away. The entire forest seemed to be watching, too—a hush falling all around.

The nymph turned her gaze upward. "My *ssssisters...*" She lifted her hands, reaching for some invisible source of comfort. Her voice came like a final hiss of steam. "I'm *ssssorry.*"

Sampson stepped toward the nymph.

Poppy's hand flew out instinctively. "What are you doing?"

Sampson looked back, his answer as clear as if he'd somehow said it aloud: *Saving her.*

"But..." Poppy looked past him to the nymph lying on the ground, her light and powers dimming. *"Why?"*

The wind tossed Sampson's mane. His expression was calm. Maybe this was his purpose, saving others. Or maybe he shared some magical bond with the nymph. But the reason, Poppy realized, didn't matter. All that mattered was that he was asking Poppy to trust him.

She took a deep breath. "Okay."

As Sampson's shadow fell over the nymph, the forest creatures broke their silence, humming a sacred forest chant.

Once, twice, three times, Sampson licked the nymph's shoulder. Each time, the wound healed a fraction more. The bleeding stopped. The skin regenerated—scales multiplying before Poppy's eyes—then knitted back together.

The nymph raised a trembling claw to her shoulder. "Lion. I owe you a debt."

Poppy moved to his side. "No more debts. No more deals. All we need is for you to give back what you've taken."

Every part of the nymph seemed to wilt with shame. "I cannot return to the Old World without the mortal magic."

"Then I'll get you different ones." Poppy could find other books, couldn't she? Ones that didn't matter as much? Ones that wouldn't change the world and history and her family? "I can go now."

A cloud crossed the moon. The nymph's gaze lifted. "There is no time."

"There has to be! Please!"

"I *musssst* go."

So that was it? The nymph would take Grandma's journal? The Narnia book? Lady Lark-Hayes's memoir, Luca's comics,

The Odyssey? Dozens of others. And Poppy, alone, would carry their memories.

The thought was a spark.

A flash of hopeful light.

Memories . . .

Poppy's eyes lifted to Sampson. He was the key. The memory of every book they'd read together . . . they were all inside him. The Keepers would see that. He could go back to the Old World with the nymph, take the place of the books.

Sampson watched Poppy carefully. He was only ever a heartbeat behind her. He would sense what she was thinking. His gaze dropped, searching the ground. When he lifted his eyes, they were aflame. Eager.

Suddenly, Poppy recoiled from the idea. "Wait . . . no. You can't. You can't go."

Sampson thumped his tail.

Poppy understood everything in his expression. The bend of his mouth. The lowering of his brow. It held a depth of sadness. But more than anything, determination.

Sampson put his forehead to hers.

Poppy dug her fingers into his mane.

She couldn't live without Sampson. And he wouldn't survive without her, would he? This life was all he'd ever known.

But what kind of life was that? Cowering in the carriage house? Quiet and careful and unseen?

Sampson flew now. He *roared*.

He'd outgrown this world.

The forest collapsed around them. There was nothing else—no searchlights, no moon, no nymph. There was only Sampson: eyes shining, mane fluttering in the restless breeze.

"I'm sorry, Sampson."

He nuzzled the crook of Poppy's neck, his breath warm against her back. Her tears wet his mane. "I'm so sorry," she whispered again.

He huffed, as if to say, *Me too.*

The nymph's voice severed the moment. "Farewell, mortal child."

"Wait!" Poppy released Sampson. "Don't leave! We have an idea!"

"I told you, there is no time—"

Poppy pushed forward. "You said your Old World Keepers can read memories, right?"

The nymph's head cocked. "Yes."

Poppy braced herself. This was going to be like plunging a dagger into her own heart. But it was the only way to save her family, to restore the lost books. "Take Sampson back with you. The stories are inside him, in his memories. Leave the other books with me."

The nymph squinted, her milky eyes swirling. "The mortal magic . . . is inside the winged lion?"

"Yes! Exactly!"

The nymph thought for a moment, then turned her gaze to Sampson. "Winged lion, do you come willingly?"

Sampson dipped his head in a nod.

Her silky voice came low. "Then do as I say."

Men's voices rang out in the distance. "There! Over there!"

Poppy's pulse thundered. "Hurry. Tell us."

"The cloud on the horizon…Do you *ssssee*?" Beyond the treetops, a sheet of dark cloud inched into view. "When it shrouds the moon, the Old World opens her doors. The lion must go then."

The cloud stretched steadily toward the eclipsed moon. It wouldn't be long. Fifteen minutes, at most.

Fifteen minutes left with Sampson.

A crack began to rend Poppy's heart—a tear she'd never be able to fix.

The nymph continued, "If a *ssssliver* of moonlight breaks the cloud, you will be too late. The threshold will close."

"The portal is only open when the cloud covers the moon. Got it." Poppy nodded. "Then Sampson goes back to the Old World. But how? Where?"

"The door through which he entered."

"The room in the manor?"

"Yes. But understand *thisss*. … . For the memory of the books, you sacrifice your memories of the Old World."

"Wait…" Poppy fell back on her heels. "I'll forget all of it? I'll…I'll forget Sampson?" It was too much. She looked at him, wishing he'd tell her it wasn't worth it.

But he huffed, urging her on.

"Penelope!" The searching men's voices grew louder, closing in. *"Penelope Woodlock!"*

"Go!" the nymph said.

"Wait!" Poppy caught the nymph's wrist, the scales sharp and cold in her hand. "When Sampson goes back to the Old World, you have to protect him. You have to help him find his place. Swear it."

The nymph's pearly gaze was level and true. "The deal is sworn."

Shadows flashed between the trees. "There!" a man said.

The nymph slipped beneath the water, slick as an eel. Poppy vaulted onto Sampson's back.

He sprang from the ground as another gunshot cracked. The bullet shattered a passing trunk, spraying splinters over Poppy. A man's voice shouted, *"What the devil—"* but distance swallowed the rest.

They broke into the clear sky.

"Head for the manor!" Poppy cried.

As Sampson flew, she kept her eyes on the cloud slipping toward the eclipsed moon. It seemed to taunt her, moving faster.

The meadow surrounding the manor came into view, blazing with movement and noise. Police cars, fire trucks, ambulances. People darted across the property like frantic insects.

A thrumming sound came from the distance, growing louder.

A helicopter appeared, its spotlight roving the woods. A muffled voice boomed from its speaker: *"Aaron Kemp, found.*

Now searching for Poppy Woodlock. Brown hair. Blue jacket. Poppy Woodlock..." The announcement repeated as the helicopter circled the manor.

Sampson pulled upright, his beating wings pushing them backward in the sky.

Poppy hugged his neck. "Don't be scared! It won't hurt you!"

The helicopter made a sharp turn toward them.

Sampson swiveled, cutting through the air in the opposite direction.

"No! Wait!" Poppy pulled on his mane to turn him back, but he wouldn't stop.

Above, the cloud grazed the edge of the moon.

Poppy pulled her phone from her pocket. If she told Mom she was at the cottage, they'd call off the search party. The helicopter would leave. The phone bobbled from her fingertips and plunged downward, tumbling through the trees.

"Sampson! Down!"

He dove, landing on the forest floor with a thud. Poppy scoured the ground on hands and knees. But the phone was impossible to find in the darkness. And they didn't have time. She climbed onto Sampson's back. "If you won't fly, you'll have to run. Head toward the—"

A voice cracked. "Poppy?"

She looked over, cold flooding her veins.

Luca.

CHAPTER THIRTY-SIX

Luca braced himself between two massive pines, his face ashen. "Poppy . . ." His breath came in a ragged gasp. "Get off that thing."

Sampson looked back at Poppy and released a quiet, curious moan.

"It's Luca," she whispered. "My brother."

It was the moment Poppy had dreamed of. Luca and Sampson. There was so much to tell. So much to explain.

She looked skyward, her heart falling. But there was no time.

Something in Luca's hand caught the moonlight. A gleaming silver whistle. He lifted it.

Poppy's hand flew up. "Luca, don't! Please!"

He hesitated. And maybe the old Luca would have let her go. But suddenly Poppy knew: This Luca, the one with fearful eyes and white socks, would never defy their parents.

She ducked to Sampson's ear. "Run!"

He charged forward.

Luca's whistle pierced the air, over and over, giving away Poppy's location.

She clung to Sampson. The forest passed in a blur. He changed directions suddenly, avoiding the men flocking toward Luca's whistle, bounding over fallen logs, skidding beneath branches.

The sky appeared through a break in the trees, revealing the cloud covering half the moon. In minutes, it would be obscured completely.

"To the back door! Stay in the trees!"

As they passed Lark-Hayes Manor, time seemed to slow. The front door was thrown wide, like a mouth gasping for air. Veins of ivy reflected the emergency lights, their waxy leaves glowing like wounds.

Someone shouted in Poppy's direction, "There! What's that?"

"Don't shoot!" Mom screamed.

Poppy and Sampson rounded the side of the house, cutting toward the back door. Sampson stared across the meadow, in the direction of the collapsed carriage house.

Grief slowed his gait.

It ached inside Poppy, too: the realization that they could never—would never—go back.

Poppy leapt down and yanked the handle of the servants' door. It stuck, unused for too long. She leveraged her foot against the jamb and pulled. The door gave, throwing her to the ground.

"Go!"

Sampson bounded inside.

The search party rounded the side of the house and spotted her. Mom. Dad. The foreman.

"Penelope!" Mom screamed. "Stop!"

Poppy ran inside and slammed the door, threw the bolt, then raced up the stairs, Sampson on her heels. They skidded to the doorway of the room where Sampson had hidden as a cub.

A sudden stillness fell all around.

Sampson sniffed at the threshold. He seemed to remember the place, his snowy wings shuddering as he crept forward.

"Sampson...," Poppy whispered. The sound of her own heartbeat filled her ears, muffling the pounding on the door downstairs.

Sampson took another slow, careful step. His front paws crossed the threshold. His wings. His tail. Tears blurred Poppy's vision. She remembered the short, tufted tail of the little cub who'd first run into this room. The knobby gray wings. The tiny kitten face.

She'd loved Sampson from that first moment.

Voices came muffled from downstairs. *"Poppy! Poppy, open up!"*

If she didn't send Sampson into this portal now, she'd never do it.

She pulled the door shut.

The banging below stopped. The house fell quiet.

Panic flooded Poppy. She hadn't even said goodbye.

"Sampson!" She swung the door open.

He stood there, his head cocked, a look of curious alarm on his face.

Poppy threw her arms around him. "Sammy. You're still here...." Her relief turned to worry. She straightened. "You're still here."

She went to the window. The roving lights of the helicopter passed over the manor and disappeared. Darkness swallowed the sky.

Poppy touched the windowpane. "The portal should be open. The nymph lied." She spun around to Sampson. "She lied and now—"

The words died on her lips.

Sampson was staring into the closet, the fur along his spine standing on end. His tail flicked.

The closet.

Poppy crossed the room, and that familiar scent grew with every step—woodsmoke and thunderstorms and cinnamon. She felt something, too. Wind. Her jacket didn't rustle; Sampson's mane didn't flutter. But some invisible force stirred around them, dry and fitful against her skin. A low, hollow moan echoed from some place unseen.

This was the door.

"Poppy!" Mom called from downstairs.

Poppy glanced back out the window. At any moment, moonlight would break through. The Old World portal would close.

"Sammy," Poppy said. "It's time."

He backed away from the closet, giving a long, low whine.

Dad's voice came. "I heard something upstairs!"

Poppy took Sampson's face and smoothed his golden mane, memorizing everything about him—his trusting amber eyes, the downy wisps of white crowning his face, the spirals of short fur on the bridge of his nose. Tears blurred her vision. "I don't care what the nymph says. I'll never forget you. You're the best thing that's ever happened to me." Poppy searched herself for a well of strength she wasn't sure existed. But if it did, she needed it now. "But you have to go."

His ears pressed back, nearly flat to his head. It'd been so long since Poppy had seen this expression on him that she almost didn't recognize it.

He was scared.

Poppy couldn't send him away like this.

"The world on the other side of this door is your new home, Sammy," she said. "It's where you belong." The words were worthless. How many times had her parents said that to her before they'd moved? When she was scared, only one thing gave her courage. "Listen. There's still one story I haven't told you yet."

Curiosity sparked in Sampson's eyes.

"Penelope!" Mom's voice echoed down the hall.

Dad called, "You're not in trouble! Come out and talk to us!"

Poppy kept her eyes locked with Sampson's. "It starts like this. . . . Four kids go through an enchanted door in a mansion." Sampson's gaze cut to the closet, just as she'd hoped. "Yes. *Exactly* like that. They get transported to Narnia, a kingdom full of magical creatures. But an evil witch tricks one of them. And just when they think all hope is lost. . .Aslan shows up."

Sampson tossed his head.

"Sampson! You don't know Aslan? He's a lion, like you! And he teaches the kids to be brave. Then in the end, he sacrifices himself to save everyone." She stroked Sampson's fleecy mane. "And I know Aslan exists, no matter what the nymph says. Because I've seen him in you."

Footfalls thundered down the hallway. "Poppy, we know you're up here!"

Poppy pressed her forehead to the wrinkled bridge of Sampson's nose. "In your new world, you won't have to hide anymore. You can be loud. You were *meant* to be loud."

She stepped back. This time, without fear or hesitation, Sampson walked inside the closet. He turned to face her.

Tears ran down Poppy's cheeks. "Find where you belong, Sampson. And if you can't find it, make it."

Sampson threw back his head and roared—filling every inch of the room, rattling the windowpanes. It shook loose all the emotions Poppy had been holding back. She lifted her face skyward, laughing and sobbing.

When Sampson stopped, Poppy knew it was time. The noise would bring the search party straight to her.

"I won't forget you, Sampson. I promise."

The last thing she saw were Sampson's golden eyes, shining against the darkness.

She shut the door between them.

Something rushed from Poppy, like one final, brilliant flash before a star dies. Her knees buckled as Mom and Dad burst into the room.

Mom scooped Poppy into her lap. "Oh, my girl, my girl. Don't ever do that again."

Dad fell over them both, wrapping them in his arms. "Are you hurt? Penelope, answer me. Are you hurt?"

Poppy shook her head.

The foreman charged into the room, gun slung over his shoulder. "Was someone with her?" He swung open the closet door, faltering. "What the devil is this?"

Poppy peered into the closet. A stack of books was piled in the center. The Lady Lark-Hayes memoir, a bunch of Luca's comics, some big novels from Dad's bookshelf.

"My mother's journal?" Mom plucked the book from the heap. Her gaze cut back to Poppy. "You brought these over here?"

"No." Poppy shook her head vigorously.

The draft from the opening door had blown something over Dad's foot. He held up a long white feather. "Where'd *this* come from?"

Poppy studied it: the pure white of the plumes, the translucent stem. It fanned wider than any bird feather, each barb as soft as whispering snow. She took it in her fingertips.

A memory rushed toward her: wind whipping all around. A crashing sea thundering below.

Something warm and heavy carried her; but it was without shape or edges, as if made of pure light. Poppy wrestled with the memory, trying to pull it into focus. But her struggle sent more ripples through the vision, pushing it further away.

Mom patted her leg. "What is it?"

Poppy pressed the feather to her cheek and reached deeper into the memory, grappling for traction. But with each heartbeat, it faded toward a dark space behind her eyes.

What is it?

The sound of the sea grew faint.

What is it?

The wind weak as breath.

What is it?

Poppy lowered the feather and let it fall from her fingertips. It whisked along the floorboards.

"I don't know," she said.

And it was true.

Chapter Thirty-Seven

ONE YEAR LATER

"Order!" Poppy banged her gavel, trying to defuse the explosive Readers Club debate. Chase Parker had just suggested that Marley Mae was the true villain of this month's book, which had nearly incited a riot with half the members. "Order!"

The bickering dissipated. The gavel had been Mrs. Bartholomew's idea. Readers Club had twenty-six members now—each one with big opinions about literature. But honestly? Their passion was the best part.

Poppy held up her palms. "I think we can agree that, villain or not, Marley Mae is awesome. Those knife skills? Come on."

A swell of agreement came from everyone in the circle. Even Chase Parker joined some kids pretending to spin invisible weapons.

"What's the next book?" someone called.

Poppy turned to Annabelle. "Secretary?"

Annabelle consulted her notes. "It's called *The Winds of Winslow County*."

"Oh! One of my favorites," Mrs. Bartholomew piped up.

Mr. Thomas was reclined next to her, twirling a feathery purple pen. "Haven't read that one." He hosted the Yo-Yo Club in his room on Wednesdays, but he usually popped into Readers Club, saying, "Just grabbing a famous brownie," and ended up staying the entire time.

"I've read it. It's really good," Poppy said, even though for some reason the memory made her strangely sad. Like a tugging attached to a string she couldn't find. "Okay." She banged the gavel. "Meeting adjourned."

As kids headed out, Annabelle called, "Remember—next week is the fourth Wednesday!"

The departing chatter turned to costume plans. On fourth Wednesdays, everyone dressed up like a character from that month's book. When Poppy had first proposed the idea, the other kids had been hesitant. But, after a little encouragement, they began to have fun with it. Fun grew into enthusiasm. Enthusiasm became...something bordering on mania. Last month, Poppy and Annabelle had stayed up until 1:00 a.m. making suits of armor with tinfoil and duct tape. The month before that, Grace Jennings had chopped her hair with kitchen scissors. The month before *that*, Nick Bray used superglue as beard adhesive and had come to school with full Merlin facial hair for three days before his mom took him to the doctor to get it removed.

Annabelle packed her notebook, then swung her bag over her shoulder. "I thought of someone who'd be good for next year's vice president." Their current VP was graduating and heading to high school.

"Who?" Poppy asked.

Annabelle's voice dropped as she gestured to someone near the door. "Meher Singh."

Poppy whispered, "The sixth grader? Sai's sister?"

"She's come to every meeting this year. Her costumes are always awesome. And she reads crazy huge books—like I'm pretty sure she read *The Odyssey*. For *fun*."

Poppy turned to see Meher ducking from the room, not talking to anyone, a book clutched to her chest. It looked familiar. "Yeah, she might be good. I'll talk to her."

"Cool. My house or yours on Friday?"

"Yours," Poppy said. Annabelle's mom stocked the pantry with so many snacks it looked like a grocery store.

"How about your house and I bring the snacks?" Annabelle always wanted to hang at Poppy's—mostly to peek at the progress on the manor. Mom was busy working her magic these days. They were far from finished, but already, when you walked through the door, it felt like a step back in time.

"Only if you bring licorice," Poppy said.

"Deal."

They thanked Mrs. B and Mr. T on their way out. In the hallway, Holden was scrubbing Doc Mimi's rolling trash can. Turned out he *was* the one who'd accidentally started the carriage house fire. But since he came forward and admitted it, instead of pressing charges, the Lark-Hayes trust gave him six hundred hours of community service. Three times the normal amount because he refused to rat out the other kids who'd trespassed with him. He'd be cleaning trash cans till the tenth grade.

Their eyes connected. Poppy gave him a weak smile, continuing down the hallway.

"I've got to admit," Holden called, "you seem like a way better president than I was."

Annabelle and Poppy looked at each other like, *Did he really just say that?*

Poppy was about to brush him off when she thought of a quote she'd copied into her fuzzy pink notebook last week:

> *That's the thing about forgiveness. You don't know if a person deserves it until you see what they do with it.*

Poppy turned and walked backward. "Next month's book is *The Winds of Winslow County*."

Holden stopped scrubbing. Gray water dribbled from his

rag. "You mean you want me to come?" His voice cracked. He cleared his throat and shrugged. "Yeah, maybe I will. You know, for old times' sake."

"Or maybe *not* like old times," Poppy said.

Holden laughed as Doc Mimi came around the corner behind him. "Come on, baby, those cans won't clean themselves."

Holden muttered an apology and went back to scrubbing.

Poppy sometimes wondered if the custodian knew how much that pep talk in the band room had meant to her. But before she could say anything, Doc Mimi winked. "Run along, Madam President. You're distracting my staff."

Poppy swung her backpack down in the cottage foyer. "Anyone home?"

"Just me," Luca called from the kitchen.

Poppy peeled off her jacket, following the scent of cooking in the kitchen. She found Luca pulling a tray of pizza bagels from the oven. He tossed it to the counter with a clatter.

Poppy reached for one and he blocked her hand.

"Not enough," he said.

"You made like forty!"

"Student council meeting."

Poppy rolled her eyes, then got a spoon and dove into the

red sauce bubbling on the stove. Grandma's journal said to let it cook for three hours—so Mom always simmered it for exactly that long. But already, it was good enough to eat like soup.

Luca arranged the pizza bagels on a platter, humming a song Poppy didn't recognize. His hair was longer than ever, brushing the bottoms of his ears, and he had this new love of wearing kerchiefs around his neck, which he claimed had started a trend at the high school. "How'd Readers Club go?" he asked.

"Great. Mom and Dad at the manor?"

"Yeah. They told me to send you over. Something about a surprise for you."

The last time they'd "surprised" Poppy was that banana-yellow dirt bike. The one she'd crashed on that horrible night of the bear hunt.

Poppy slipped back into her jacket and grabbed the bear spray, which she was supposed to carry everywhere now. The incident with the grizzly last year had her parents spooked, even though it couldn't possibly happen again. Grizzlies didn't actually live in Oregon. That bear had come from a private zoo up north, who'd set it free so they could collect the insurance money. Luckily, the rangers had found her and the cubs, tranquilized them, and transported them safely to a zoo in San Diego.

"Hey, Weasel," Luca called. Poppy turned and he tossed her a pizza bagel. "Never say I gave you nothing."

Poppy considered riding her dirt bike to the manor, but the warbling birds and whispering pines drew her onto the path by foot.

Lately, she only rode the bike when she needed to clear her head. Sometimes she ended up at the burned-down carriage house. But she never lingered there long. It was still charred and disturbing, untouched since the fire, and it made her sad to think about how much time she'd spent there alone.

Other days, she ended up at the cliffs. The roaring waves reminded her of a memory just out of reach. It frustrated her. Unsettled her. But kept calling her back.

Luca must have texted their parents, because they were waiting on the front steps when Poppy arrived. Lark-Hayes Manor looked so different now—the moss stripped away, the windows gleaming and shutters painted.

She remembered the quote that had drawn her to explore the manor last year, about quiet things keeping the best secrets. That might still be true. But apparently Lark-Hayes Manor hadn't wanted to keep its secrets forever. Because now, it looked open and inviting and proud.

Poppy crunched down the gravel drive. "What's the surprise? My birthday isn't for six months."

"Wait, what?" Dad said. "Shoot, Cordelia. How did we get it so wrong?"

Mom swatted him, then clasped her hands beneath her chin. "No special occasion. We just know you'll love this."

Dad covered Poppy's eyes as Mom led her by the hand.

She'd grown to know the feel of the manor. The damp, timeworn air. The scarred floorboards warmed by the skylight windows. The pipes that clicked and groaned.

She knew, even with her eyes closed, that they were passing beneath the staircase—mahogany Mom had finished with a stain recipe from 1880. The freshly plastered walls were covered in portraits, the spindly tables set with antiques Mom had collected from around the country.

They stopped in what felt like a doorway.

"Ready?" Mom said. "One ... two ..."

Three. Dad's hands lifted.

Poppy gasped.

She'd seen the library a hundred times, but never like this. Hundreds of books filled the two-story shelves—all with fraying spines and linen covers. Four rolling ladders lined the walls, and with the velvet drapes drawn, the crystal chandelier cast a warm, fluttering glow over it all.

"Is it bookworm approved?" Mom asked.

"Approved?" Poppy swept into the room and spread her arms. The smell of old books had to be the best scent in the world. "I want to *live* here." She moved along the shelves, admiring the novels. One caught her eye—the only one that didn't look a hundred years old: a dark spine with a gold symbol. She drew the book from the shelf. The cover was embossed with that same image, but this one spanned the width of the cover—

A lion. A golden lion with *wings* lifted above its head.

A memory flickered—a light struggling through fractured darkness. "Where'd these books come from?"

"Private collections, museums, antique dealers. I curated the entire collection myself so they'd be true to the time period." Mom glanced over. "I don't recognize that one, though. What's the title?"

"It doesn't have one." Poppy traced the cover with her fingertips. The gold leaf was strangely warm to the touch, the coarse linen the color of crushed wild berries, like the ones growing behind the burned-down carriage house.

Poppy opened the book, its spine crackling as if it'd never been read. A scent wafted from the pages. Familiar. She inhaled deeper—searching for its place in her memory. It took her somewhere rich and full of earth, like pines in the rain. But it was more than that. . . .

It was cinnamon.

And thunderstorms.

And woodsmoke.

The darkness inside Poppy burst into a thousand shards.

The book tumbled from her fingertips, but before it hit the ground, a single word escaped her lips: a whisper, a shout, a shattering light—

"Sampson."

AUTHOR'S NOTE

The day I submitted *The Lion of Lark-Hayes Manor* for publication, I went into labor with my third child. It felt like such beautiful symmetry: two of my babies making their debuts together. It *had* to be a sign. I joked with my agent that I wasn't sure which endeavor had taken more out of me. And though I thought that was the extent of the synchronicity, I soon learned it was just the beginning.

Because three hours later, I gave birth. Naomi was born with paralyzed vocal cords—a rare condition impacting fewer than one in a million babies. We have no explanation for it, no cure, no genetic or gestational component to shed further light. It just is.

I wrote a book about a girl finding her voice; I gave birth to a girl without one.

The irony felt so deliberate and cruel, for weeks I couldn't think about it. I nearly pulled my book from submission. One night, beneath the dim lights of the newborn intensive care unit, I watched Naomi breathe to the rhythm of the ventilator. It was the evening before her tracheotomy—a surgery that would give her a stable airway but more fully steal her ability to vocalize. I heard the rumble of the sliding glass door, the squeak of sneakers as a nurse joined me.

I didn't lift my head. "How can I care for a baby who can't cry?" I asked.

The response that came will stay with me forever: "You'll have to change the way you listen."

I was terrified to bring Naomi home. It would have been so easy to fail her. But I'll tell you what: Even from another room, my ear can pick up the wheezing sound of her cry. A change in her breathing wakes me from a dead sleep. She is communicative and emotive and brilliant, but she hasn't magically learned to vocalize. *I've* learned to listen.

There's a chance my daughter's vocal cords spontaneously recover some day. Until then, it doesn't mean she has nothing to say. I think of the final lines from Poppy's favorite storybook:

> *"She knows*
> *she makes the world beautiful*
> *when she blooms in her own time."*

The Lion of Lark-Hayes Manor is about a lion learning to roar, a young girl fighting to be heard. Since the day of its conception, my hope was that a child would see themselves in these pages and find that courage. But Naomi has taught me something it seems Mr. Thomas already knew:

Some voices take longer to find than others.

Until then, it's up to us to change the way we listen.

ACKNOWLEDGMENTS

Immeasurable gratitude:

To my life's coauthor, Hunter Hartman, for your support and sacrifice and unfaltering faith in me. To my mom, Lezlie Evans: beautiful writer, sharp-eyed editor, and patient mentor. I couldn't have made it a single step in this journey without you. To my dad, John Evans, for hyping every amateur novel I wrote.

To my thoughtful and brilliant agent, Molly O'Neill: endlessly generous of your time and talent and energy. Your belief in my stories kept me going. And to my film agent, Berni Barta, whom I feel thrilled to be associated with.

To my insightful and gentle editor, Ruqayyah Daud, for championing and honing this novel. Your vision turned my dream into reality, and I am deeply, forever grateful. And to the entire Little, Brown Books for Young Readers team: Patrick Hulse, Sasha Illingworth, Jake Regier, Andy Ball, Patricia Alvarado, Daniel Lupo, Barbara Perris, Bill Grace, Andie Divelbiss, Emilie Polster, Savannah Kennelly, Marisa Russell, Christie Michel, Amber Mercado, Victoria Stapleton, Megan Tingley, Jackie Engel, Shawn Foster, and Danielle Cantarella. I cannot overstate how honored I am that such talented professionals worked on my little story.

To *Lion*'s artist, Christopher Cyr. The rich and meticulous way you brought this book to life is nothing short of perfection.

To my writing group and treasured friends, Teri Christopherson, Melanie Jacobson, Brittany Larsen, Tiffany Odekirk, and Jen White: Your fingerprints are on every page. Finding you all is one of my favorite miracles.

To Ann Marie Stephens and Valerie Patterson for your invaluable feedback and encouragement. And to the rest of the Sisters of the Pen, particularly Erin Teagan, Ellen Braff, and Corey Wetzel, for allowing me to be an honorary member when I was nothing but a girl with a sluggish laptop and a dream.

To Janet Constantino and Luz Harris for loving my kids whenever I was discovering other worlds.

To my siblings, Andrew Evans, Katie Parkinson, Megan Evans, Daniel Evans, and Nathan Evans, all of whom encouraged or plotted with me at some point, and each of whom is a better writer than I.

To my late aunt Lynne for the advice to "write one page a day, and you'll have a whole book in a year." Thank you for leaving out the part about revising said book.

And most especially to my babies: Scarlett, who inspired all the best parts of Poppy; Asher, my fierce and loving little lion; and Naomi, my Little Tree. I wrote every word with you three in mind.